Crossings $12.99

LIKE A WATERED GARDEN

Like a Watered Garden

A Novel

Patti Hill

BETHANY HOUSE PUBLISHERS

Minneapolis, Minnesota

Like a Watered Garden
Copyright © 2005
Patti Hill

Cover design by Zandrah Kurland, Koechel Peterson & Associates

Published by Bethany House Publishers
11400 Hampshire Avenue South
Bloomington, Minnesota 55438

Bethany House Publishers is a division of
Baker Publishing Group, Grand Rapids, Michigan.

Printed in the United States of America

ISBN 0-7394-4922-2

TO MY FATHER,

the gardener,

AND HIS SON,

the true vine

And the Lord will guide you continually,
and satisfy your desire with good things,
and make your bones strong;
and you shall be like a watered garden,
like a spring of water,
whose waters fail not.

ISAIAH 58:11 RSV

MAY 2

Cloudless and warm and breezy. Added montbretia (Lucifer) to bed below southern porch. Planted a dozen bulbs with compost and mulched with cedar. Hope south-facing bed gives winter shelter.

I received a box of flowers from my dead husband.

That's a stretch. They weren't flowers at all but a dozen montbretia bulbs that looked like hazelnuts with ponytails. Blooms wouldn't show up until July, I figured, if they showed up at all. The UPS man had hidden the box under the welcome mat in a clumsy attempt at security. It amused me until I remembered I had ordered nothing from Burpee's. Within a heartbeat, I knew the flowers—because that was what he had intended them to be—were from Scott.

I knew with great certainty the very day my husband had made the order. The autumn valley had looked like a grade school rendering with the crayons pressed so hard no white showed through. The golden ash trees lining our street shimmered below a cerulean sky. Pots of orange and rust and yellow chrysanthemums lined the porches of Victorian houses painted the extravagant colors of memories. On any other day, the scene would have seemed gaudy. But not that day. The day was electric, charged by the crisp snap in the air. It seemed perfectly normal for the colors to glow from within.

I'd laughed at the Weather Service's blundered forecast of bitter temperatures and gloomy skies but then thought better of ignoring the warning altogether. I washed the breakfast dishes and went out to the garden to tuck in the flower beds for winter.

Scott found me cutting coneflowers. "Love you," he said and kissed my cheek before leaving with a friend to train for yet another masochistic bike race, probably the Thankless Turkey Tour. I didn't expect to see him before supper or the end of the USC-UCLA football game.

By midmorning, it was warm enough to discard my sweatshirt. I finished cutting back the perennials and worked at laying a heavy blanket of mulch to shelter the plants during the coming winter. Then I raced against the setting sun to add compost to the vegetable garden. As I turned over the last spade of soil, the sun dipped below the plateaus. The dry air of western Colorado relinquished the day's warmth without one bit of struggle.

I slipped a sweatshirt back over my head just as Scott pushed his bike through the side gate. His face was flushed from the last leg of his ride, the twenty miles from the Timeout Sports Grille to home. His gray hair stood in disorderly shafts from sweating under his helmet all day, and while I hoped he had combed his hair before entering the restaurant, I knew better. Scott raised his eyebrows and flashed a mischievous grin. I was in trouble.

"Aha," he said, pulling the Burpee Seeds and Plants catalog from the stack of mail under his arm. "I have intercepted that which tempts you beyond your power to resist. Now we can afford to eat this winter, and Ky can get new cleats, and I can finally get a high-performing, distortion-reducing Fat Lady driver with a zirconium soleplate."

He had a point about the flower thing. Dahlias, irises, peonies, roses—or any other flower. My hobby had turned into an obsession and then into a business, which thrilled Scott. He liked the prospect of reversing the flow of resources back into our bank account. For every special occasion, romantic or not, he presented me with books on small business management, and once he even packed my bags to send me to a cash flow seminar in Denver. I knew he really believed in me when I came home to find a truck in the driveway with *Perennially Yours, Mibby Garrett, Garden Designer* painted on the door and a box of matching pea-green business cards on the driver's seat. The red bucket of daisies on the truck's cab gave the vehicle its name, the Daisy Mobile.

And yet he still protested, however gently, each new flower addition that encroached his lawn. It was all a part of our marriage dance, the one that questioned and valued our differences. He claimed to be protecting the dog's right to his personal space. In response, I declared a patch of lawn the "poop deck," no flowers allowed. It seemed like the fair thing to do.

Usually I took Scott's ribbing about my obsession for what it was, a not-too-serious-but-could-you-please-show-some-restraint plea for moderation. But that day, standing in the garden with scratches up and down my arms and cedar mulch embedded in my knees, I didn't appreciate his exaggeration at all.

I jabbed the shovel blade into the ground and sighed. Scott stepped behind me, probably afraid I'd whack him with the shovel, and wrapped his arms around my waist. I pressed the shovel in deeper, tightening my stomach muscles against the warmth of his arms.

"Mibby, I didn't mean it." His breath filled my ear and poured onto my cheek. He held out the catalog. "You can buy a dozen of everything in here if you want. I'm sorry."

Of course, it was clear to me later that I was the one who should have apologized. But I didn't.

"You should be sorry," I said, walking out of his embrace and into the house. It was time to start dinner.

After I'd coaxed a simmer from the spaghetti sauce, I found Scott looking through the catalog on the porch. The light from the kitchen window boxed him in a yellow glow. Showered and combed, he looked more like the steadfast banker I'd married. He made room for me on the wicker loveseat and gave me a cautious smile.

"See anything you like?" I asked, crossing my arms and leaning against the railing of the porch.

He held up a picture of fiery red blossoms arching along a stem. "These look like montbretia, but they're calling them *Cro*—"

"*Crocosmia*," I said, trying to sound indifferent. "Montbretia is its common name."

"Want some?"

"Maybe."

I left the porch to take the last bag of clippings to the compost pile. Scott walked with me.

"Montbretia prefers a milder climate," I said.

"So do you, but look how well you're doing."

"You'd probably be wasting your money."

Since that day I've spent many hollow hours trying to remember why I was so rough on him. Surely something else, something hurtful and consequential, had triggered my irritation and justified its endurance. Had I resented Scott for leaving me with all the gardening chores? Had he begged out of attending a jamboree fund-raising meeting and asked me to go in his place? Had he eaten the last pecan sandy and put the empty bag back in the pantry? Those were the worst things I could think of Scott doing, and even for me; they were trite. What clung most ardently to my memory was regret. I remembered wanting to tell him how hot he looked in his snug bicycle shorts. But I didn't.

Scott was killed the next day, hit by a truck whose driver didn't see him pedal into the intersection on his way to work. I'd squandered the last hours of our lives together nurturing my annoyance with coarse grit sandpaper and all the while thinking I had the luxury of time to smooth the agitation with an indulgent polishing of steel wool.

Getting flowers from my dead husband was what I classified as a "whammy o' grief." After Scott's accident I worked very hard to avoid them. I stayed away from people, places, and things that could collapse the fragile composure I'd constructed. It wasn't easy.

Grief is an unfamiliar room on a moonless night. You move slowly, cautiously. Your arms reach out, swaying from side to side to find the oak dresser. Your feet slide along the carpet, feeling for the leg of a chair or a chest of blankets. The light switch is never where you remember. Someone has moved the rocker.

Whammy.

All of my planning and sidestepping hadn't prepared me for flowers from Scott. *Whammy*.

I took the box of montbretia into the basement, where I could wail without distracting passing motorists. I lay there, face down in a pile of laundry, until my sobs mellowed into sighs and my sinuses felt like they had been packed with a king-sized comforter. I realized it was almost time for my son, Ky, to come home from school, so I blew my nose and moved to the back porch, where sun and air would dry me out. While waiting for Ky, I fell asleep.

"Mom?"

I popped up like a mom-in-the-box ready to deliver the after-school litany.

"How was school? Do you have any homework? What do I have to sign?"

Ky reached out to touch my cheek; his blue-gray eyes dancing with mischief. "Mom, you look like a waffle."

I rubbed my cheek. Sure enough, my nap in the wicker chair had left me marked. Embossed or not, I couldn't let him distract me from the one bit of motherly behavior I still performed with proficiency.

"Kyle," I said, slowly enunciating his given name, "what do you have for homework?"

He headed for the back door and the refrigerator. "Not much. I'll do it after I clear the poop deck and mow the lawn." He stopped halfway through the door. "Well, I'll probably have to do it after practice. But I don't have much."

The screen door slammed. I heard the quick opening and closing of the refrigerator. There was nothing inside to satisfy a thirteen-year-old's growing body—only blue Kool-Aid, milk, and a tub of margarine. My stomach turned in shame. Ky bounded from the house carrying half a package of saltines and headed for the tool shed. The next day I'd go to the grocery store, I told myself, ready or not.

Louise Giovanelli came through the back gate just as I was watering the montbretia. She carried a napkin-covered basket that matched her crisply pressed navy capri pants and sailor-collared shirt.

"Mibby," she called, pulling out each vowel like taffy, "it's lemon scone day!"

Louise's bed-and-breakfast, the Garden House, was across the alley from my house. On Wednesdays, she baked lemon scones saturated with sweet cream butter. If her guests were the least bit health conscious, there were leftovers for her less discriminating neighbors—namely me.

Louise humphed herself onto the bottom stair of the porch, cradling the basket on her lap. Before she had time to gather a thought, Blink rested his chin on her knee and twitched his nose at the basket. Louise moved one stair higher. Blink sat on his haunches and made Louise the object of his devotion. She rose another step.

"Sugar baby, for heaven's sake, what are you planting now?" she asked in the velvet timbre of her Louisiana drawl.

"I'm planting Lucifer," I said, referring to the variety name of the montbretia. I knew Louise would love the idea of putting the devil in a hole. I didn't dare tell her the bulbs had come from Scott. I was having enough trouble breathing around the emotion in my throat. I turned away from the narrowing of her deep blue eyes, knowing she had noticed the puffs of flesh under my eyes but wouldn't ask. That was why I loved Louise.

"Oh, really?" she said, twisting her blond pageboy off her neck. "Ready for a break? I could use a cold drink."

Since Scott's death, Louise had made it her job to call on me at least once a day. A well-heeled debutante thirty-something years past, she always thought up a bona fide reason for coming. Lemon scones were one of her best, but the raspberry dream muffins from her Monday menu also earned her an enthusiastic welcome. Her imagination was challenged on days her guests ate to the last crumb. Then she came with questions like, "Mibby, how do you get the li'l ol' bugs out of the window on your stove?" That one had kept us occupied for almost two hours as we read the owner's manual and tried to remove parts of the stove. We finally agreed to let the bugs mummify where they'd fallen.

Louise came to make sure my boat was still tied to the dock, that the knot hadn't loosened and set me adrift. She tightened the knot with love, southern style—indulgent and usually fattening.

Only after Louise and I had downed our drinks and were chewing on ice cubes did Blink give up his post and trot down the garden path to the poop deck.

Ky came out of the house dressed for baseball practice. "Blink, I just cleaned that!"

Grass stains colored the knees of his uniform, and a wide stripe of red clay smudged the left hip. I tried to remember the last time I'd done the laundry. I couldn't. Six months after Scott's death, I was still surprised by the normal events of an ordered life, like Ky going off to baseball practice or Louise measuring out the ingredients for her scones.

How can such ordinary things keep going on when I've been cemented in place for so long?

Louise handed Ky a scone. "Have you had dinner, hon?"

"I'm eating at Salvador's house." He turned to me. "Mom, Salvador's dad will drive us to practice and bring us home."

When he leaned close to kiss me good-bye, I made a mental note to do the laundry.

"Mibby?" Louise said after Ky left, watching the ice swirl in the bottom of her glass. "Are you fixin' to let your hair grow?"

I swept loose strands of hair out of my eyes and refastened them with a butterfly clip. "I haven't decided."

The line of questioning made me nervous. Other seemingly innocent inquiries about my hair had led to a frenetic perm and a misadventure with a sun-streaking kit, all at the hands of Louise.

"Some wispy bangs would soften your forehead. Do you have some scissors handy?"

I promised her I'd think about it. Before she walked back across the alley, Louise gathered my hands and pressed them to her heart. Our foreheads touched as she prayed, "Sweet Jesus, shelter this precious child with your everlasting arms. Amen."

She left when she saw I wouldn't drift away.

After a shower, I slipped into one of Scott's T-shirts I'd scavenged from his laundry basket after his funeral. I breathed deeply as I pulled it over my head, hoping to evoke his presence with a few drops of dried sweat and some sloughed skin cells. But sleeping in the shirt for six months had diminished its magic.

Blink and I shared lemon scones in front of the television in my bedroom. I chased mine with the last of the blue Kool-Aid and added the empty glass to the growing collection on my nightstand.

Six o'clock. The hour of coming home. I upped the volume on the television to mask the sound of my neighbors slamming their car doors as they arrived home from work. But even over the din of soft drink commercials, the sound of closing doors coughed for my attention. Unwittingly, my heart pounded a welcoming beat to each coming-home noise they sounded.

Opie was explaining to Andy Griffith his earnest need for a huntin' dawg when Ky slammed the front door and clicked the deadbolt into place. The stairs creaked loudly as he bounded up. He dropped his duffel bag and cleats in front of my grandmother's pink damask chair. Before I could protest, he raised his hands in surrender.

"I know! Don't sit down until you take a shower."

"And put those clothes in the washing machine."

He came from the shower to the doorway of my room with his sandy hair slicked back. I wanted to invite him in; I wanted to hold him tightly in my arms and smell that warm place behind his ear.

If he took one step toward me . . .

"I'm going to do my homework now," he said, leaving for his room with the last scone and a glass of water.

After the late local news, I checked on Ky. Blink raised his head from Ky's belly when I moved closer to listen for breathing. So still. His right arm was draped over his forehead with his palm open to the ceiling like he was shielding his eyes from the sun. I touched his palm. Although his fingers closed against the tickle, he didn't wake. Alive. He slept on top of the covers, his young boy body hot from forging the man body within.

I moved his book bag from the foot of his bed to the middle of the doorway where he wouldn't miss it. By loading his bag at night, Ky gained two minutes of sleep each morning, something his growing body coveted more than food. It took him twenty-three minutes from alarm to out the door. No more, no less. In that time he fixed his own breakfast of instant oatmeal and juice. My only morning job was to send him off with a prayer for protection and a quick kiss.

I studied the gallery of Ky's dragon art spotlighted by the hallway light. His latest dragon creature lay on his desk waiting to be added to the wall. It dripped blood from the corner of its mouth and held a sinewy carcass in bloodstained claws. Those were new details. I promised myself I'd talk to him about the gore.

Blink followed me into my bedroom and waited patiently while I spread the sheet on my side of the bed. After I crawled into Scott's place, the dog hopped up and nestled against my back. Soon his breathing beat out a rhythm deep and even. Blink and David Letterman lulled me into a shallow sleep.

MAY

3

Too hot for May, low 90s. Hosta leaves almost completely unfurled. Hope they bloom this year. Trying something new in pots by front door. No more geraniums! I'm tired of fighting budworms. Giving upright fuchsia a chance at center stage with some pansies, nasturtiums, and dwarf marguerites as supporting cast.

Margaret gasped when I unsheathed the pruning shears. "What are you going to do with those?"

Margaret had called early Monday about her Don Juan roses. She said two of the five weren't doing well, especially the one on the end, and wanted me to take a look. She had understated the first plant's distress. Mostly bare and brown, the rose had only two canes supporting leaves, and those were twisted and anemic. None of the usual villains seemed guilty of the injury. No insect borer holes. No spider mites. Not even a dusting of powdery mildew.

The split-rail fence along Margaret's front yard bent from the burden of the four other Don Juan roses. A profusion of burgundy-tinted leaves and sprays of eager buds testified to the plants' health and care, with only the slightest dulling of leaves on the second rose. No big worry there.

I slipped the shears back into place before I turned to answer Margaret. The morning sun glinted off the sequined clips holding an éclair twist of gray hair on each side of her head. She held her hands over her heart as she waited for my response. Tiny beads of sweat collected in the coarse hairs of her upper lip. I resisted the urge to check my own lip.

"I just need to nick the bark a little to look for living tissue," I said.

Blink, my business partner, lifted his head from the grass and narrowed his eyes. It was the same look he had given me when I'd put diet dog food in his bowl.

"Will it hurt the plant?" she asked.

I looked to Blink for support, but he had already rolled onto his side and into dreamland. "No, I just need a little peek. The plant won't even notice." That was true.

I started with small nicks high on the central leader, looking for the greenish tissue of life. Nothing. I worked my way down the canes to the base of the plant. Only the two canes with the pathetic leaves had a hint of living tissue.

"Well . . ." I said, sliding my shears back into their sheath, "there's a tiny bit of life in these two canes."

"That's wonderful," she said through a relieved sigh.

I hadn't intended to encourage her. "Margaret, that really isn't enough to support the plant. Let me dig it out for you."

"It's a little soon for that, don't you think?" She flipped a dismissive wrist, her red fingernails fanning the air. "We can always hope for a miracle."

She agreed to let me remove the dead canes after I promised to call the county extension agent about her rose. "You know, Mibby, them roses are very special to me." She raised her eyes, and I looked up, too. Wispy clouds stretched across the corners of the sky like cobwebs. A smile deepened the creases around her eyes and sparked the light within. "Come in for some iced tea when you're done."

Margaret was one of my maintenance customers. I did the fussy work in her garden—clearing away plant debris and deadheading spent flowers from her perennial bed. It took about five minutes every other week. I mostly drank iced tea or coffee in her kitchen while we talked about our sons—hers, a successful fifty-four-year-old dentist, married to his third wife, who happened to be a gold digger. Mine, a thirteen-year-old second baseman who longed to hit a home run. Her son sent me a check each month to keep his mother out of the hot sun, but Margaret was smart enough to do her gardening in the early morning hours before the sun was up. She said she'd rather I had the money than her son's floozy.

My twenty maintenance customers were a study in humanity with their individual endearments and foibles, such as Mr. Chandler the neatnik, Mrs. Pierson, who stopped gardening after a bout of skin cancer, and Roseanne, the lady of the manor. When I'd started my garden design business, I'd hoped my maintenance accounts would become unnecessary, but new clients weren't coming fast enough. As far as designers went, I was at the bottom of the food chain. Clients called me for a specific need, maybe a showcase perennial border or a splash of color by the front door. But I'd also designed vegetable gardens and flowerpots for outdoor weddings. Most of my work came to me by word of mouth.

I wished my customers would start talking.

Blink was snoring in the shade of Margaret's honey locust tree when I stepped into the cooled air of her house. Goose bumps rose on my arms and intensified the sting from the scratches I'd gotten wrestling the dead canes into her garbage can.

Margaret counted the wounds on my arms and legs before turning my chin to get a better look at the scratch along my right cheek. "It looks like there's still some fight in ol' Don Juan yet. You better clean these out. I'll get some ointment."

When she was satisfied my wounds had been treated, she served the promised iced tea in a tall jelly glass. I drank half of it straight down. She refilled my glass, and I watched the icy moons tumble and crowd back to the top of the glass.

Margaret's kitchen was function over fashion. One narrow counter held a chipped porcelain sink. The refrigerator and stove, evidently afterthoughts, stood in tight formation along the adjacent wall. Margaret and I sat at a chrome and laminate table dotted with cigarette burns—more where I sat, because it was Quentin's old seat. A wall of windows looked out on her iris beds. The bearded ladies stood frozen in their regal postures as though posing for an unseen artist. Blink, unimpressed by the company he kept, stretched in his sleep.

Margaret turned her glass in the puddle it had left on the table. Only the clatter of the evaporative cooler and the muffled voices from a faraway radio filled the silence until she spoke. "Quentin gave me them roses on our fiftieth wedding anniversary, one for each decade we was married. He scratched himself up pretty good, too, when he planted them. He was so proud of himself, finding them Don Juan roses. That's what I called him, my Don Juan."

The roses were aptly named. Like the famous lover, they blazed red with passion and climbed vigorously to be noticed by their admirers. Quentin must have lit a fire in Margaret.

She leaned across the table, resting her pudgy hand over mine. Her thumbnail was painted apricot, while all the other nails glowed cherry. "How are you doing?"

Most people didn't want the answer to that question. As the widow, it was my job to paste a smile on my face, square my shoulders, and free them from worry. "Better every day," I'd say. That was not a total lie. I *was* better than the day I had the flu so bad I vomited blood. I *was* better than the day my water broke and I almost delivered Ky in the pickle aisle at the grocery store. And I *was* better than the day I realized that the pain of loss would own me forever.

But when Margaret invited me into her cool kitchen and poured me a glass of iced tea and planted herself in a chair as if she had found her final resting place and then asked me how I was doing, she really wanted to know. I had an answer ready.

"Some days are better than others."

On better days I didn't have to remind myself to breathe. On better days I was completely dressed before I had the urge to crawl back into bed and turn into a rock. On a better than best day, I read with interest a recipe on a soup can and clipped it off to save for later. Yes, some days were better than others.

She stopped turning her glass and found me with her milky blue eyes, waiting for more, but I didn't trust myself to continue. I studied my fingerprints on the frosty glass instead.

Her voice was lower when she continued. "I'm going to tell you something you won't believe, but it's completely true. Someday you'll get red-hot angry with yourself."

Someday?

My chair scraped, then caught on the cracked linoleum.

"You'll cry yourself to sleep because you didn't think about Scott for one whole hour."

Impossible.

I poured the iced tea into the sink and set the glass down a little too hard on the counter.

"Then you'll go a few hours or most of a day without thinking about him, and you'll think you've forgotten him."

Never.

I made a beeline for the screen door but stopped short. I

wanted to be gone but not rude, not to Margaret. I watched Blink roll onto his back and stretch.

Margaret got out of her chair and leaned against the doorframe to watch Blink sleep. "I want you to know this, because it will make you crazy. But it shouldn't. It just means that your mind has decided to go on, even if your heart hasn't."

I pushed through the door.

"Thanks, Margaret. I really enjoyed—" enjoyed what? The intrusion?—"the iced tea."

Margaret and Blink followed me to the bottom step. "It doesn't mean you love him less. I still love my Quentin." Her hand was on my arm. "And wonder of wonders, my ol' heart longs to love again. Ain't that something?"

"Come on, Blink. It's time to go bye-bye."

"Now, don't you forget to call the extension agent about ol' Don Juan," she called as I pulled Blink to the truck.

"Don't worry. I won't."

Blink sneezed, and the wind pushed the shower back into the cab of the truck.

"Blink!"

He looked at me before squeezing his head back out the passenger's side window, which had never opened completely. I pressed his rump to the seat. "Sit down, Blink." His rump bounced off the seat like he'd sat on hot metal. Having a dog for a business partner had its difficulties. But if I insisted on leaving the window up, he'd have dissolved the partnership for sure.

Leaving Margaret's neighborhood of rectangular houses, I pulled onto the business loop that funneled interstate traffic through the heart of Orchard City, a name created for promotional brochures meant to draw people to this barren valley in the mid-1800s. Fortunately, some visionaries and irrigation engineers, but mostly guys with shovels, had made the name prophetic.

Most of the businesses along the highway had been built during the aesthetically-starved era of the mining booms in the fifties and seventies. They were graciously grandfathered into the landscaping ordinances that required green space for all commercial properties. Skirts of asphalt or concrete reached from the foundations to the curbs of used-car lots and motels. An occasional tree grew courageously from a hole in the concrete. But most often, harried business owners opted for decorative rocks enhanced by larger decorative rocks and gnarled juniper logs. It was a plant-lover's nightmare, but its severity had a bright side. It served to filter out the less adventurous from discovering the more beautiful parts of Orchard City and staying.

When I turned off the highway and onto the road leading to the western region of town, the miracle that water brought to the desert unfolded. A cross-hatching of irrigation canals carried life to the lush pastures supporting herds of cattle and fields of alfalfa and hay, orchards of fruit, and vineyards.

Everything in Orchard City was a ten-minute drive from the center of town, edging up to twelve as the traffic in the growing community increased. That meant Blink's rump was in my face from Margaret's house on the south side of the river to Walled Garden Nursery on the western edge of the city, more than twenty minutes. I pulled into the shady parking lot and waited for the post-ignition shimmy of the Daisy Mobile to stop. Blink headed straight for the fountain inside the front gate for a long drink. Reloading.

Walled Garden Nursery started as an adobe house on ten acres. Judith, the owner, built a six-foot-tall textured wall around the house to mimic the enclosed patios of Mexico. Once inside the gate, customers walked on tiled pathways through the tables of bedding plants and perennials that were her specialty. Baskets of flowers hung from the lath shade structure that covered the patio area, and running fountains provided shopping music for the customers. The house included Judith's office and a gift shop for gourmet gardeners.

The patio hummed with urgency. Gardeners eager to beat the intense heat of summer reached over tables laden with plants for the best petunias or columbines. I wound my way to Judith's office through a traffic jam of red wagons loaded with vegetables and flowers. She sat at her desk eating a hamburger with one hand and signing paychecks with the other. I moved a pile of plant catalogs from a chair and plopped down in front of the fan. She didn't look up.

"I'll be done in just a minute," she said. Damp curls striped with blond and gray clung to Judith's neck as she double-checked the figures on the computer screen before she signed the checks.

I kicked off my Birkenstocks and made myself at home. She pressed the last bite of hamburger into her mouth and pushed herself away from the large oak desk. "Why didn't you say something, girl? I thought you were a . . ."

This was where Judith usually slipped in a colorful adjective, but she let *salesman* stand alone. Blink trotted into the office and rested his head on her lap. Judith gave his ears an enthusiastic scratch as she slipped him a French fry.

"You spoil that dog rotten," I said, wiggling my toes in the breeze of the fan.

A little frown creased Judith's face as she looked me over. "Goodness gracious, what happened to you?"

I ran my fingers along the scratch on my face. The welt rose thick and hot from the corner of my right eye to my jaw. "I fought the rose and the rose won."

She handed me a message from a faded Adidas shoebox labeled *Mibby* that sat on the corner of her desk. "Be sure to wear sunscreen on that until it heals. Redheads scar real easy."

I rubbed a bare spot in my left eyebrow. *Yes, I know.*

I'd first worked for Judith part time when Ky had gone off to kindergarten. It was the best way to get acquainted with the plants that thrived in this red rock country. I rarely brought home a complete paycheck, but I did get the yard landscaped at an employee's discount. After a couple of years, she asked me to try designing for the customers. Cottage gardens congested with nostalgic favorites such as hollyhock and lavender and daylilies were getting popular, but folks needed help creating the happy-accident-of-nature look. I loved the challenge. My first designs were embarrassing, but I got better. It was Judith who had convinced Scott I had the talent to be on my own. Now she directed requests for small garden designs to Mibby Garrett at Perennially Yours.

"This guy has called a couple of times. Ben something," Judith said. She put on her tattered straw hat and snuffed out her cigarette. "He seems a little anxious to get some roses planted. It might be a nice in-and-out job for you."

They were never in-and-out jobs, but it was pointless to contradict her. I stuffed the pink paper into my pocket.

She pointed a knowing finger at my nose. "Now, Mibby," she scolded. "Don't put off calling this guy."

Dismissed, I collected and paid for some annuals to plant in my own flowerpots by the front door. I didn't really feel like doing it, but the empty pots were a constant reminder that things were not normal, and at least for Ky, I tried to do normal things. Before I left the garden center, I put a sold tag on a Don Juan rosebush for Margaret, just in case. I found Blink watering an arborvitae.

The direct route back to my house ran straight from the garden center to the historic district near downtown. But I took a small detour east on Carpenter Avenue, south on Dominguez, west on

Otto—to avoid the long light at Ninth—and a couple turns later, I was on my street, Crawford Avenue. The houses there reflected the eclectic tastes and budgets of early homebuilders in the West. Some, like Louise, made their homes into charming bed-and-breakfast inns catering to the slower-paced visitors to our valley. A few of the smaller homes in the neighborhood were rentals that received varying degrees of care.

Our house was one of the sensible western Victorians dressed for every day. Louise said it was sitting around in its underwear—but not the mostly-for-show kind. Our house wore tan BVDs with a tasteful trim of evergreen and barberry. No lace. Five windows and one door spaced evenly in two rows created the façade. Like me, it had a lopsided roofline and an unpretentious front porch.

Out of some romantic delusion about quaintness and old homes, Scott and I had purchased the house when we first moved to Orchard City. A succession of owners had covered up its straightforward charm with dark wood paneling and gold shag carpet. Most of the windows were painted shut. The previous owner let her son paint all of the ceilings black and each door a color usually reserved for bus stop benches. Somewhere in its history, the kitchen went Mediterranean with glazed tiles, dark walnut cabinets, and orange swirl countertops. The appliances occupied two rooms and the porch. Preparing a holiday meal qualified as aerobic exercise.

The only gleam of beauty in the place was the grand oak staircase that had remarkably escaped any attempts at modernization. Countless hands had polished the newel-post to a warm patina as their owners whipped over the bottom stair. The real estate agent knew he had a sale when Scott lovingly inspected each baluster as we ascended to the second floor. For me, it was the creaking of the stairs under my feet. The sound reminded me of my grandmother's heavy steps at the end of the day and the deep-throated hymns she sang as she lumbered by my door on her way to bed.

After we moved in, Scott and I focused most of our time and resources into the house, starting and stopping as our fortunes ebbed and flowed. At first, the results were functional only. The foundation had to be wrestled back from the termites. The plumbing, electrical, and heating systems all needed to be replaced long before the money was available. To protect the aging clapboard siding the first winter, we painted it a hummingbird green we'd found in the bargain bin at Kmart. The people across the street moved the next weekend.

Priorities shifted our goals. When we found out Ky was on the way, it became very important to insulate. We rushed to refinish the floors when he started crawling. Blink made it necessary to go outside and build a solid fence.

In a lot of ways, remaking the house made our marriage. As walls were removed to unclutter the floor plan, Scott and I shed the habits of singleness to build a relationship of openness and function. Paint colors from opposite sides of the spectrum turned into a sensible antique white as we learned to compromise. It took trust to yield to each other's flights of whimsy, which meant we ended up with akimbo shower tiles and a door stained the color of railroad ties. These mistakes became the things we cherished most, because they represented the risk and reward of trusting someone with your heart. The house became more a part of us, the Garrett family, than anyone else. It reflected our movements and our tastes. We made it to fit us.

We saved the kitchen and a small addition with a wraparound porch until last. Scott worked with Droop, our carpenter, and his crew after work and on Saturdays, but the work halted while we waited for the cabinets to arrive from Denver. I was using plywood counters over sawhorses and cooking oatmeal on a Coleman stove when the police came to the door to tell me about Scott. I thought it was Droop with the new cabinets.

I burned the oatmeal.

Blink was as eager to get out of the truck as he had been to get in. He raced past me to the front door. While I finagled the old lock, he danced from one foot to the other anticipating his crunchy Fido food. Inside, I sorted through the mail. I put a pastel envelope into a shoebox above the refrigerator. Everything else had the disposable look of glossy paper. I pushed the play button on the flashing answering machine and looked for a piece of paper and a pencil.

Beep. "Mibby. Margot. Call me." *Click*. I laid down the pencil and waited for the mechanical voice to tell me the day and time she had called. "Thursday, one twenty-three P.M." Twelve twenty-three California time. She had called during her lunch hour. I didn't like calling her at the hospital. Each time I did, a new secretary grilled me for my true identity and intent before taking a message.

Beep. "Mibby." My sister again. "This is your weekly reminder to rejoin the land of the living." *Click*. "Thursday, one twenty-four P.M."

"Thanks, Margot." I rubbed my divided brow for the second time that day.

Beep. "Mrs. Garrett, this is Mrs. Friedlander, Ky's homeroom teacher. Please call me about Ky's midterm grades." She left her school and home phone numbers. I played the message again. Mrs. Friedlander's tone was businesslike, pleasant. I looked at my watch. Two-twenty. They weren't out of school yet. I made a mental note to talk to Ky about the message.

I pulled the pink message slip from my pocket and smoothed it on the plywood counter. It always took a little pep talk to make the first contact with a potential client.

You love your work, and you're good at it. You have three, no, two and a half years to start making a profit. Call this person or fill out an application at McDonald's.

The doorbell rang. I hesitated; I didn't want to lose my momentum. But it could've been Louise with the day's leftovers.

The porch was empty. But a small car with a lawnmower muffler pulled away from the curb as I opened the door. The car raced down the street, slowing only slightly for the stop sign at the corner. It looked like the paint had baked off the trunk and roof, leaving a faded band of yellow on the sides. Boxes and layers of clothing in the back seat obscured the person driving. A post stuck out the passenger window like a lance. Wrong address? I looked around the porch to see if the person had left anything. A brochure or a payment?

A delicate gold identification bracelet lay in an open swirl on the welcome mat. Two scrolled initials—A. G.—filled the small oval charm. The clasp was broken. It looked like it had caught on the doorknob. That meant the person had left quickly. But did it mean they were trying to open the door? I went back into the house and set the deadbolt. I wrapped the chain around my wrist. It slipped easily over my hand.

Just great. An Amazon warrior is stalking me.

I checked my watch. Fifteen minutes until Ky's dismissal bell rang. I slipped the bracelet into my pocket. Time enough for another phone call or two.

Ben *something* turned out to be Ben Martin. He answered on the seventh ring. I heard his hello as I put the phone in the cradle. I snatched it up again only to hear the dial tone. I considered throwing away his phone number.

McDonald's.

He answered after the first ring. "Yeah." His yeah said I'd better have a good reason for calling.

"Mr. Martin?"

"No." Silence. "Yeah."

McDonald's.

"Mr. Martin, this is Mibby Garrett of Perennially Yours Garden Designs."

"What are you selling?"

He had personality *and* charm.

McDonald's.

"Judith at Walled Garden Nursery gave me your name and number. She said you needed a rose garden designed. Do I have the right person?" *Breathe.*

Mr. Martin had to think about that. "Yes. Look, Libby—"

I almost let it slip. Chances were I'd never meet this man. But old habits die hard. "*Mmmm*ibby," I hummed into the phone.

"*Mm*ibby?"

"Yes, *Mm*ibby."

The air seeped out of his bluster. "I thought you were a telemarketer. They've called a lot today."

I considered asking for his wife. It was usually the women who had seen a glossy magazine spread of a cottage garden and called me. Before I could ask, Mr. Martin got down to business.

"When can you come?"

We settled on a ten-o'clock meeting the next morning, and I planned to take Blink in case Mr. Martin mistook me for an encyclopedia salesman. Blink could sneeze on him for me.

Next, I called the county extension service and left a message for Albert, the staff horticulturist. If anyone would know what was wrong with Margaret's rose, Albert would.

Phone calls done, I left the house to meet Ky. I walked in and out of the shade of the old ash trees. My T-shirt was sticking to my back by the time I crossed the street to the school.

The dismissal bell rang. Ky squinted as he walked into the

bright sun. When he saw me, he flashed a worried look back at the school and strode toward me with his head down. He turned for home. I fell in beside him. He shifted his book bag to his other shoulder.

"Is everything okay?" I asked.

"Yeah."

"Good."

"What are you doing here?" he asked.

I usually met Ky closer to home, within sight of the busy intersection he had to cross.

I wasn't ready to tell him about the visitor who had spooked me, so I said, "It's such a beautiful day, I thought I'd get a little exercise."

He finally looked at me. "You've been pruning roses again," he said with a smile.

Ky had inherited this generosity from his father, the willingness to forgive easily. I'd committed the cardinal sin of mothers of middle school boys. I showed up uninvited to escort him home without a functional purpose for being there. No orthodontist appointment. No post-school music lesson. His charity deserved something in kind. I asked him, "Ky, where would you like me to meet you?"

"Whadd'ya mean?"

"I mean when I walk to meet you after school," I said.

He watched his feet hit the pavement. "Maybe you could wait for me at home."

After Scott's accident, Ky had stopped riding his bike to school. He'd decided this on his own. I'm sure it was a favor to me.

"Maybe next year."

He started to protest, "Mom . . ." but let it fade. After a few more beats, he changed the subject. "I have a game at five."

This news altered my plans for a leisurely afternoon. As soon as we got home, I put his uniform in the washing machine and started the shortest cycle before ordering a pizza. The socks were damp dry when we heard Salvador's cleats clacking across the porch.

Ky threw the socks in his duffel bag and looked at my bare feet. "Maybe you could come next time?"

"You better get going. We'll talk—"

But he had already pulled the door closed hard on his way out to the car. I reopened it and yelled, "Wear your seatbelt!"

That was motherly and caring, wasn't it?

After he left, I showered and settled in front of the television. Louise slipped in the back door with a basket of apple cinnamon muffins with bonus nuts. I showed her the bracelet and told her about the car speeding away. We listed everyone we knew who had a name beginning with *A*—Agnes Humphrey and Angie Mangold and Alberto Martinez and Albert Strait from the extension office. Small list, no matches.

"Your last name starts with a *G*," Louise said. Her eyebrows rose in speculation. "Maybe it's a long lost—very large—relative coming to bring you money."

I thought about my dead father and grandmother, my still-adolescent mother weaving seashell necklaces on the Santa Monica pier, and my sister, Margot, whom Louise declared tighter than a girdle at a potluck supper.

"I don't think so."

No matter. It was time for *The Barefoot Contessa*, our favorite cooking show. When it was over, Louise got up to leave. "Sweet pea, remember, you are precious in His sight. He will shelter you under His wings."

Precious me had sent my son to his game in a damp and dingy uniform. I'd be lucky if God didn't hit me with one of His wings.

By the time I'd remembered Mrs. Freeloader's phone call, Ky was in a deep funk over a lost baseball game. Worse yet, his error had allowed the winning run. It wasn't the right time to talk to him about school.

MAY

4

Possibility of 93° today. Ugh. Bitterroot doesn't seem to mind—wears a thick wreath of pink flowers. Pruned back viburnum. Seems early. Will miss spicy fragrance. Roses starting to bloom. Sun Runner already has spider mites—leaves stippled and webs present. Is it going to be one of those summers?

While drinking my morning coffee on the back porch, I thought back on the day I'd watched my mother pack for her trip to Washington, D.C. She'd filled her suitcase with jeans and embroidered Mexican blouses. As she stuffed her underwear into the gaps around her tops, she explained her mission to Margot and me.

"I'm doing this for you girls," she said, gathering toiletries from the bathroom. "We're getting close to the deadline, and the Equal Rights Amendment will die if we don't force an indefinite extension for ratification. Thousands and thousands—maybe a hundred thousand—women will march on Washington when we put out the call. Your lives will be so much better. No shackles, no limitations."

Mother dropped her brush on the thick carpet. The bristles held long strands of red hair that matched mine. I pushed the brush under the bed with my foot.

"Will you be gone long?" I asked.

"No, baby. Just until the amendment is ratified."

My sister reached under the bed for the brush and laid it in my mother's suitcase. When my mother turned to gather her sweatshirts, Margot stuck her tongue out at me. I was too busy wondering why mother needed sweatshirts in August to care.

Margot let the screen door slam behind her when she joined me on the porch later. I held my tears like they were the last two caramels from my Christmas stocking, knowing I would savor them later in a secret place. My mother and her friend pulled away from the curb in a convertible Mustang the color of a flame. I sent her a silent plea full of promises of good behavior. It was a silver thread that I tied to the bumper. The end of the thread flew through my fingers when the car turned the corner and my mother waved without looking back.

Margot socked me in the arm with her paralyzer punch, the fist with one knuckle extended to meet the bone of my arm. A sharp pain raced to my fingertips and shocked them into numbness.

"You aren't crying, are you?" Margot asked.

Tears pressed for release, but I refused them. "No way."

"Good. She isn't worth it." Margot returned to *The Galloping Gourmet*. I ran the eight blocks to my grandmother's garden.

My grandmother found me between the rows of corn making mud pudding with my tears. She settled onto the soft earth and pulled me into her lap. The smell of peach jam that clung to her apron reopened the floodgates. I sobbed until I'd tied a new silver thread, this one a bit thinner, to my grandma.

She opened her hanky, spat on the corner, and worked patiently at the muddy crust on my face. "Jesus cried in a garden," she said.

"Did His mama leave, too?"

"No, but His mama couldn't help Him."

"Was His daddy working?" My father was a fireman. The world crumbled when he left for his shift and had to be rebuilt when he returned.

"Yes. He was working." She gathered my hair into a ponytail and secured it with a rubber band from her pocket. "I just wanted you to know that Jesus understands what it feels like to be all alone." She cupped my chin in her hands and looked over her glasses at me, so I stretched a closed-mouthed grin over my teeth. It was enough.

"I have to check my jam, see if the jars sealed." Grandma struggled to her feet. "Come in when you're ready."

Horned tomato worms guarded the entrance to my grandmother's garden. My sister, squeamish about bugs big enough to ride, stayed outside the rows of tomatoes and zucchinis and lettuce. I was eternally grateful for the respite, however short.

I lay there watching the corn tassels paint the sky blue until I heard my sister call.

"I know you're in there!"

If I lie very, very still . . .

"Bring me some strawberries!"

"Why should I?" I clamped my hand over my mouth.

Silence.

"I'm coming in!"

I jumped up to flee. The rock hit me above my left eye. It took twelve stitches to close the gash.

The small disaster gave me hope. I wished upon three stars and a rabbit's foot that my mother would race home, for she was always her most tender when she fussed over my wounds. I imagined her telling the woman in the orange car to turn around immediately. And when she arrived home, no matter how late it was, she would come up the stairs to put a cool cloth on my throbbing head and sing about mockingbirds and diamonds.

I watched the roses on the wallpaper fade to smudges and then disappear with the darkness. I fell asleep waiting for her footsteps on the stairs.

I considered calling Margot back before I left for my appointment with Ben Martin. I played with the gap in my eyebrow while listening to the weather report. Another record-breaker. I grabbed my clipboard and called Blink to the truck. He didn't come.

I found him watching Louise's guests eating breakfast under the wisteria arbor. The man and woman wore skimpy running clothes and efficient hairstyles. They ate yogurt sprinkled with granola instead of Louise's Friday delight, caramel pecan sticky buns. That meant Louise had leftovers. I apologized to the couple for Blink's attentiveness, but they seemed pleased with his company. They explained how they missed Forest and Stream. I assumed they missed their dogs, not a magazine.

Louise came out with a pitcher of orange juice. "Mibby, do you have time for breakfast?" She frowned at Blink.

I looked at my watch. Mr. Martin lived in a rural area almost five miles to the north. I had about ten minutes before I had to coax Blink away from his new friends. I shot Blink a warning glance and followed Louise into her kitchen.

Every room in Louise's house was decorated with a flower theme, excluding her husband's den, of course. Only cattails and mallards graced Manley's hallowed walls. The kitchen was the sunflower room. I'd helped her hang the black-and-white gingham wallpaper bordered with a garland of golden sunflowers. It had been the supreme test of our friendship. Matching seams meant different things to Louise and me. A bouquet of sunflowers sat on the kitchen table, where a cup of coffee and a prayer of forgiveness had reinstated our friendship.

The fact that Louise and I were friends was its own kind of miracle. We were a study in contrasts, especially in the revealing light of morning. The differences began with how we viewed clothing. Louise wore outfits. Everything from earrings to socks was carefully coordinated to a theme or color. A butterfly print dress required dangling—never studded—butterfly earrings and a tiny butterfly decal on her left thumbnail. The shade of amethyst precisely matched the delicate purple of the crease-pressed camp shirt. The socks matched, too.

I subscribed to the indigo rule of fashion. I wore denim every day; it went with everything. I only started wearing socks that matched my T-shirts due to Louise's influence. I owned a pair of everyday Birkenstocks and a dress-up pair of Birkenstocks. They were suitable for shorts, pants, and skirts, which meant I wore them to church.

I had never seen Louise without makeup, and her hair was always doing something appropriate. She liked jewel tones, so her face resembled a stained glass window lit from within. I kept a tub of Carmex in my pocket to keep it warm and squishy. I loved the way it felt on my cracked lips. When Scott was alive, I occasionally wore mascara and Nudie-Cutie lip gloss to church and Christmas parties—but only because he'd suggested it.

Louise was born with straight hair asking for permission to curl. My hair? I had surrendered control of my rebellious locks to Louise on several occasions with the promise of carefree maintenance. But really, how could a woman with submissive blond hair understand the willful defiance of my chili powder hair? My head was subdivided into regions of wavy, straight, coarse, and fine hair. For years, I folded, stapled, and mutilated it into compliance. I was done with all of that. It was on its way to a perpetual French braid.

Louise saw the world through eyes the color of a high mountain lake. I looked through a muddy puddle. She was the poster child for southern complexion, conforming pleasantly to all references to cream and fruit. I was a ginger-spotted pink cheeks bird. We had one thing in common, though. Our body shapes qualified us for a fruit salad. Louise was an orange; I was a pear.

In her sunflower kitchen, Louise leaned toward me. "Just between you, me, and the lamppost, those folks out there are nuttier than Aunt Pansy's fruitcake."

She wrapped a sticky bun in a gingham napkin and put it in a basket with a banana. "They brought their own food, towels, and sheets. Isn't that a little weird?"

"Totally."

"I've got just the thing for your scratch." She pulled a white tube out of her junk drawer and smeared the soothing ointment along my cheek. It felt better immediately.

She pushed my bangs out of my eyes. "Are you fixin' to wear a hat today, sugar?"

"I have one in the truck." Did I? I wasn't sure. I headed for the door.

"Mibby?"

I stopped.

"You will know the truth, and the truth will set you free. Jesus said that."

Yikes!

I got my hat from the house before I left.

I pulled over to the side of the road and double-checked the address. This was it. The house stood—or did it float?—forty feet from the road. A narrow deck with a low railing skirted the house. Three steps supported on cinderblocks led to the front door. The structure looked like a houseboat temporarily moored for repairs—

and it needed some. I could tell the house had once been a haughty shade of pink from the shadows left by the shutters, but a sinister brown peeked through the curled flakes of faded pink, threatening to reclaim its territory. Several panes were missing from one of the windows. I checked the address again.

If the house was needy, the yard was destitute. The lawn looked like an abandoned pasture. Mallow was more prevalent than bluegrass or rye. A line of junipers lapped at the front deck like frozen waves. Mice, not halibut, inhabited those waves. Dead patches showed where the mice had chewed through the bark last winter. I shuddered. The skeletal remains of a barberry shrub, or something related to it, marked the end of the driveway. I counted three large cottonwoods, two in the back and one in the front. They had lost their stately forms to disease, and dead branches hung precariously over the house. Even in their poor condition, the trees were the jewels of the landscape for the shade they provided.

Blink followed me eagerly to the front door but balked at the stairs. I listened for a radio or voices. Nothing. I tapped the screen door lightly and waited. I tapped a little harder and then opened the screen door to knock on the wooden door. The screen door twisted out of my hand and fell to the deck.

"That worthless door." I recognized Mr. Martin's voice behind me. "Just leave it where it fell."

Mr. Martin wiped his hands down the front of his shirt, and they left smudges of pale paint on his T-shirt. He offered his right hand. "I'm Ben Martin."

Ben Martin was a whole lot younger than I had expected him to be. This was not your typical rose gardener. He looked to be my age, maybe younger, much taller. Although his hair was hidden under a ball cap, I could tell it was closely trimmed. He hadn't shaved in a couple of days, but his beard didn't hide the square line of his jaw. He wore cowboy boots with his cutoff sweat pants.

The legs above the boots were tanned and muscled. Blink trotted off toward the junipers.

Always start with the obvious. "Painting?"

"This pink has got to go," he said. His eyes were two Oreo cookies floating in milk.

"I like the color you've chosen." I pointed at his shirt and introduced myself. He frowned at my cheek. "It's nothing," I said. "Just a battle I lost with a rosebush."

"Hope you won the war."

"Not yet."

I handed Mr. Martin the Perennially Yours brochure I gave to new clients. He did what most of my clients do. He folded it in half and put it in his pocket. In a couple of days it would be nothing but paper pulp in the lint trap of his dryer. If Scott had been there, I would have said, *I told you so*.

Mr. Martin took me to his backyard through a chain link gate wired open. He closed his paint supplies against the drying heat while I looked around. A small sprinkler coaxed a new growth of green out of the lawn. Shaded by one of the healthier cottonwoods, remnants of the lawn had survived the imposed drought. Beyond the chain link fence stood a metal outbuilding. An older truck filled with boxes and bedroom furniture was parked inside. Blink investigated a row of three mismatched wooden sheds.

His property bordered the unirrigated region of the valley. The view, unencumbered by buildings or trees, was expansive. Orchard City sat just east of the apex in the horseshoe-shaped Grand Valley. To the northeast, rolling hills of Mancos shale reached for the Book Cliffs that rose two thousand feet above the valley floor. Barren from erosion, the rippled slopes resembled a shelf of books when the sun cast shadows on the ridges. In the morning light, they looked more like a continuous row of Mayan temples.

To the southeast, the world's largest flat-topped mountain

loomed six thousand feet over the valley. That day a few cottony clouds had collected around its top like leaves at the edge of a pond.

The Colorado Plateau walled us in along the southwest rim of the valley. Its shear cliffs blushed pink from iron-rich sandstone. A juniper-piñon forest greened the flat surfaces like sprinkles on a Bundt cake. I wondered if he had bought this place for the view.

I worked the dry soil of his yard with my shoe. "Mr. Martin—"

"Ben," he interrupted. Pale flesh radiated from the corners of his eyes. It matched the pale ring of flesh around his wedding finger.

"Ben, how can I help you?"

"I want to plant some roses."

He needed more than roses. "Where?"

"Over here. Under the bedroom window."

He led the way to a window on the far end of the house where a cottonwood cast a dense shadow.

"This isn't a good place for roses," I said.

Ben gestured to the sprinkler watering a patch of lawn. "I'll make sure they get water until I install a sprinkler system."

"It's not that," I countered. "It's the tree. Roses need a lot of sun to be happy."

"Are you sure?"

I assured him roses planted in the shade would disappoint him. "They'd be scraggily and stingy bloomers."

"They have to go here," he said. "My wife always planted a rose first thing when we moved into a new place, right under our bedroom window." His voice broke; my heart responded with a warning beat. Whammy alert.

Ben watched the sprinkler with his fists deep in his pockets. He drew in a breath and continued slowly. "We moved a lot. She said it felt more like home with a rosebush under the bedroom window. She loved the way they smelled." He told me he'd be right back and went into the house. This was my chance to leave. I looked for Blink. He was nowhere in sight. Typical.

Ben returned with a large loose-leaf notebook. "This is her scrapbook. It has all the roses she planted and where. I want to put them all right here." He handed me the scrapbook and spread his hands to mark acceptable boundaries for the rose bed.

He stopped talking. We stood there wondering who would say the forbidden words first: *dead, was, sorry, lonely, remember*. Not me. I called for Blink and started for the gate.

"I have plenty to get your plan started. Let me go home and mull this over."

Ben walked beside me wearing the universal look of the flummoxed male. I used my clipboard to shield my eyes and scanned the horizon for Blink. A ditch on the edge of the property looked like a happy hunting ground for dogs. I yelled in that direction.

"Blink!"

Best friend? I don't think so.

"I'll contact you in a few days, maybe a week," I said and walked faster. "Then I'll measure the yard and prepare a proposal drawing. Blink!" *I hope you like your new master*. "If you like it—the plan—I'll draw a final working plan and send you a bill."

I stopped at the door of my truck. Ben looked past me into the cab, counting empty Starbucks cups, no doubt. I grabbed the door handle. "Does that work for you?"

He tilted his head toward the cab. "The dog's right there."

Blink was sleeping on the seat. I pushed him to his side of the cab and turned the ignition.

Ben bent to speak to me. His voice came from a deep place. "It's been a long time since the funeral. I really need to get this done." He coughed into his hand. "It's what she would have wanted."

"Bye for now," I said. I ground the gears into reverse, pinging pebbles against the underside of the truck all the way down the driveway. From the road I saw Ben, hands on hips, watching me.

McDonald's, here I come!

I drove toward the airport and down a dirt road into barren Mancos slopes. I put my head on the steering wheel for a good cry. It seemed like I'd been caught in a strange subculture of death that recognized me as one of their own. They came at me with their unsolicited wisdom and tried to proselytize me into the fold. First Margaret, and now one of their fairest sons wanted a memorial garden. I was a magnet for death.

To prove my continued participation in life, to Blink anyway, I ate Louise's sticky bun all by myself. Blink's revenge was a puddle of drool on the passenger's seat.

When I first met Roseanne Mitchell, I wanted to dislike her. Perfect body—long and fluid. Perfect face—symmetrical and as smooth as a river stone. Perfect life—which for me meant having a living husband. Innovative hybridization would have been required to include Roseanne in a fruit salad with Louise and me, say a cross between a banana and an Elberta peach—the late summer variety with no stone and the sweetest, most rosy flesh.

If her baby girl, Phoebe, napped on the days I came, she worked alongside me, asking questions as we went and putting her slender fingers to any task I did. I almost felt guilty taking money from her, especially when she padded the check and wrote a note saying, "Mibby, you were here a lot longer than for the time you billed me. Take Ky to the movies. Love, Roseanne."

Roseanne lived in one of the most exclusive neighborhoods in the valley; exclusive not because it was situated for optimal views, but because the residents were determined to make it so. The houses rose conspicuously from the former farmland like the hotels on a Monopoly game board. In time, the trees and shrubs, I knew, would soften their arrogance.

While I worked at Roseanne's house, Blink had to stay in the truck. Her neighbor, Mr. Carpenter, was the subdivision's covenants enforcer. Evidently, the pastoral scene the developers strived for didn't include dogs sleeping in the shade. Blink worked his jowls, chewing a pitiful whine as I gathered my tools.

"Don't sass at me, Blink, or I'm going to fire you for sure." I worried a little about the revenge he would exact for this abandonment, so I gave him the chew bone I kept in the glove compartment for such an emergency.

Roseanne lifted the sunglasses from my nose. "Have you been crying?"

If they weren't going to hide my blotchy eyes, there was no sense looking at the world through smudged lenses. I put the sunglasses in my pocket. "I'm okay."

Roseanne studied me with chestnut eyes flecked with gold while I trimmed the spent blossoms off a Korean lilac.

"Really?" she asked.

She sat on the steps of the gazebo, a giant in a fairyland village she had built for her daughter while the baby was still in utero.

"Yep," I said without looking at her. Roseanne didn't go places uninvited, so I relaxed and moved on to a flowering almond to prune a few dead twigs. Roseanne started pulling seedlings of European bird cherry that peppered the shrub beds. Left to their ambition, they'd start their own woodland. That wouldn't do.

Phoebe's fairy village sat in a forest of trees Roseanne and I had chosen for their varied foliage and blossoms. Roseanne celebrated every inch of growth. "Check the growth on that crabapple," she'd say. "I think it's already grown a few feet." It was hard to disdain that kind of commitment to life and its triumphs.

Brick paths wound past the tiny cottage, general store, gazebo, and post office of a village scaled to fit a seven-year-old. By the time Phoebe was ready for her reign in six years, the trees would shade the paths.

When Roseanne had showed me the plans before they were finalized, I had suggested adding a chapel. Her anger had struck with a fierce quickness. "Over my dead body," she said before she packed up her annoyance and softened her face to say, "I'm sorry, Mibby. Thanks for the suggestion." I fretted over her anger, wondering how the thought of a little white chapel nestled in a copse of trees could have enflamed her.

"Has Ky gotten that home run yet?" she asked. When I told her no, she said with the confidence of a prophet, "He will. I just know he will." And I believed her.

We worked our way past the gazebo to the cottage. Tender pink roses the size of ping-pong balls climbed up a side trellis. They would reach the roof by August. I snipped off a few blossoms that had bleached white in the sun.

"Should I cut down these delphiniums?"

"There you go again," I scolded lightly. "You're determined to make this harder than it has to be."

Roseanne looked like a little girl left out of a playground game of hopscotch. Her sensitivity surprised me.

"Not yet," I said evenly, "but when you do, snip the spike off just below the lowest blossom."

She moved on to the potted flowers on the cottage's porch. "Were you crying about Scott?" she asked, removing the crumpled blossoms of a geranium.

I had to think about that for a minute. I wanted to answer yes, but honestly, that wasn't it. I didn't want to tell her I was getting tired of death's company, so I blamed it on hormones.

She leaned back on her heels. "I wish my husband . . ." she started but stopped to brood over her wish. The breeze played with her cinnamon hair.

"Roseanne?"

"Do you ever think you're better off alone?"

When I'd found myself appreciating how easy it was to make the bed or clean the bathroom or control the remote, at least the one in the bedroom, without Scott in the house, my efficiency had sickened me. "No, not ever."

Roseanne smiled tightly; her face flushed. "I think I'll go check on Phoebe."

Later, she pressed a department store bag into my arms. "I was cleaning out my closet yesterday. I thought these would look better on you."

I hoped they weren't maternity clothes.

"There's a Rockies cap in there, too, for Ky. Someone gave it to Daniel at the office."

A delicate sadness weighted her eyes. I wondered if I'd just imagined that she'd hesitated slightly before saying her husband's name. As Blink and I drove back toward town past alfalfa fields and horse pastures, it dawned on me that Roseanne was asking the question of herself: Would *she* be better off without Daniel?

Grief had plunked me to the bottom of a dank well where my own pain spoke back to me in an endless echo, drowning out the pain of others. I pledged to myself that I'd pay more attention to Roseanne on my next visit.

The phone rang as I followed Blink into the house.

"Mibby, hon, I almost hung up." It was Louise. She sounded agitated. "Those granola eaters just left, and you won't believe what they did." She paused to let me ask the obvious question. "They stole the robes!"

I tried to picture Mr. and Mrs. Granola tiptoeing out of Louise's house with bulky terry cloth robes stuffed under their running clothes. Louise could exaggerate, so I quizzed her on all the likely places the robes could be hiding. She had checked them all.

"Let's pray for them." Louise ushered me into a holy place with her soft, earnest voice. "Dear Father, those poor people just can't know what they've done. They're tryin' so hard to fill up those lonesome ol' places with expensive cotton robes. Prick their consciences, Lord, when they wear those robes, so they'll know they've done something naughty. And have them return the robes to me freshly laundered."

Amen.

"How was your appointment?" she asked.

I told her about Ben's houseboat and that he wanted a memorial rose garden for his wife. Louise waited patiently for the rest of the story, so I had to tell her about my hasty retreat.

"Now he knows he's hired the handicapped," she said.

I told her I wasn't sure I was going back.

"Mibby?" I waited for the "I wonder" to follow, the open-ended musing Louise frequently used to quicken my conscience.

"You know, Mibby," she started slowly, "it's like Ben is that ol' beaten and robbed man lyin' mostly dead on the road to Jericho. He just needs a little help binding his wounds. You're right, though. It will cost you something, just like it did the Samaritan, if you decide to go back."

Here it comes.

"I wonder what would have become of that man if the Samaritan hadn't come along."

I had brought Ben's scrapbook home, so I was destined to return to the pink houseboat no matter who benefited most from the work. Since I had the scrapbook and he had handed it to me,

I felt I had permission to look through it. I took it out to the back porch with a cup of coffee. It was too hot for the birds to sing, so I returned to the air-conditioned house.

The notebook was blue and white with bold collegian letters spelling out "United States Air Force Academy." The scuffed vinyl was split at the corners, revealing its cardboard structure. I opened to the first page. The title, "The Many and Varid Homes of Second Lieutenant and Mrs. Ben Martin," was printed in black marker. The carefully formed letters stood like snowmen along a straight line, their bottoms flattened. Mrs. Martin had left the *e* out of *varied* but got *lieutenant* correct.

The next page featured a photograph of their first home and was dated July 19, 1990. Ben had his arms around the waist of a blond-haired woman who smiled but looked at something to the side of the camera. Ben looked directly into the camera with a smile big enough to overexpose the film. Her hair hung loose to her shoulders, where it softly turned under. She wore an oversized white T-shirt. The front was splattered with mud. Ben's hair stood at attention above his forehead. They were barefooted. Ben and his wife leaned against an ivory-colored clapboard house below a window. A small rosebush with two lavender blossoms grew by their feet. The caption under the picture read, "Fairchild Air Force Base, Spokane, Washington, Angel Face."

The Martins had lived in Florida next, MacDill Air Force Base. By then, Ben was a first lieutenant. The couple crouched beside their painted cinderblock house. The photograph caught only the corner of a louvered glass window, and palm frond fingers reached into the frame. A trellis stood behind a puny rosebush with one stretching cane. The small flower was pale pink. Ben wore the look of a honey *do* husband. A large bandage covered the back of his hand. Mrs. Martin wore the victorious grin of the honey *done* wife. Her face was turned into the sun, away from the camera. There was tight, efficient handwriting in the corner of the page. "Let me go on record saying this is the most evil plant that ever grew. Planted only for the love of Jenny." The rose was a climbing Cécile Brünner.

By the time the Martins had arrived in Georgia, Ben was a captain and Jenny had a perm of boisterous curls framing her face. She seemed to be smiling politely at a bug crawling through the grass. Ben wore leather gardening gloves. A hose lay coiled at his feet. The new rose was between them. The white tennis ball–sized blossoms nestled into the dark, glossy leaves of White Lightnin'.

Over the next three pages, Ben became a major and Jenny's hair got shorter and shorter. She planted a deep yellow rose in Texas, another red in Utah, and a salmon pink in New Jersey. By the time they got to California, Jenny stood alone by a Sheer Bliss rose, unsmiling. Ben was also missing from Wisconsin, where Jenny held a bare root rose in front of a Christmas tree. In her lettering she wrote, "Ben ordered Buffalo Gal from duty in Germany." A thick sheaf of blank pages waited at the back of the scrapbook for more pictures.

I closed the scrapbook knowing I would design the rose garden Ben wanted.

Ky waved with exaggerated sweeps from a block away. I'd moved our meeting place back to the original corner. He approved.

"Mom!" he called from the opposite side of the street. "I kicked a goal today." His cap was pushed back from his face, and his toes hung over the curb. A tight formation of cars sped by.

I waved him back. He looked at his feet and inched away from the curb. When he looked up, his smile had faded.

We walked home in silence after the first round of obligatory questions. Everything and everyone was fine at George C. Parker Middle School. These questions were meant to build rapport with Ky before I asked him about the real school issue. I had learned this technique from watching Oprah.

"Ky," I said, wading cautiously into the unknown waters. "Mrs. Freesomething called about your midterm grades the other day."

"Friedlander," he corrected me.

"She wants me to call her, but I wanted to talk to you first."

"So?"

I sharpened my words against his insolence. "Do you have them?"

"What?"

"Your midterms, Ky." I leaned hard on each word. "Do you have your midterm grades in your book bag?"

"That woman is such a—" There is only one word a thirteen-year-old boy would put on the end of that sentence, so I interrupted him. One problem at a time.

"Kyle," I said much louder than I'd intended, "what's going on at school?"

He walked faster. "I'm not getting an A in math, all right?"

That was news. He had excelled in math since kindergarten.

What would Scott say?

"That's okay," I said.

"Okay?" He was incredulous. "I don't think so. I just have to try harder. That's all."

What would Scott say to that?

"Do you understand the concepts?"

We stood face to face at the sidewalk leading to the front door.

"Look, Mom, there's no reason to worry." He sounded so much like Scott. "We just did a bunch of new stuff. I didn't get it at first, but now I do." He started for the front door. This would have been a good place to drop the subject, but I've never been good at that.

"Could it be all the time you're spending at the ball field?"

Ky stopped with one hand on the doorknob. "I'll do it," he said, just this side of control. "You don't have to call her. I'll do it."

The door banged against the wall as he pushed it open. I listened from the front porch as he pounded his way up the stairs and slammed the door to his room.

I turned toward the street in time to see the same car from the day before speed away again. All I could muster was a mild annoyance. I didn't have room for fear among the disappointment and anger of the day.

I screamed my full fury at Scott into a hill of mildewy towels in the basement. "You should be here!"

I heard Ky's steps on the stairs as I stuffed a bundle of towels into the washer. He apologized and so did I. He walked easily into my embrace and stayed willingly. The warm spot behind his ear stored the exertion from the lunchtime soccer game, sharp and sweet. He promised to let me know if things got tough again and reassured me math was going well. I mentally crossed Mrs. Freeloader off my phone call list.

I stayed in the basement to fold the contents of the dryer. Later, I found Ky staring into the fridge holding a pad of paper. He was making a shopping list. It was my turn to make a promise.

"I'll go tomorrow."

MAY 5

Hot and clear — expecting mid 90s today. Wind last night dropped a zillion seeds from neighbor's Siberian elm. Argh! Spent over an hour scooping and sweeping seeds in yard. Vacuum? Considering arboricide. Added some asparagus fern to front pots for fluff. Robins tending nest in crotch of honey locust. Hope Capone the gangsta cat doesn't find them.

I hadn't dreamed about Scott in months.

In the first few weeks after the accident, he had come to me often in my dreams to say good-bye and to reassure me I'd do a good job with Ky. I considered the dreams a gift from God. They gave me a chance to hear Scott's voice and to smell his aftershave, even if his words didn't have their desired effect. In my dreams, he was always dressed in his bank clothes, a pressed shirt and trousers with just the right amount of break over the shoe. It made me wonder who was doing his ironing.

I stopped having the dreams when I told Louise about them. She had chided me about sleeping in late. But they were morning dreams, I told her, dropped on my pillow like the morning paper. I had to read every line. Evidently, sharing that bit of information canceled my subscription.

The dream that woke me that morning was very different. Scott and I were at a Renaissance fair with brightly colored banners snapping in the breeze. People pressed by us wearing the garb of the fourteenth century—ladies in billowy dresses and men cinched into velvet tunics. Musicians played breathy melodies on recorders while drummers laid down beats like stepping-stones for the dancers to follow.

Scott was dressed as a jousting knight—lance in one hand and feathered helmet in the other. Dark waves of hair hung to his shoulders; a well-trimmed goatee circled his mouth. His armor was definitely starched. I wore denim shorts and a T-shirt, of course.

If Scott had mounted a white stallion and rode off into the forest, the dream would have made perfect sense. But it didn't happen that way.

"Why didn't you tell me? Why didn't you tell me?" I kept shouting at Scott without waiting for an answer. The rage rose from my belly and burned its way out of my chest. It gained momentum on every unnamed disappointment it touched. I was overwhelmed with a sense of betrayal, but I didn't know its source.

Even through dream's fog, I knew my anger wasn't right. It was the kind of anger women hurled with futility at their husbands who had squandered their wages on ale and cockfights, not on decorated knights. Scott had done nothing to deserve my scorn. I searched the faces of the revelers around me, hoping their judgment would cool my fire, but they were too deep in their merriment to notice. And strangest of all, I was trying to get away from him, even though my dream mind said, *Go back, go back to him.*

Scott caught me from behind. I pulled at his arms to release his grasp, but my grip slipped on his armor. He turned me roughly to face him and dropped to his knees. His hot breath warmed my belly; his tears wet my top.

"I am so sorry, Mibby. Please, please forgive me," he pleaded.

I ran my hands through his hair still sweaty from the helmet. Lords and ladies walked around us like we were a badly placed signpost. My dream mind pleaded with me to forgive him, to steal this forbidden moment of togetherness at any cost. I bent to kiss the top of his head.

The cries of a robin pair woke me. Probably Capone, my neighbor's cat, raiding a nest.

I brought my dream to the surface like a pearl diver and dropped the treasure into a small boat rolling with the waves. I pulled the covers over my head and went down into the murky water for more, but the dream of Scott was replaced with a dream of a picnic with neighbors I didn't know. Faceless people in plaid shirts drank iced tea and turned hot dogs on a grill. I couldn't breathe. No one seemed to notice. When I resurfaced into wakefulness, I gulped for air to fill my burning lungs.

All through my first cup of coffee and long after I was squeaky clean from a shower, I turned the first dream over in my mind, looking for meaning in the jumble of events. I'd never been that angry with Scott in real life. He had never done anything to deserve such wrath, especially from me, at least not when he was alive.

I dropped another dustpan of elm seeds into the trashcan and stopped to watch a robin collect mulch fibers for his love nest. Last night's wind had sent a snowstorm of the papery seeds into my yard, and they'd collected like snowdrifts at the bases of plants and along the brick path. Even my neighbor's half-dead Siberian elm tree produced copious seeds each spring. Scott and I had offered to have it cut down at our expense, but Mr. Stewart wouldn't hear of it.

"Mibby? Hello?" Louise called over the fence to announce her arrival. She poked her head inside the gate. "I heard you cursin' Harold's elm tree, so I knew you were up. Is it safe to come in?" She walked down the path, her hands disappointingly empty.

"Sorry, Blink," she said, opening her hands just out of Blink's reach. "I sent all my blueberry streusel muffins fishing with Manley." Blink nuzzled her pockets but returned to his third nap of the morning without a prize.

It was bird theme day. A row of appliquéd birdhouses bordered the hem of Louise's chambray dress, and a pair of calico sparrows perched on her pockets. From each earlobe, enameled bluebirds swung frantically. Despite her support of local birdlife, a robin complained about her intrusion. I dropped another dustpan of elm seeds into the trashcan.

"Are you going to catch elm seeds all day?"

The branches of Mr. Stewart's tree were still heavy with the remaining seeds. A breeze rattled the treetop, and another swarm of seeds headed earthward. I closed the lid of the trashcan and topped it with my dustpan.

"I'm just waiting for Ky to get up," I said, "so we can go grocery shopping." I believed there was strength in numbers.

The warming earth sent another breeze to foretell of the day's coming heat. Louise brushed away the honey locust's caterpillar flowers before she settled on the bench. I checked the location of the nest overhead and joined her.

"Why don't you go now, beat the rush?" she said. "I'll stay with Ky. You do have coffee, don't you?"

When I hesitated, Louise pouted. "Don't you trust me?"

I hugged my knees to my chest. "It's not that."

She slid in close and wrapped her arms around me. I leaned into her, a hard-boiled egg balanced on the big end. I concentrated on breathing evenly, hoping the rhythm would lull my tears to sleep. When Louise finally spoke, her voice startled me.

"I didn't go to the grocery store for a whole year after Kevin died. I just never knew who I'd run into." I lifted my head to look at her. Louise rarely spoke about her son. She never talked about the time after his death.

"I know. It seems crazy."

No, it doesn't.

"I got so tired of people asking me how I was and then scrutinizin' me for signs of weakness. I told Manley to plan on burying a very skinny Louise. I'd starve before I went shopping again." She gave me a private smile. "Like that would happen."

She closed her eyes and lifted her face to the breeze. "Manley came to me after the anniversary of Kevin's death. He looked just awful. Tears ran down his cheeks, and his shoulders shook so. He said he needed my help. I'd reduced that strong man to a sobbin' glob of Jell-O. He had been working his job and running the house and carrying the same crushing burden of grief I carried. But I hid under Mammy's quilt." Louise's eyelashes were wet. "I asked Jesus to tell me what to do, but I'm not sure I believed He would."

I straightened.

"Yes, you better make yourself comfy," she said, using her fingers to wipe the tears from her face. "Now that I'm rolling, this here's at least a three-point sermon. Maybe more. That was just the introduction."

Louise's sermons were short, dramatic, and powerful. Customized for her audience of one—me—they always hit home. After a good sermon, I felt different. Sometimes I felt like the healing light of heaven had warmed my soul; sometimes I felt a gentle arm around my shoulders guiding me in a new direction; sometimes I felt the pain of a swift kick to the derriere. It was good to be sitting down. Besides, as long as Louise talked, I was sitting in my garden, not pushing a cart around a grocery store.

"Should I take notes?" I asked.

"No, just remember the high points." She held up a blue-painted fingernail. "Point one. Maybe folks weren't scrutinizin' me at all. Maybe they were loving me the best they could. Maybe that searching look on their faces was just an earnest desire to let me know they cared."

A new direction piece? I usually needed time to think about those, but Louise didn't slow the pace. She added another finger and took a deep breath. "I did hear Jesus talk to me through the Hallelujah Hannah's Good News Radio Show a few days later." She shifted her drawl to the backroads of Alabama. "Hannah said, 'To be like Jeezus, y'all must love yore neighbah befo' thay loves yew.'"

A love piece. I started to feel the healing warmth of heaven. "Bring it on home, sistah."

"Point three," she said, wagging her fingers at me. "To be like Jesus, my own dear Savior, a man of sorrows and familiar with suffering, I needed to love the shoppers first, even in my grief."

I told her about the hoards of people who had given me doleful looks and asked me how I was doing. "I'm tired, Louise."

"I know. I know." And she did. Louise had lost her ten-year-old son to cancer after a three-year battle. "Those folks are just trying to be kind. They don't know what to say or how to say it, but they don't want you to think they've forgotten Scott or how much you two meant to each other. They just don't know when to stop."

Louise dug a tissue out of her pocket and dabbed below her eyes, checking the white tissue for errant mascara.

"Lovin' the folks at the store first was just a way of deflecting people's attention," she said. "If they asked me how I was, I'd say, 'Just fine' and ask them about their lives. How's Joe? What's new with Moe? Tell me what Curly's doing. But doing it changed my heart. It was my way of telling folks they mattered, too. It also told them they weren't responsible for my happiness. They seemed genuinely relieved about that."

Louise pulled my head to her shoulder, cupping my cheek in her hand. "I saved my honesty for my dear friend Regina. We became the Hoot 'n' Holler Choir. Whenever that dark cloud of despair overtook me, she hooted words of understanding while I hollered at God for what I thought was unfair treatment." She kissed my hair. "You can save your honesty for me, Mibby. I'll hoot *and* holler for you, if that's what you need. Okay? Jesus and I can handle it."

I nodded into her hand.

"Besides," she said, "I don't think you want to bury a skinny Ky."

A swift kick.

Ouch.

Only the stouthearted and desperate go grocery shopping on a Saturday morning, but I didn't miss the rush as Louise had promised. I found a parking space in the hinterlands with the other eager beavers. None of us wanted to be there, so it was all business. I pulled out the list Ky had started. Apples. Cereal. Glow Green Lime Puffs? *I don't think so.* I grabbed a couple of asparagus ferns instead. They would look great with the upright fuchsias in the pots.

I scanned each aisle for familiar faces and prayed, partly because I wanted to follow Louise's example of love and partly because I feared I couldn't. The coast was clear in the canned goods aisle. After putting six cans of cheese ravioli in my cart, I passed a young woman studying a can of white hominy.

She wore her black hair clipped tight to the nape of her neck and longer in the front. Her hair curtained her face until she tucked it behind her ear. A row of silver earrings lined her earlobe, and a tiny garnet stud nestled into the fold of one nostril. I had a hard time picturing the sleek beauty scooping hominy onto her plate beside a breaded pork chop. She looked up as I passed but returned quickly to reading the can. There was something about her that seemed familiar, but I doubted she was anyone I knew.

My favorite Aretha Franklin song came on over the store's speakers. I was spelling R-E-S-P-E-C-T along with Aretha when I pushed my cart past Earring Girl in the frozen food aisle. Her cart was still empty. As I reached for a frozen pizza, she said, "The other one's better." She sounded a little breathless.

I took two of the pizzas she had recommended and added them to the cart. "Thanks."

As I checked the fat content of hot dogs in the deli case, the girl picked up a package of bacon. "Who knows what they put in those things," she said, nodding at the all-meat franks.

She looked at the bacon in her own hand and dropped it. "Gross!"

A blush rose from deep under her black shell, past a trio of blue stars tattooed at the base of her throat, all the way up her alabaster forehead. She looked nervously over both shoulders, as if the undercover nutrition police patrolled the store, and pushed her empty cart down the snack aisle.

Although Ky had many snack items on the list, I skipped that aisle and went on to the cleaning supplies. No one had ever died from a lack of Yellow Bomber Snack Corn. I picked up a box of laundry detergent, strangely missing from the list, and headed for the pet food aisle. I wrestled a fifty-pound bag of Doggie Delights into the cart and tossed in a bag of cheese-flavored treats. I needed to get back on Blink's good side. I only had the bakery and dairy aisles to go before I could declare this a whammy-free shopping trip. I whispered a prayer of thanks.

"Mibby! How *are* you?" Carrie Hightower, captain of the neighborhood watch, was loading hoagie buns into her cart when I turned the corner. Her tethered sunglasses pressed painfully into my chest as she embraced me.

Louise would ask me about the friends I'd seen and how the encounters had gone, so I tried to follow her advice. "I'm good—fine, really."

"Really?" she asked, creasing her forehead in concern.

I dismissed the question with a flip of my wrist. "Really, I mean it. I'm good." *Move it along, girl.* "But how is that daughter of yours?" *What's her name?* "Is she playing varsity this spring?"

That was all it took to get Carrie talking. While she gave the dramatic details of the latest tennis championship match, I watched Earring Girl squeeze loaves of French bread behind her. The girl put the French bread back and read with great intensity the labels on the bran muffins, raising her eyes in my direction several times before moving on to the blueberry muffins.

When Carrie paused, I said, "Oh, really?" Then I heard about the incompetent official who had stolen the tournament from Vanessa with bad calls.

Vanessa!

Earring Girl studied a package of frosted Danish. She looked up but quickly dodged my gaze. Her cart was still empty.

Like a sunrise on an overcast morning, it slowly dawned on me that Earring Girl was following me. "It was so nice talking to you, Carrie. Say hello to Vanessa."

I headed directly for the checkout counter, feigning nonchalance as I looked through the shoppers for the girl. I'd lost her. I threw a package of Oreos and a bag of Snickers from an end display into the cart to appease Ky and paid for the groceries.

When I unlocked the door of the Daisy Mobile and reached for my groceries, they weren't there. I'd left the cart at the checkout counter. I considered going back for the sake of my starving child.

Earring Girl trotted toward me, waving and shouting. "Wait, I have to talk to you!"

I completely disagreed with her. I backed out of the parking space and headed in the opposite direction. Just a few parking spaces away, I passed the primer-and-yellow car. It had gold on blue California plates, but I was moving too fast to read the numbers. The lance still jutted out the passenger window.

A lance?

Louise had left a note taped to the screen door saying Ky had a game at ten. He would be home by noon. Ky had added a postscript. "Can Salvador spend the night?"

I took the calendar from the kitchen wall and laid it on the dining room table, Garrett Family Central. I'd have Ky write in all his game dates and times when he got home.

There was a message on the answering machine from the grocery store telling me they had my groceries in the refrigerator. "Please come get them by eleven."

I looked at my watch. Ten fifty-seven.

I closed all the shades and locked the doors. I slumped into Scott's chair in the living room just to wonder when my sanity might return. There was no reason Earring Girl or an Amazon warrior would be stalking me. The girl was just being helpful. She'd probably run out to tell me I'd left my groceries behind. I just didn't hear the end of her sentence. "Wait, I have to talk to you . . . about your groceries." That was it. Hadn't she been friendly all through the store, pointing out the good pizza and questioning the origin of the hot dogs? Maybe she was lonely, new to town, and just needed to make human contact.

The primer and yellow car? Orchard City was still small enough to run into the same people—or cars—around town. Besides, Earring Girl probably drove something avant-garde, like a convertible

Karmann Ghia. Lime green. Hundred to one, she had just arrived for the summer semester at the college to study art.

Feeling stupid was so much better than feeling afraid. Like everything else since Scott had died, I'd underestimated how vulnerable his absence had made me feel. I closed my eyes and let the deep cushions of his chair cradle me. My last thought before I fell asleep was a question I'd asked myself as a reflex to loneliness since my husband's death.

When did Scott say he'd be home?

The two boys stood over me like vultures. "What's for lunch?" they asked. They wore baggy shorts and T-shirts that almost matched, not their uniforms.

"How long have you been home?" I asked.

How long have I been sleeping?

Ky sat on the arm of the chair. "Salvador's mom just dropped us off." He kicked the chair with his heel to some internal rhythm. "So, what's for lunch?"

I greeted Salvador, hoping I'd get more information from him. "Why aren't you wearing your uniform, Salvador?"

"We didn't have a game," he said as if he was reminding me the sky was blue or it was air that we breathed. You should know this stuff, Mrs. G.

I looked at Ky. "You didn't have a—"

"Don't worry, Mom. Salvador and I made lots of money selling drugs, so you don't have to worry about money no more."

There's nothing quite as difficult as getting a straight answer from an adolescent boy about his whereabouts. I gave him the evil squint. He stopped kicking. "We worked the snack bar."

Uh-oh. Parents were expected to work alongside their kids at the snack bar to make it a safe and profitable experience. My absence put me on the blacklist for sure.

"It's okay, Mom. I told them you had things to do."

I walked into the kitchen later to hear Salvador talking to his mother, Janine, on the phone. He assured her I was awake and seemed okay. And no, we hadn't had lunch yet.

Janine and I had been friends since the boys were in a preschool playgroup together. We enjoyed joking that the boys had two mothers and really couldn't tell which home they were in most of the time. When Scott died, Janine and Emilio opened their arms and their home to Ky even more. But Janine withdrew from our friendship. I was hurt at first, but really, it was a relief. Janine fancied herself an amateur psychologist.

"Does your mom want to talk to me?" I asked.

"Mom, do you want to talk to Mrs. G?" He put his hand over the mouthpiece. "She says she has to go somewhere."

The boys and I crammed into the truck and headed for the grocery store. Fortunately, the store clerks had been too busy to reshelve my groceries. It was a small victory going back to the grocery store to reclaim my groceries, and it felt good. I hadn't been whammied at all. I'd just let my imagination get away from me. Giddy with my modest triumph, I invited Salvador to spend the night and promised a gourmet microwave meal.

Ben answered the phone on the first ring. I'd hoped for an answering machine. I reminded him who I was and things got quiet.

He finally said, "I was worried about you."

I wasn't expecting concern. "I just overreacted. I do that sometimes."

"I'd understand if you don't want to do the job." Ben sighed into the phone. "The place is in pretty bad shape."

"I've seen worse." That wasn't true. "It's just that I'm a little sensitive, I guess. Anyway, I wanted you to know I have your scrapbook."

"You can drop it in the mail."

Mailing the scrapbook seemed like the easiest thing to do. But then I remembered Louise talking about binding wounds, and I could smell the grease at McDonald's.

"Ben," I started again. "I'm a widow." *That explains everything, doesn't it?*

Silence.

"It hasn't been that long." *I'm still in the raw zone.*

Silence.

"November." *Has it been that long?*

"I'm real sorry, Mibby."

If he hadn't said that with such knowing; if he hadn't said my name without stumbling over the *M,* I could have put that odd scrapbook in a box and dropped it into the nearest mailbox. *Adiós amigo!*

We arranged another meeting for after lunch on Monday. I promised to bring the scrapbook.

Surviving two trips to the grocery store had provided enough inspiration for me to set the table, shake the salad makings out of the bag, and listen for the beep of the microwave. The lasagna simmered and steamed all the way to the table. Betty Crocker would have been so proud, and Ky was pleased but polite enough not to say anything about the rarity of a real meal in front of Salvador. After dinner, the boys and I played a cutthroat game of Monopoly. The phone rang just as I was forced to sell my last hotel. Salvador and Ky exchanged looks of conspiratorial glee as I left the table. It was Louise.

"Can I bring a movie and some popcorn over? Manley isn't home yet and that young couple in the Lilac Room is . . . well . . . quite vocal."

Louise came to the back door in her pink chenille robe and matching slippers. Her hair, pulled into a ponytail on top of her head, bounced with every gesture. One look at Louise and the boys retreated to Ky's room.

I reported to Louise that I'd called Ben, and I even told her about my conversation with Carrie at the grocery store.

"When you're able to love people like Jesus, Mibby, it means you're healing," she said.

Is that what I'd done?

I didn't tell her about Earring Girl. The whole thing embarrassed me terribly. I decided to save that story for our rocking chair days. We'd need a good laugh. I asked Louise to help me measure Ben's yard on Monday.

"You know, I just love Oreo cookies," she said, doing jumping jacks with her eyebrows.

I walked Louise to the alley gate after the movie. She scuffed across the alley but stopped short of her gate. The light from her back porch outlined her shape and gleamed off her golden ponytail. She looked like a Roman fountain.

"Mibby girl," she called through the darkness, "I'm so proud of you. Jeezus loves yew!"

There is an irksome tension between joy and grieving. Life had brought me an answered prayer for love in the grocery store, a child's appreciation, and a friend's kind words. I should have savored it all, but pleasure for a widow is like an old boyfriend at a high school reunion. He is unreasonably handsome now that his frame is padded with muscles and a little indulgence. But the boyfriend—joy—is from a life that used to be, and it feels like a betrayal to her husband's memory to indulge in his company. After all, it was her husband who had soothed her when the car accident was her fault. Her husband was the man who told her to breathe when she wanted narcotics at the birth of their son. And her husband was the man who never complained about the goo she slathered on her feet at night. For all of that, and so much more, misery alone chaperoned my heart. Joy would have to ask someone else to dance.

I knocked softly on Ky's door before I pushed it open. A swaying beam of light on the wall of a blanket tent meant someone was still awake. Blink lay on the floor by the bed. His eyes followed me as I moved to the tent, but he remained hunkered down. It was Blink's way of telling me to leave him be.

"Hello," I whispered.

Ky pushed his head out from the blanket. Salvador's feet didn't move on the pillow beside Ky. "I'm reading a really good book," he whispered back.

I was relieved to see there were no pictures in the book. "Ky, did you mark the calendar?"

"I forgot, sorry."

"Tomorrow, then." I kissed his sticky forehead. "Church tomorrow, too. Love you."

"I love you, too." I was almost out the door when he added, "Mom, the lasagna was good."

Before going upstairs to bed, I checked the locks on each door and window, working from the back of the house to the front. I don't know why I looked out the peephole of the front door, but there was Earring Girl chewing her bottom lip with her fist raised to knock.

I screamed and clicked the deadbolt into place and slapped the porch light off.

Why is it still so bright?

The lamp! I lunged for it, but my foot caught on the rug, and I went sprawling onto the lamp table. The lamp finally blinked off when it hit the floor with a crash.

Don't knock. Don't knock. Don't knock.

Blink eagerly clomped down the stairs to survey the damage. Ky and Salvador padded halfway down the stairs. Ky pushed past Salvador but stopped a couple of steps later when he saw my face.

"What is it, Mom?"

I didn't know what would be worse, explaining Earring Girl or hearing a knock. I put my finger to my lips. The boys responded by sitting down on the stairs. I waved them back upstairs. When they hesitated, I scowled and gave them an authoritative point upward. It worked.

Don't knock. Don't knock. Don't knock.

I crawled back to the window and peeked around the edge of the curtain. The girl was gone. Blink gave a half-hearted bark and headed back to bed. I followed him up the stairs. The boys were all atwitter, more from the adventure than from fear, so I told them it had been an intoxicated person at the wrong door.

"Shouldn't we call the police?" Ky asked.

Officer, Earring Girl is nicing me to death.

I shook one, then two sleeping pills into my hand and washed them down with Kool-Aid.

MAY

6

Cottonwoods and tamarisk fully leafed out along the river. River running high and fast for so early in May. In the low 90s again. Drought?

I used to envy people in the witness protection program. I imagined them at a hidden laboratory in the Nevada desert getting full makeovers: a little liposuction from the thighs, a New York hairstyle, and a brand-new name, one that didn't require exposition. But after one whole day of looking over my shoulder for Earring Girl, I was almost willing to live with my hips. Almost.

At any moment, I knew, Earring Girl could knock on the door and demand to see the contents of my refrigerator or pop out of a shrub to take my picture eating preservative-laden processed food. Although I tried to imagine a less ridiculous scenario, I couldn't.

This girl wanted to talk to me. Had she come all the way from California to do so? Maybe she needed to talk to me about a violet I had sold her mother ten years ago. "It just isn't looking well," she would tell me, wringing her hands and insisting on a cure. I've always found passive-aggressive types so dishonest and irritating. Or maybe the girl was selling encyclopedias, but she was too embarrassed to come out and say so. I was angry with her for being persistent yet so ineffectual.

Whatever.

Until I knew what she wanted, I was determined to keep her away from Ky. I planned to be unavailable to her until he returned to school the next day.

The sleeping pills left my system magically at 12:28 in the afternoon. One instant I was asleep, the next I was wide awake, dreamless and fully oxygenated. I found Ky and Salvador eating cheese ravioli on the sofa watching *Blazing Saddles*, not for the first time.

"Ravioli for breakfast?" I asked, separating the curtains to look up and down the street.

"This is lunch, Mom."

Sure enough. Two bowls with crusted cornflakes sat on the coffee table next to a carton of milk. "Ky, did anyone come to the door this morning?"

He loaded another ravioli into his mouth and pushed it into his cheek. "Just Louise," he said without looking at me.

Louise had come to walk to church with us. I knew I should call her to let her know I was okay, but she probably wasn't home yet. I hoped Earring Girl was a late sleeper, too. But I felt certain she would be at the door soon.

"Let's go ride our bikes by the river," I said.

Salvador lowered his spoonful of ravioli back into the bowl and looked at Ky, then me. "Right now?"

"We're watching this," Ky said, still staring at the television.

I pressed the TV's power button. "Let's go."

It was a race. I wanted to get out of the house before Earring Girl returned, so I assigned the boys jobs while I got dressed. Ky inflated tires and loaded the bikes into the back of the Daisy

Mobile. I sent Salvador into the kitchen to call his mom and to find some nutritious snacks to take along. He packed Snickers and Oreos, two of the four basic food groups: chocolate with nuts and chocolate without nuts. I filled three water bottles and grabbed a bowl for Blink. Ky remembered the helmets.

There was nothing I could do as a widow that didn't carry with it a memory to prick my heart. Even something as simple as a family outing to the river came embedded with a thousand rituals to remind me a beloved player was missing.

Blink tapped out a dance of joy with his claws on the truck bed. When he saw me, he froze. His eyes watched me without blinking. This was where Scott would have agitated Blink into a deeper frenzy with his "Wanna go bye-bye?" chant until the dog nearly exploded with rapture before we ever left the driveway. Evidently, the baton had been passed to me as acting alpha male of the pack. Blink worked his mouth impatiently and moaned pitifully. The boys stood motionless beside the truck. I apologized silently to Blink and got in the truck. The boys slid in beside me. We were turning out of the alley when they clicked their seatbelts. I watched the mirrors for any sign of the yellow-and-primer car.

Clouds dotted the sky like popcorn spilled across a blue floor. The day was bright and too hot for early May. We drove along with the windows down. The air stirred up the dirt inside the cab to stick to our sweaty skin and fill our mouths with a fine grit. Ky had to move his knees whenever I shifted into fourth gear.

"Mom, maybe we could use Dad's Yukon next time."

I hadn't driven Scott's car since his accident. It was cluttered with his debris. Business cards. Mentos. CDs. Besides, its behemoth proportions made it impossible to park. I kept my eyes on the road and lied ever so whitely.

"Maybe."

I parked the Daisy Mobile in the last available space at the river trail parking lot. A pair of in-line skaters sat on a stone bench strapping padding onto their elbows and knees. Under a cottonwood tree, a father adjusted the helmet of a toddler perched on the back of his bicycle. Blink whined for his leash. Long-time trail buddies, Blink and I moved along at a comfortable pace. Usually Scott had ridden maniacally with Ky. Things had to be different.

"Ky, I need you and Salvador to stay in sight today."

"Why? What could happen?"

Earring Girl could pierce your ears repeatedly with a rusty needle.

"It would just make me more comfortable to have you near. The river's running pretty fast."

The threat from the river was real enough. Local television stations ran public service announcements each spring warning people to stay out of the river. Its muddy waters ran deceptively smooth, hiding rocks and trees below the surface, where people had been pinned by the current.

"We aren't going *in* the river," he complained.

Of course not. No one planned to go into the river, but things could happen. Highly improbable—yet definitely conceivable to mothers—chains of events pulled children into the river. But males don't have good imaginations when it comes to mortality, so I changed my tactic. I pleaded.

"Pl*eeease* stay in my sight."

Ky and Salvador turned a curve into a tamarisk grove approximately five seconds after we had started down the trail. I pressed hard against the pedals to catch up, but Blink balked at the pace. My rational mind argued against any real threat from Earring Girl. The trail was busy with weekend users. Besides, she would have to catch them first. Still, she was out there somewhere.

Trusting God to protect my son was the hardest kind of faith for me. It was one thing to entrust myself into His care, but Ky? Wasn't that my job? More and more, Ky was removing himself from my protection, defiantly pressing the bounds of independence wider and wider, and I was left clinging to my puny faith.

"Lord," I prayed, "protect him."

By the time I found the boys reading about great horned owls at the Audubon kiosk, I'd worked up a boiling resentment of Earring Girl. She had ruined my Sunday outing by turning a leisurely ride into a spiraling descent into paranoia. I'd looked for Earring Girl behind every bench, rock, and tree trunk. I had even checked the stalls of the bathroom for platform shoes. When we stopped for a snack, I'd sat with my back to the river like a nervous gunslinger. Pedaling back toward the truck, I made a pact to confront Earring Girl and tell her to get lost. I practiced scolding her in my mind, even stooping to use coarse language to drive my point home. I almost believed I would.

After we dropped Salvador off at his house, I suggested to Ky that we go out for dinner.

"I have homework, Mom."

"You have to eat." This was an impossible piece of logic for a growing boy to argue against. "Where do you want to go?"

"Hotdog Hut."

I remembered Earring Girl saying, *"Who knows what they put in those things."*

I said, "Regular or foot long?"

I lingered over my hotdog as long as I could, even considered ordering another. "What do you want for dessert?"

Ky pushed the empty plastic basket to the end of the table and popped a sugar packet into his mouth, paper and all. "I need to do my homework."

After we got home, Ky went to his room, closed the door, and turned on his stereo. I did the same. I listened to the Beach Boys while lying on my bed. If Earring Girl came, I didn't want to hear her. Instead, I imagined impossible movements to the music. It was a great mind workout.

MAY

7

Cloudy, windy, and cold! Only 49° at midmorning. Brr. Such is life in the high desert. Ordering new brand of seeds for cilantro (La Cocina Seeds from New Mexico). Catalog says they'll tolerate the heat. We'll see. Worried about one of the green ash trees near street. Some bare branches. Borers?

I startled awake. I wasn't sure why. I listened for Ky, but I heard the back screen door slam instead. The clock read 6:01. Too early for Ky, or was it? The door slammed shut again. In or out? I decided to be cautious.

I slid Scott's oversized driver out of his golf bag that leaned in the corner of the bedroom. I tightened my grip on the club and stepped into the hall, sliding along the bare planks without lifting my feet. Walking noiselessly in the old house was impossible, but I had learned from many wintertime hide-and-seek games with Ky to avoid shifts in weight and to keep to the edges of the hall.

The shuffling of feet in the kitchen sent a resonant creak through the house too heavy to be Ky. Blink's wet nose hit the back of my left thigh when I stopped to listen. I stifled a gasp with my hand. Blink and I shared a look of concern. He whined softly and turned back to the bedroom and my side of the bed. So much for my canine security system.

Reason told me to join him under the quilt. But my reason wasn't gripping the Fat Lady golf club with white knuckles or building a case for justifiable battery against Earring Girl. That was who it had to be. I wanted to give her a scare, and I was counting on the really big golf club to do it.

I leaned into Ky's room. He lay on top of a nest of bedding, his chest rising and falling with a low snore. I shifted into she-bear mode. If I'd had claws, I would have sharpened them on the newel-post right there and then. Instead, I tightened my grip on the club. I pulled Ky's door shut before lowering myself slowly onto the first step. I waited and listened.

I'm not loving this, Lord. Please help me.

The busy movement in the kitchen continued. Earring Girl certainly wasn't concerned about being discovered.

I leaned against the wall, slowly shifting my weight from step to step. Just as I eased my foot onto the entryway floor, I considered the possibility that the intruder was not Earring Girl at all. Perhaps I was headed for a confrontation with an escaped prisoner desperate for food and money.

The intruder released a rumbling belch. Only three steps away, the front door beckoned me to walk out. But no self-respecting she-bear would leave her cub. I considered returning to the bedroom. Would the intruder follow me to Ky? I had to call for help.

Lord?

We had two phones downstairs: one in the kitchen and one in the new family room. I continued my slide down the hall to the half bath under the stairs, where I stopped again to listen. Metal clanked against metal. I was outgunned.

Gun?! Lord!

I peeked around the corner into the family room. The phone

sat on a small table on the other side of the room. The handset wasn't in its base. It sat on a bench below the window, fully visible from the kitchen.

The family room was part of the new addition. Scott had insisted on those engineered squeak-free floor joists, so I was able to walk silently to the edge of the wall separating the family room from the kitchen. I should have been thankful, but bubbling along with my fear was resentment at Scott for not being there. I waited again, wanting desperately to hear the screen door open and close. I heard a phlegmy cough instead and more clinking of metal. I held my breath and looked into the kitchen.

The intruder grunted and scuffed behind the makeshift island, out of sight, on the floor. I started to wonder what he was doing down there but stopped myself. I didn't want to know. I wanted to be under the quilt with Blink. I crawled to the phone. Just as I reached for it, I heard a loud thud followed by a familiar voice and a heartfelt expletive.

I looked cautiously over the island to find the man who matched the voice under the sink. The fleshy backside of Droop Ingram rose out of his sagging jeans like the twin moons of Mars. Identity confirmed, Droop backed from under the kitchen sink slowly. As our carpenter-in-residence, I'd seen Droop—more of him than I really wanted—backing out of crawl spaces, looking for errant vents, and just getting a closer look.

"Droop?"

Another loud thud.

Droop backed from under the two-by-four temporary platform rubbing his head. "You scared the bejeebies out of me, Mibby." He pulled off his painter's cap. The tanned dome of his scalp was fringed with silvery hair pulled back into a braid. He straightened and hiked his jeans. A canvas bag of tools lay open at his feet.

"Goin' golfin' this morning?" he asked, looking me up and

down. "I recommend you wear some pants."

Good advice for someone wearing only an oversized T-shirt.

I returned downstairs dressed in overalls and a yellow tee. A denim cap hid my hair. Droop had a cup of coffee with cream and sugar waiting for me, just the way I liked it. He also explained his presence. His current remodeling job had stalled when the cabinets got stranded in Omaha. The delay had given him time to come back to us.

"I thought you'd be gone by now," he said.

"At six?"

He looked at the kitchen clock. "Did they go and change the time again?"

"Last month."

"That explains a lot." Droop pulled up his sleeve, but only a band of pale skin circled his wrist. "Gee, I'm sorry. I was just trying to get an early start." He swirled the last of the coffee in his cup. "I wanted to surprise you."

I assured him he had. This was not the first time Droop had surprised me. He'd been the last name on the list of contractors we collected from friends and Scott's clients. The two of us walked him through the old kitchen and the adjoining enclosed porch until Droop spat his chew into a paper cup. That was when I decided it was time to weed the garden. An hour later, Scott brought the bid to me written on the back of a receipt from Budget Valley Lumber Yard. To my utter disbelief, Scott had hired him.

The next day, Droop let himself in the back door at seven o'clock, carrying a sledgehammer. By seven twenty-two, I knew how he'd earned his nickname. I knew by lunchtime that he was a skilled craftsman when he ripped open the lath-and-plaster walls without shorting out the electricity or flooding the porch.

He worked from seven to four, taking a full hour at noon to

lunch at home with Honey, his wife. After a week of being dressed by seven, I gave him a key—no invitations or knocking required. The work pace slowed when Scott joined Droop on Saturdays. Usually they swapped fishing stories, and the next thing I knew, they had loaded up the SUV with poles and bait.

Droop set his empty coffee cup on the island. "Well, I . . ."

I took his cup to the sink.

"Ya know, I . . ." he started again.

"Droop, do you need a check?"

"Heck no, I don't need no money. I just need to get this here job done. It's been hanging over my head." He rubbed the place over his heart. "Do you mind me being here and all?"

He'll never know how relieved I was that he was there and an escaped prisoner was not. "I am getting tired of picking splinters out of my feet," I joked.

Ky came into the kitchen carrying his school bag just as Droop and I returned from inventorying supplies in the garage. Ky smiled broadly at the man. "Maybe we could go fishing sometime."

Droop lowered his head and swallowed hard before answering. "It would be a privilege, young man."

Albert Strait held a magnifying lens to his right eye to look at the crispy leaves of Margaret's Don Juan rose. I watched the top of his bald head for five minutes while he turned the branch from front to back to front again, looking for signs of disease or pests. His slender, beaklike nose, long neck, and deliberate movements gave him a definite turtle quality. Albert returned the lens to its leather case and snapped the case closed. He sucked on his unlit pipe to think. I studied a poster, "The Life Cycle of the Coddling Moth." When he cleared his throat, I knew he was ready to talk pathology.

"Any sign of a borer?" he asked.

"No."

"Is she overwatering?"

"No."

"Drought?"

"No, the soil is well aerated and moist."

Albert raised his eyes to the ceiling and stroked his outstretched neck as if reaching for another line of questions to solve the puzzle, but he looked like a turtle reaching for a succulent leaf, so I calculated the age of my Birkenstocks to keep from snickering.

"Go back to your client's house and look at the crown of the plant, just at the soil level where the roots flare out from the base. Nip the bark there to see if there's black streaking in the woody tissue. You'll be looking for the effects of verticillium, a fungus capable of this kind of damage."

I started to ask him what to do about verti-whatever, but he raised his hand to stop me.

"We'll cross that road when we come to it."

He put the ailing leaves into a plastic bag and sealed the bag with a twist tie from his pencil drawer. "It would certainly be worth your while to take my class on the pathology of roses, Mrs. Garrett."

Thank you very much, Bertle the Turtle.

Louise laid a white kitchen towel on the seat of the Daisy Mobile before sitting beside me. "Raspberry Dream Muffins," she said, waving a grease-spotted bag before my eyes.

I'd eaten less nutritious lunches. Blink pressed his nose against the rear window of the truck. He would know soon enough that I wasn't in a sharing mood.

Louise wore her official garden designer's assistant outfit, dark indigo jeans tucked into bright yellow Wellingtons, a hand-painted sweatshirt with garden angels tending their hollyhocks, and watering-can earrings dangling from each ear.

"Mibby, what's that stickin' out of your hat?"

It had taken thirteen bobby pins and half a can of hairspray to tame my hair. "A ponytail."

"Must be a sad little pony with a tail like that."

Louise told me about her latest guests, Harland and Gayla Lundquist. They were in town visiting their newest grandbaby. The daughter-in-law had shooed them out of the house at six-thirty the night before when the baby went to bed.

"They came back to the house lookin' lower than snakes in a ditch," she said. "So Manley and I played pinochle with them until midnight. Such delightful people. They're leaving after their afternoon visit with the baby."

I told Louise about Droop's early morning visit.

"So," she asked, "did the fat lady swing?"

Groan.

The radio confirmed what I was seeing. A ceiling of steel-gray clouds had blown into the valley sometime during the night on a wind that now churned the trees into a wild dance. The wind also brought cooler temperatures, a welcome relief from the hot spring.

Margaret, her neighbor Walter, and Louise watched from the house as I dug around the base of the dead rose. A steady wind pelted my face with dust, and an occasional twig from a nearby globe willow hit my head. I pulled the collar of my jacket up over my ears. Goose bumps rose on my bare legs.

The crown of the rose looked dead, but so did the rest of the plant. No spongy tissue, no discoloration. The soil under the plant looked dark, like it had been watered recently. I smiled, thinking of Margaret's tender care to its last gasping breath. Then I did something gardeners all over the world do. I gathered a handful of soil and raised it to my nose to smell it. Margaret's soil didn't smell like the rich humus of a healthy garden. It smelled like the inside of my grandmother's garage.

Inside, Margaret poured a cup of coffee and joined Walter, Louise, and me at the table. She sat on the edge of her seat.

"It's petroleum of some kind," I told her. "It's in the soil of the neighboring rose, too, and that rose's symptoms have gotten worse."

"Petroleum?" asked Margaret. "On two of my roses? Oil? Where in the world did that come from?"

"Maybe someone changed their oil by the curb or—"

"Somebody poured oil on my roses? Why would they do such a thing?"

"I know who did it, and I know why."

We all looked at Walter.

His bottom lip pressed forward. "It's those hoodlums from the school. I've seen them stop in front of Margaret's house to light their cigarettes."

"That doesn't mean they poured oil on her roses, Walter," Louise said.

He hit the table with his open hand. "I wouldn't put it past them. They cursed at me something awful when I told them to go smoke their cigarettes somewhere else."

"Do you remember anyone working on their car in front of your house?"

Margaret looked into that faraway place where memories go to hide. "Nope," she said. "I don't remember nothing like that." Tears threatened to spill out of her eyes.

Louise moved quickly to her side and put her arm around Margaret's shoulders. "Well, now, it looks like we have a mystery and a loving Father all at the same time. Let's ask Him for help." Louise and Margaret bowed their heads to pray. I watched Walter stare out the window until his eyes darted to me. He bowed his head but didn't close his eyes. I joined the prayer as Louise said, "In Jesus' name, amen."

I arranged a time with Margaret to come back to plant two new rosebushes. "I'll replace the soil, too."

Margaret lowered her voice and smiled conspiratorially. "Just bill my daughter-in-law, the floozy."

When we got to the highway, Louise asked the question that swam around in my own head. "If the oil had been poured on the roses at the same time, wouldn't they have died at the same time?"

Probably.

Louise took Ben's hand when I introduced them and stepped in closer. He didn't flinch.

"Mibby tells me she's designin' a rose garden for y'all—a beautiful place where you can cherish your wife's memory."

Geez, Louise.

Ben held her gaze. "Yes," he said finally. "Her name was Jenny."

Louise smiled broadly. "How beautiful."

With that, I started to breathe again. I grabbed my clipboard and zipped up my jacket. Time to go to work.

The house wore a new coat of buttercream paint. Bare wood showed through on the trim where Ben had sanded in preparation for the paint.

He asked, "Can you suggest a color for the trim?"

"Do you have a favorite color?" countered Louise.

He didn't even have to think about it. "Blue."

"Why, that would look simply *dee*vine, Ben."

"Your scratch looks a lot better," Ben said to me.

A blush warmed my face. *Where did that come from?*

Memories and our attempts to keep them fresh are not completely accurate or rational. I knew that well. I was the one sleeping in a T-shirt that hadn't been washed in months. That was why I'd decided not to push onto Ben the botanical worth of sunlight for roses. His garden had nothing to do with prize-winning roses. It was to be a bookmark for a favorite passage in a beloved novel. But as we stood there, he asked me how much sun roses needed.

"Roses need at least a half day's sunlight to bloom well."

Ben studied the area. He looked up at the cottonwood that shaded the small yard and made an arc with his arm through the sky in what I knew was the sun's summer path. Louise and I watched him. He had replaced his painting clothes with slim-cut Levi's, a white T-shirt, and an unbuttoned flannel shirt that whipped around him in the wind. His face was clean-shaven, revealing a sliver of a scar on his jaw. Louise tried to get my attention with little coughs, but I ignored her. I didn't need to see her face to know her eyebrows were jumping overtime, and I was trying to keep the visit professional.

Ben walked to the fence opposite the bedroom window. "So they would have to go here?"

"Is that all right with you?"

"I'll be able to see them from the bedroom. That might actually be better."

"Do you want a place to sit in the garden?" I asked.

"Why, it wouldn't be a memorial garden without a bench," Louise said.

I shot her a warning look. She ignored me. "The whole point of a memorial garden is to be close to your memories."

Is it?

"That might be nice." A smile creased the corners of Ben's eyes. "Can you get garden benches with cupholders?" Scott had asked me the same question when I mentioned a bench for our garden. It's a guy thing.

Ben went into the house while Louise and I measured the yard. She held one end of the measuring tape and called off the feet and inches while I wrote the dimensions and drew a rough sketch. The wind carried the sweet smell of rain. It also made it difficult to manage the papers on my clipboard. Louise sidled in.

"Should we come back when the wind is calmer?"

McDonald's called my name. "No, I would like to get this done."

"Good." She rubbed her hands together greedily. "I'm happier than a one-eyed dog in a meat market."

I didn't have to ask her what she meant. She'd said the same thing about Steve the plumber and Jake the tile guy. Oddly, I felt the same disloyalty at letting myself appreciate Ben as I had when Louise and I had giggled over the subcontractors remodeling her bathroom. Only then, Scott had still been with me. His absence had done nothing to diminish his claim to my heart.

"Let's get this done before the rain comes," I said.

I drew in the cottonwood, including the reach of its shade, and noted where the windows were on the back of the house. Next came the hardest part of the design process, figuring out what the client really wanted. I hoped Ben knew.

Ben poured coffee into delicate china cups with saucers for Louise and me, a large ceramic mug for him. We sat at a round wooden table painted daffodil yellow. The color echoed its excitement on the cabinets and the refrigerator.

One end of the living room was visible from the kitchen. Stacks of magazines and books anchored each seat, and crocheted pillows deflated with wear were propped in the corners of two chairs facing a television. Family pictures filled every available tabletop space and wreathed doorways and windows. Proud families in front of shiny vehicles. A young baseball player kneeling with his bat and ball. Many brides and grooms and graduates with mortarboards. This wasn't your typical bachelor pad.

Even more incongruous was a wooden shelf above the kitchen table. It held a collection of salt and pepper shakers—pink pigs from Iowa, cowboy boots from Wyoming, and pineapples from Hawaii.

Ben sat down with a plate of Oreo cookies. He must have seen me looking at the collection. "My grandmother wanted a pair of shakers from every state, but my grandfather died before they got to visit all of them. I sent her the pineapples and the scallops when I was stationed in Hawaii and Florida. Jenny found the beehive shakers in Utah to complete her collection."

"This was your grandparents' house?" asked Louise.

He told us it had been left to him when his grandmother died the year before. That explained the decorating. He planned on moving to Orchard City with Jenny when he had left the military.

One cup of coffee turned into two as I asked Ben questions about the garden and took notes. When I had to write or sketch, Ben and Louise talked. He told her about the summers he had spent in Orchard City. Each of his five siblings had taken turns enjoying an exclusive two-week stay at Grammy and Grampy's place.

Then he turned to more current events with a little help from Louise. He had left the Air Force when Jenny died, but he'd had plans to do so earlier. After he told us that, Ben leaned back in his chair and crossed his arms over his chest, the male signal for "No more questions, please." I hoped he didn't mind a few more about the garden.

"A couple of the roses are climbers," I said. "They'll need some support. A trellis or an arbor would do the trick. Which do you prefer?"

He rubbed his chin in concentration. "An arbor. My wife always wanted one."

"Maybe you could put the bench under it," Louise suggested.

When Ben offered to make another pot of coffee, I looked at my watch. Ky would be home in five minutes. Once again, I was leaving Ben's in a rush. I promised him I'd have a plan in a week or so. To my surprise, Blink came when I called.

Ben shook my hand before I could get in the truck. He leaned in and whispered, "Thanks for bringing Louise."

Inside the truck Louise rested her head against the door and closed her eyes. "Mibby," she said without opening her eyes, "Ben's nice."

By the time we reached the highway, her soft snores filled the cab.

"Mibby, you slow this contraption down this minute. Ky will be just fine."

I pressed the brakes hard in front of Louise's walk. She snapped her seatbelt open and scrambled out the door.

Ky had never come home to an empty house before. Guilt and fear played king of the mountain in my stomach. I pushed aside images of Ky running out of the house with his hair flaming but couldn't dethrone the deeper ache presented by a lonely boy wondering why his mother had abandoned him.

I prayed Droop was still in the kitchen, but his truck wasn't in its usual place at the curb. My worst fears were realized in that moment. The primer-and-yellow car was!

Ky sat with Earring Girl on the front steps eating ice cream. No time for a pretty parking job. I locked the brakes into a slide that stopped when the truck tapped the bumper of Earring Girl's car.

Blink trotted past me to greet Ky. For once I was glad he didn't stick to his training. If Ky was in danger, Blink would know it. Ky waved broadly when he saw me, but the look on my face stopped him short. He met me halfway down the front walk, speaking softly so the girl couldn't hear. "Mom, she isn't a stranger."

I looked past him to Earring Girl, whose cone dripped pink drops onto the front steps. Blink lapped them up and watched her cone attentively. Perhaps he feared Ky would drown in pink ice cream.

Earring Girl stood up slowly and held her oversized purse protectively. Her eyes were red and puffy. She swallowed hard. It was good to know that I could make the girl flinch; there was nothing I wanted more.

I kept my eyes on her as I spoke to Ky. "I want you to go into the house and let me talk to—"

"Andrea," he said. "She's really nice, Mom. She bought me some ice cream and gave me a ride home."

"You got in the car with her?" As soon as I'd said it, I knew I was headed down the wrong road. We'd review stranger safety later. "Ky, let me talk to her alone for a minute."

"Why?" he asked, holding his ground. "She's just being friendly."

To be fair, he didn't know about the girl's visits to the house or our encounter at the grocery store. He was just embarrassed by his hysterical mother.

"I've met Andrea before. I think she wants to talk to me about something."

Ky looked dubious but went into the house. I turned to Andrea and willed myself to become Medusa with a ponytail of writhing snakes.

"Who are you, and why are you here?"

"Ky's a neat kid. He's really tenderhearted." Unlike you, she added with her eyes.

I repeated my questions.

"I didn't mean to scare you or bother you. I came here looking for my father."

"Your father? He's not here." I turned for the front door, but she caught my arm.

"I know. I kept waiting for him to show up, but when he didn't . . ."

"You expected your father to show up here?"

Andrea studied me hard. "You don't know about me, do you?"

I don't know why, but the question quickened my pulse. She didn't wait for my answer.

"My father is, was, your husband, Mrs. Garrett."

I can only explain what happened next by the spider-in-the-shower phenomenon—stomp now, check for venom later. I slapped the girl hard across her cheek.

She held her cheek with one hand and backed into the porch railing for support and to gain a margin of safety. I was instantly ashamed of myself for hitting her but didn't say so. I was too busy doing the arithmetic. The girl had to be in her early twenties. Scott would have been fifty in January. Even for the mathematically challenged, it subtracted out with plenty of sperm and opportunity. But there was more to this than biology.

Scott would have told me.

"Did you tell Ky your story?" *Fairy tale? Fantasy? Lie?*

"No, and he didn't ask. I just asked him where his dad was."

"I don't know what kind of sick joke this is for you." My voice wavered under the weight of her deception, so I bolstered it with anger and trudged ahead. "But I want no part of it. If I see you again, I'll call the police. Now, go."

"Mrs. Garrett—" she started, but I closed the front door on her. I watched through the peephole as she drove away in her car.

Ky sat on the floor, his back to an open window, his face

hidden in his arms. "I can't believe you hit her." He looked up. "You hit her," he said again to make it more believable. But apparently it didn't, so he stomped up the stairs repeating his accusation. "You hit her. You hit her."

I followed him to his room, but he had locked his door.

"Ky, I'm so sorry." And I was. "Come down to the kitchen when you're ready. I'll start dinner."

I busied myself preparing dinner. I needed to do something—anything—to keep from thinking about the girl's words, but Droop had stripped the kitchen of all but the most important element, the sink. I rummaged through a few boxes he had filled with cooking utensils in the dining room until I found the saucepan but returned it when I couldn't find the stove. I called Pizza Man.

The message light blinked on the answering machine. I ignored it. Whoever had left the message wouldn't want to talk to me in this state. Instead, I read a note from Droop nailed to the wall: "I knocked off early since I came at six. I promise to be here at the real seven tomorrow. D.D."—short for his full name, Droopy Drawers.

Fine.

I took my pruning saw out to the garden to remove old branches from an overgrown lilac. I hacked at the lower branches with more force than was needed. My intent was to improve air circulation to prevent powdery mildew. By the time I stopped, air circulation was the least of the plant's problems. It was now knee high with barely enough leaves for photosynthesis.

A soft rain wetted the garden and released the thick scent of humus. I lay with my face to the sky, trying to reconnect all my frayed ends. When that got tiresome, I counted the droplets of rain that tapped my face. Ky found me hugging a bundle of branches.

"Did I tell you she has a picture of Dad when he had long hair and a funny beard?"

MAY 8

Flutterby roses opening with lemon yellow blossoms that change to salmon and to almost white as it fades. What a show! Elm seeds gooey mess from rain. Weapon of choice, shovel. Still cooler—around 75°. Better.

Droop poured me a cup of coffee when I shuffled into the kitchen just after eight. Ky had stopped by my room to kiss me good-bye and receive his benediction. He seemed eager and happy about the day ahead of him, so I offered a prayer of thanks for that, too.

"Good party last night?" Droop asked.

"No, movie. Late show."

"If you say so."

Only Jimmy Stewart and Henry Fonda could vouch for me, and they weren't talking.

"How'd the conference go with Ky's teacher?" he asked.

"Conference?"

"She left a message on the phone."

Beep. "Mrs. Garrett, this is Mrs. Friedlander calling again. I'll be in my room until five o'clock tonight. Please come so we can discuss Ky's work." Ky had lied to me—and I'd wanted to believe him. It took too much energy to do otherwise.

Beep. "This is Judith. Have another referral for you. If the address I have for her turns out to be the cemetery, I wouldn't be surprised. Anyway, it's here for you."

Cemetery? I should be taking notes.

Beep. "Ky, dude? Sal. Pick you up at five for practice." I left that message on the phone for Ky to find later.

I left my coffee in the kitchen and headed for the garden, hoping to find grace for a mother who had taken the easy way out. I found piles of soggy elm seeds instead. With each scrape of the shovel, I flogged myself with another accusation.

Scrape. *You're too crazy to be a mother*. Scrape. *You don't deserve a kid like Ky*. Scrape. *Scott wouldn't lose control like this*. Scrape. *Would he?* Scrape. *For crying out loud, get it together!* Getting it together seemed a little ambitious at the moment. Maybe I'd just be Ky's mom again.

Louise pushed through the gate wearing one of the terry cloth robes she provided for guests. A second robe was draped over her head, veil style. She looked like the patron saint of terry cloth. She was smiling her I've-got-a-secret smile. Her cheeks pushed her eyes into half moons.

"You will never, never, ever guess what Federal Express brought me this mornin'." She waited and rolled her blue eyes skyward.

I was in no mood to play guessing games with Saint Louise. I should have suggested she come back later. I scraped my shovel along the path to scoop up a load of elm seeds.

"Tell me," I said flatly.

"No, you have to guess."

Sometimes it was all I could do to keep from torpedoing her indomitable spirit. "Look, Louise . . ."

Her smile dimmed, and she pulled the robe off her head. "I can see I'm going to have to tell you. Remember the granola eaters with the sticky fingers? They sent the robes back with a note that said they were sorry. You can't outrun the Holy Spirit, Mibby."

How I envied Louise. Her God was at her beck and call twenty-four hours a day, running interference and retrieving her robes. He cared deeply about the details of her life and seemed determined to make her His poster child for grace. What about me? Maybe it was up to me to be the spokeswoman for the forgotten. After all, He'd allowed my life to slip through His fingers and shatter, hadn't He?

Blink greeted Louise from behind with his version of a handshake. She let out a yelp and threw him a Magnum P. I. muffin—a carrot muffin packed with nuts, raisins, and pineapple hunks—not chunks—from her pocket. I watched Blink gulp it down. Jealousy didn't help my attitude.

Louise took off her robe and inspected the damage. A smudge of dog snot and rich soil marked the spot. The gardener in me was proud, but I apologized to her for the mess.

"Nothin' a little bleach can't help."

We were drinking coffee on the back steps when Louise asked, "Mibby, what do you think about Ben?"

"What do you mean?"

"Do you think he's nice?"

Sometimes I thought Louise was stuck in the sixth grade. "Sure, he's nice." *Very nice.*

I didn't mean to think about how nice his hand had felt when I'd shaken it at the end of our meeting. But it had felt nice—so nice that my heart had almost exploded, which made me feel incredibly guilty. I whispered an apology to Scott. Margaret had been right. My body had a mind of its own, evidently closer to the primal end of the scale.

Louise took a breath like a child preparing to dive for the quarter on the bottom of the pool. I knew she was going to suggest something painful, like plucking my eyebrows or waxing my legs, so I went on the offensive.

"Louise, I need to plant Margaret's roses and start on Ben's plan. Gotta go."

She asked me to find out from Margaret exactly when she'd noticed the roses suffering. Louise had a theory. "Get me dates."

The phone rang as I passed through the dining room. It was Andrea.

"Don't hang up!" she begged.

I tried to sound like a vice-principal. "What do you want?"

Andrea told me she only wanted some information about Scott—family, health, interests. It would fill in some holes for her. Then she started to catalog all the reasons I should meet her. "I don't want anything from you. I'll leave after we talk. I don't have much time. Please. You're the only one who can tell me what I need to know. I'll never contact you again. I can prove I'm his daughter."

Bingo.

She was here to claim Scott's estate. I needed to see her proof, so I agreed to meet her in the park at eleven. That gave me enough time to replace Margaret's roses before I met with Andrea. I planned on telling her that Scott had the measles when he was seven, period.

Once I dug out Margaret's Don Juan roses, I continued digging until the mechanical smell of petroleum was replaced by the sweet smell of damp earth. Then I shoveled out six more inches just to be sure. I bagged the soil with plans to ask Bertle the Turtle what to do with the contaminated soil. I looked forward to telling him it wasn't a fungal disease at all but a crime against botany, which was more than just a little sad.

Walter stopped by while I was digging to tell me he'd seen the hoodlums smoking their filthy cigarettes that morning. "There's nothing good about them punks."

"Did they stop in front of Margaret's house?"

"Not today. They saw me watching them."

Walter had his mind made up, but I wasn't so sure about his theory. Vandalism wasn't a crime of logic. Whoever had killed these beautiful roses, loved and nurtured by a gentle spirit of a woman, felt completely justified in doing so. No reason needed. I had to wonder if the vandals were watching me as I worked. Were they planning another raid?

As I loaded my tools into the truck, Margaret brought out a glass of iced tea and a bowl of water for Blink. He watched me over the edge of the bowl as he lapped the water.

"How long will it take for the new roses to catch up with the old ones?" Margaret asked.

"With your magic touch? Three to four years."

"That's not so bad."

"Margaret," I said, remembering Louise's request for information, "can you remember when you first noticed the roses were having trouble?"

"I know exactly," she said. "I wrote it down on the calendar. You never know when you might need information like that."

I followed Margaret into her kitchen. Blink made trails on the screen door with his wet muzzle as he watched us. Margaret took her calendar off the wall. Each square was filled with penciled notations. "Car stalled at 12th and Peach. New refrigerator bulb. Fertilized lawn."

She scanned the squares with a magenta fingernail. Only her thumbnail glowed orange. "I've learned to write everything down.

My mind is like a steel trap, you know. One that's sprung, that is." She gave me a quick wink. "Here it is. April second. 'New growth on Don Juan twisted and brown.'"

She found the note about the second Don Juan a month later on April thirtieth. I wrote the dates on a piece of paper and put them in my pocket. Blink barked to hurry me along, and I obliged. To reward my compliance, he sneezed before we got in the truck.

Good boy.

I pulled Scott's Yukon to the curb behind Andrea's car but didn't get out right away. It had been a big mistake to drive Scott's car. I had to stop twice on the way for a park-and-blubber break. My eyes felt woolly and hot. The black Yukon was meant to make me incognito. If I had to strong-arm Andrea's birth certificate away from her, I wanted something less conspicuous than a pea-green truck as a getaway car. Sitting at the curb, I thought it might have been better to write Andrea a check for the balance in my savings account. At least she could buy herself a nice blouse. At Wal-Mart.

Andrea's car turned out to be a 1970s Toyota. The "lance" was the neck of a cello case. The fat end rested in the back window. Andrea had removed the headrest of the passenger seat, so the cello angled out the window. A maple bonsai tree sat on the passenger seat. Quarter-sized maple leaves, perfectly formed, covered the eighteen-inch-tall tree, but the new leaves were a lighter green, edging too close to yellow. A beach towel wrapped around its container held the tree in the center of a box. I felt like Gulliver looking upon a Lilliputian's prized tree.

"It's been in the family for a long time. Someone got it for a graduation present. It's almost thirty years old," said Andrea from behind me.

"It's beautiful."

"I have to get it to a permanent home. It's already showing signs of stress."

Andrea led me to a picnic table under an ancient cottonwood. She wore the same crumpled purple shell and black shorts she had had on the day before. The park was quiet. A young mother pushed her toddler in a swing, and a woman in a business suit read under the picnic pavilion. I was relieved to see that Andrea didn't have a red imprint of my hand on her cheek. But she did have dark shadows under her eyes.

When someone you love dies, you spend the rest of your life looking for him in the way someone laughs behind you at a ball-game, or leans on his hand as he talks, or pushes his hair back from his forehead. It's the heart's way of keeping the hope alive that he is not gone forever. Scott was all around me, hidden in the folds of other people's lives.

I studied Andrea for an echo of Scott. Her eyes were too dark, almost black, and much too round and liquid to be from Scott. Her nose was too delicate, long and slender with a slight bump, hardly noticeable. Her mouth was thin, barely there. That was Scott's mouth, maybe.

She lifted a Campbell's chicken noodle soup box from the bench to the table. The corners had been taped more than once and one of the flaps was missing. *Personal* was written on the side in black marker. She opened the flaps and stopped.

"I found this box under my moth—" She hesitated, looked up into the branches of the tree, and bit her lip. "Well, I guess it was my grandmother's bed."

If it was important to make such a distinction, she didn't tell me why.

"It was after graduation," she said. "I had to move out of the house so the new renters could move in. There were so many things to sort through." She turned her eyes to me. "I almost threw it away without looking inside."

Andrea fingered the contents of the box. "There are almost three hundred letters and cards in here, all of them addressed to me from a man who signed them 'love Daddy.' That really confused me—'to Andrea, love Daddy'. I didn't have a daddy. Although I know. . ." She swallowed hard and held my gaze. "Although I know now that my grandmother made the whole story up. She'd told me all along that my father left before I was born, so I didn't ask her about him until I got older. Then she had to get more creative, I guess. My grandmother told me that my father was a guy she'd met in the season of her breathless passion. And when she'd caught her breath and her belly had started to swell, he packed his bags." Andrea smiled at the memory, then sighed and wiped her face with her hands.

It was getting harder and harder to keep the characters of Andrea's crazy soap opera straight. So far, there was a grandmother with an identity crisis making up stories about a boyfriend who was afraid of commitment. But what did that have to do with Scott? And who was her real mother? Despite my best efforts to remain detached and objective, my chest tightened around a growing dread.

Andrea continued, "Saying that out loud makes the whole story sound stupid, but you had to know my grandmother. She was so exuberant, so alive and so beautiful. It was totally believable that she was my mother and especially that she was vulnerable to seasons of passion. I saw it every day in the way she lived and painted. I never questioned her."

Maybe Andrea's curiosity had been satisfied. Mine wasn't, so I surrendered to the frustration, letting it sharpen the edge of my voice. "This isn't making any sense to me."

"You're right. I'm babbling. I'm so sorry." Andrea reached out to touch my hand, but I recoiled. She didn't even blink. "From where you're sitting, this must seem totally bizarre."

She reached out again, and I let her fingers rest on my hand. "Maybe you should just forget everything I've said. I'll back up a bit; see if that helps."

When I sighed, she promised to make it short.

"I was raised by a woman I thought was my mother, but she was actually my grandmother. All I know of my mother and father is in these letters written by a man who signed his name as Daddy. The return addresses are from Scott Garrett, no street address, just a P.O. box. I was having trouble finding my real mother, my grandmother's daughter, so I decided to look for my dad. At least I had a name and a city to find him. That's why I'm here."

The dread I'd sheltered in my chest was now a freight train, horn blaring, closing in fast. "There must be ten Scott Garretts in Orchard City. How can you be sure it's my Scott?"

Andrea laid a square photograph on the table in front of me. "I found this picture and a marriage certificate in the bottom of the box."

In the photograph, a young Scott, my Scott, sat in a lawn chair on a green lawn. The fading light of sunset colored him with a rosy glow. A dark-haired pregnant woman sat beside him. It was too much to hope that she suffered from malnutrition. Andrea was in there, I knew, sleeping peacefully. The woman held a sparkler at arm's length and smiled tightly at the camera. Scott had wavy hair to his shoulders and a goatee—just like the knight in my dream. I shuddered.

"Are you okay?" Andrea asked.

Absolutely not. "Is this your mother?"

"I think so."

"You think so?"

She took a deep breath and crossed her arms. Her forehead

creased with worry. She probably thought I would hit her again. I had an urgent need for more facts.

"When was this picture taken?"

"This looks like a Fourth of July celebration. I was born a few days later on the seventh."

Scott was young in the picture but not a boy. "What year was this?"

"1982. When did you two get married?"

"1988."

"I was six."

She was six, and I was married, maybe, to someone who had forgotten to tell me he'd been married before. "Can I see the marriage certificate?"

The certificate was white with blue print made official-looking by the old English typeface. State of California. County of San Diego. The typewriter used to fill in the blanks had an old ribbon and an *e* that dipped below the line. The marriage had taken place at the Little Ivy Wedding Chapel in San Diego, presided over by Reverend Frederick T. Mackley, retired, on May 20, 1982. A wave of dizziness lifted, tilted, and then dropped the world around me. I looked at the picture again. Did Scott look happy? Did he adore the swollen woman?

"Do you want to see my birth certificate?" asked Andrea.

So much like a self-absorbed girl to think this is all about her.

"I want to see a divorce decree."

"I know this is hard."

This from someone who wanted to pick up my life and spill it across the floor. "You do not know. You do not know anything, little girl." I stood to leave.

Andrea stood, too. "Don't go. I'm sorry. I just need to know things about my dad to fill in some holes. I would especially like to know if he had any health problems or mental illnesses."

"You're talking about my husband, not some anonymous health report."

"Whether you like it or not, I'm talking about my father, who wrote me a whole boxful of letters and gave me half his genes." Andrea set her shoulders and crossed her arms. "Are you willing to help me or not?"

If I said no, would this be the end of it? I doubted it. She wanted something else. Maybe money to buy a new car.

"Why are you really here?"

"I wanted to find my—"

"Why are you really here?" I repeated. "What is it you want?"

"I wanted to find my father. I promised myself I'd look for him when I graduated. That's why I'm here, Mrs. Garrett. I thought I was going to find my father. But I was too late." She stopped to take a deep breath and let it out slowly. When she continued, her voice was taut but even. "So I'm willing to settle for a few bits and pieces. Is that something you can do for me?"

"Scott was healthy."

"Did he like lettuce on his peanut butter and jelly sandwiches?"

Scott had insisted on two crisp leaves of lettuce on his peanut butter and jelly sandwiches. I'd always thought it was weird.

"I don't have time for this," I said and got up to leave, determined to make it to the Yukon.

Andrea stopped me with a hand on my arm. "What would you want Ky to know about you?"

I shook her arm free and strode on.

She caught up with me and matched my stride. "Mrs. Garrett, I'm so sorry for upsetting you, especially now. I'm truly sorry. But you are the only person who can tell me who my father was."

That might have been true before I'd met Andrea, when I'd thought I knew the man I was grieving. But suddenly I wasn't sure I'd known him at all. When I stopped to unlock the car door,

Andrea pressed the Campbell's box into my arms.

"Take this. Read the letters. You'll see why I need to talk to you."

"I really don't have time."

"I don't, either. I need to get back to find a job and get ready for an audition. I'll call you tomorrow," she said and turned to leave.

No one had ever mistaken me for a NASCAR driver, but the Yukon's tires squealed on the switchbacks climbing to the top of the Colorado National Monument. I accelerated on the straightaways and braked hard on the tight turns. Ky would be home from school in a couple of hours, and I needed a place to scream without being heard. I knew just the place.

I parked at Cold Shivers Point and walked through the twisted junipers to the canyon's rim. Two thousand feet below, a dry streambed creased the canyon's red floor. A pair of juncos darted by, and the trill of a canyon wren's song echoed off the stone walls. Beyond the canyon, the Grand Valley stretched broad and even to the Grand Mesa. The immensity of the landscape had comforted me many times, but that day the expanse only verified my fear. I railed at an unhearing and unseeing Scott.

"You should have told me! Look at this mess. I have a crazy girl hounding me for information and whatever else she can milk from me. And just how am I supposed to explain all this to your son? Really, Scott, how should I explain to him that a stranger has come to disrupt and destroy us? Thanks a lot, Scott. Just thanks a lot."

I sank to the ground, but my anger was not spent.

"You should have told me. You should have told me!" The more I scolded, the hotter my anger grew, the more poisonous my sarcasm became. "Who will come looking for you next year, Scott? A son born to a teller? Twins coming to ask you to coach their soccer team? Or maybe a busload of women—"

"That's enough," I interrupted myself. There was no sense in making things up when all that was true was disturbing enough. But as angry as I was, more than anything I wanted Scott near, or to at least have a sense of his nearness, which only awakened my regret.

I regretted not having a gravesite to visit. Everything that had made cremation seem like the most practical choice escaped me now. There was no tombstone to touch or shady knoll to visit. Grieving was for the living, but I had no place to meet my memories.

And I regretted not asking Scott about his life before me. But why would I have done that? I had lost so much by the time I'd met Scott. My father. My grandmother. And my mother, I supposed. He had seemed so content to sooth my wounds, and I had been content to let him.

And now I added meeting with Earring Girl in the park to my long list of regrets. Until I'd seen the documents and the picture, she was just a crazy kid. Now, she was a menacing force with the power to unravel my life.

And while I was at it, I regretted asking my best friend's ex-boyfriend to the Sadie Hawkins dance when I was in the eleventh grade. I couldn't even remember his name, but I remembered leaning against the gym wall with him watching Linda dance with her new boyfriend. My date and I left after two songs, and he cried the whole way home.

The sound of voices coming down the trail interrupted my internal diatribe. Beyond the piñons, a woman's tense voice insisted that Tyler stay with her. Two women with three small children came into view: one child in a stroller, another in a backpack, and a sullen boy, probably Tyler, who held the hand of one of the women.

The scene worked to remind me that not all of what I believed about Scott had been tarnished. He'd adored Ky and me. The truth of it was in everything he'd done and said. It was in the way he preferred our company to anyone else's, and in the way he cheered us on to bigger dreams, and in his devotion to praying for our every need. Those were the things I couldn't argue against. As for the rest of it—another wife and a child left behind—I spoke once more to the shimmering waves of air above the valley.

"Scott, I am so disappointed in you."

On the way back to the Yukon, I vowed never to leave Ky alone again. It was too risky with Andrea around. Until she was back in California, I would stick to Ky like red on a rose. Andrea had claimed she wanted information, but I couldn't chance that she didn't want more. I decided to go on the offensive. I needed to know more about the dark-haired woman in the photograph and the claim she had on Scott's estate. The thought of a first wife on my doorstep made me entertain thoughts of moving to the Canadian wilderness without leaving a forwarding address, but I quickly dismissed the idea. The growing season was too short above the Arctic Circle, and I doubted they played organized baseball.

I delivered a pep talk into the rearview mirror.

"You've got to pull it together for Ky. Get normal. Do normal things. And for heaven's sake, act normal. Be the mother you used to be."

Louise sat on an overturned bucket in the middle of my kitchen telling Droop about the granola eaters. From the looks of it, Louise was yammering and Droop was doing his best to keep working. All I wanted to do was read a letter or two from Andrea's box. Droop slid a trowel along a drywall joint, feathering the joint compound until it nearly disappeared. The line would completely disappear with a coat of paint—he was that good. Neither of them had noticed me, so I tiptoed through the dining room toward the stairs.

"No kidding," Droop said with a yawn. "Are you going to press charges?"

"Heavens no! I'll leave justice up to the Lord. After all, they did return the robes as white as lilies."

I was almost to the stairs when Louise spotted me down the hall. "There you are," she said.

I must have worn my weariness like a cheap pair of pantyhose.

"Oh, Mibby. You look lower than a duck in Death Valley. But that don't matter. I have a surprise for you. Let's go!"

Going anywhere was the last thing I wanted to do, but acquiescing to Louise was as normal as it got. I excused myself to wash my face but really to hide the box of pictures and letters. The box was too tall to put under my bed, so I shoved it under the guest bed, where it would be safe from curious eyes.

Droop shot me a look of gratitude as I opened the door for Louise. Whatever she had in mind had to be better than thinking about Scott and another woman—or worse. I hoped the field trip had something to do with chocolate. It usually did.

"I'll keep an eye open for Ky," Droop said.

That stopped me in my tracks. I told Louise I had to be home to meet Ky no matter what.

"No problem," she said. "We have plenty of time. I'll have you back in a jiff."

Louise insisted on driving. "That truck of yours waggles my innards." Her driving made me nervous. I wasn't at all sure she could see past her Cadillac's hood ornament, but she insisted glasses were for grandmas and engineers.

"Mibby, have you had a chance to talk to Margaret? I'm dyin' to test my theory."

I fished the paper out of my pocket and read the dates to Louise.

"Open this," she replied, handing over her planner, "and see what part of the moon's cycle occurred on those dates. There's a calendar in the front."

I counted back from the dates Margaret had given me. "Both of those dates are about ten days after the dark of the moon. If you're thinking that the vandals are waiting for the darkest night to cover their dirty work, this would work out right. It would take that long for the poisoning to show up."

"Glory be! Looks like we're going to have ourselves a stakeout." Before I could ask Louise what she meant, she said, "Here we are, Virginia's Oasis of Beauty."

I was a little disappointed it wasn't the chocolate shop, but when Louise was right, she was right. I needed a haircut.

"Louise, honey, I love those earrings," said the proprietor, Virginia. "You look positively wild with passion in your jungle wear."

Virginia looked wild in her own rendition of jungle wear—over-the-ankle spiked snakeskin heels added four inches to her height and lengthened her legs below the matching red skirt. She wore a red tank top under a black vinyl vest. Thanks to polyvinyl chloride, no animals had been killed or injured to dress Virginia. To top it all off, she had lots and lots of coal black hair standing at unnatural angles all over her head. Louise looked tame by comparison. Her jungle print dress and macaw earrings had come straight out of the J. C. Penney catalog. The friends chatted happily about each other's outfits while I plotted an escape route.

"This is the girl I told you about—Mibby."

Virginia held me by the shoulders at arm's length. "Oh my goodness. You are a pretty thing. I can't wait to get my hands into your hair." She said it with such conviction, I followed her to the shampoo sink.

In front of the mirror, Virginia listened carefully as I explained I was growing my hair out to all one length. She even nodded enthusiastically when I told her I was ready for an easier hairstyle. It was possible she wasn't listening at all, but the clicking of her bracelets kept me under her spell.

"You have a small head," she said, pulling a comb through my wet hair. "You'll want a little lift to keep your head in proportion with your body."

I have a small head?

"I suggest we cut some wispy bangs to soften your forehead, and you should keep the layers until your hair is a little longer. Besides, you're getting a little old for butterfly clips." She pulled her glasses down her nose and caught my eyes in the mirror. "Trust me."

Trust you? Of course I will. My head is too small, and I'm too old to wear butterflies. I obviously need help.

"You have great color and such a pretty face. We need to get your hair to complement your assets, honey."

When I left the shop a half hour later, I looked like I wore a helmet with the Rock of Gibraltar jutting out of my forehead. To keep from crying, I breathed deeply. I assured myself that shampoo would fix everything. Maybe. I prayed I wouldn't see anyone I knew before I had a chance to wash it.

God doesn't answer all of our prayers with a yes.

"Mom, what happened to your head?"

I put the last of the Oreos onto a plate for Ky and Salvador. "Does my head look a little small to you?"

"No, not small." He seemed to be picking his words carefully. "Fluffy—and big."

Salvador talked around the cookie in his mouth. "My mom cried when that happened to her."

Plenty of time for that. "How are the cookies, boys?"

I could feel Ky watching me as I tidied up after dinner and told him his clean uniform was hanging in his closet. Perhaps he was watching for signs I'd put my rudder back in the water for good, that I was back on the list of people he could count on. More than anything I wanted that to be true.

He stopped at the doorway to ask, "Is everything okay, Mom?"

"I thought I'd come to your game tonight."

A smile of sweet pleasure lit Ky's face. I almost sobbed with shame.

"Are you going to wear a hat?" he asked.

"Definitely."

After he left, I clicked off the motherly things I'd done that afternoon. Washed Ky's uniform. Arranged cookies on a plate. Poured the milk. Grilled hamburgers. It wasn't so hard. Now I had plans to watch his baseball game and talk to him about his schoolwork.

Almost there.

People who don't believe in miracles should watch a Little League baseball game. Every player comes to the field with a dream—some modest, most not—that makes him alert to the possibilities.

The night was cold. Barbed. Spring had lost its fingerhold completely in the dry desert air. Despite down jackets and stocking caps, the wind and the accompanying chill encased us all in a muffled misery. The players wrapped their arms within the hems of their jerseys and did a two-step shuffle to keep warm. Cheeks reddened; lips tinted blue. But the hot dogs peppered with red clay from the infield still rivaled duck à l'orange. The pleasure of some things can't be diminished by a schizophrenic season like spring.

Ky struck out twice and popped an infield fly to the shortstop before he connected with a low outside pitch in the sixth inning. There were two runners on the bases—first and third—and two outs. The ping of the metal bat sounded different, clear and resonant.

Over the wall, Lord. Over the wall.

In the grand scheme of things, a home run doesn't measure up to the discovery of the smallpox vaccine or landing on the moon. Humanity is neither saved nor injured by a ball flying over a fence. But the thirteen-year-old boy who hits it moves from hoping to knowing glorious things are possible. And the mother who prayed sees the face of God in her son's purest joy.

Later, when the obligatory team celebration at Baskin-Robbins was over, Ky and I lay on his bed recounting the miracle.

"Did you see the look on the pitcher's face?" he asked.

"He was shocked," I answered.

"It cleared the fence by a mile."

"No, it was by two miles."

Our eyes met, and we agreed silently to accept this exaggeration as fact. Why not?

"Did you see the coach?"

"Yep, he was doing his one-legged happy dance."

We laughed as we pictured Salvador's dad hopping from one foot to the other in front of the dugout.

"It was so cool."

"It was," I agreed.

One more motherly thing to do before I accomplished my goals—talk to Ky about school. I waited, though, wanting to put a little time between the thrill of victory and the agony of defeat.

Ky turned to the wall and pulled his comforter up to his ears. "Mom, I'm really tired."

I looked at my watch. Ten forty-two. "You should be. It's late." There would be time to talk about school in the morning. He needed his rest. I rose and kissed him at his hairline. His damp hair still smelled sweet from shampoo. "Good night, sweetie."

"Good night, Mom."

I flipped off the light at the door.

"Mom?"

I turned and leaned against the doorframe to listen, happy to delay the ending of the day. "Yeah?"

"You don't have to be afraid of Andrea."

Adolescent children can be so exasperating. In one declarative sentence, he had let me know I was as transparent as a freshly cleaned window.

"I don't? Well, of course I don't. I mean, I'm not, afraid of Andrea, that is."

Ky spoke like someone stepping through shards of glass with bare feet. "I know she's from Dad's first family, Mom. It's okay. Kinda weird, but okay. I'd like to tell her stuff about Dad. That's why she came. Do you think we'll see her again?"

"I don't know, Ky."

"Could we try to find her?" He was insistent now, sitting up and wide awake. "She said she was staying down by the river, at the state park."

A cold finger of fear ran along my spine. Dos Rios State Park was a popular spot for fishing and picnicking adjacent to the riverfront trail. By day, the protected eddies and channels of the river provided a sanctuary for migratory birds and gave folks a wooded place to walk, jog, bike, and skate. The rabbit brush and tamarisk would have given Andrea a hidden place to park and sleep. But at night, the riverfront wore a different face. Transients gathered under the bridges for shelter and camped along the banks. Most were people just trying to find their way in the world. Some were ruthless. It wasn't a place for a young woman to be after dark.

"I think she's sleeping in her car," Ky added. "She says she gets pretty cold at night."

We dressed in sweats, parkas, and stocking caps. The nighttime temperatures were in the midforties, cool for May but downright frigid for someone sleeping in her car. Ky invited Blink into the cab of the Daisy Mobile. I almost protested. Blink cocked his head in an effort to look innocent and sat like a gentleman between us. That wouldn't last long, I knew, but if trouble came, I would need Blink to be his most obnoxious. Not that he would actually bite anyone, but I could probably count on him to release one of his gelatinous sneezes.

"Windows up. Doors locked," I ordered. Blink complained with a pitiful whine. "Sorry, Blink. This is serious." He panted in my face, the canine equivalent of backtalk. When I ignored him, he turned to look out the windshield.

Only a few cars were on the street as we drove under the amber-colored streetlights toward the river. My heart fluttered in my chest. I considered turning around. "We might not find her, Ky. But she's smart. She's probably found a warm place to stay. We'll drive through the park. Then we're going right home."

"Maybe we should pray."

"I'll drive. You pray."

Ky bowed his head and closed his eyes. We rode in silence past banks, churches, and convenience stores. He fingered his flashlight nervously. With the heater going and Blink panting his excitement, the windows started to fog. I cracked my window and Blink thanked me with a wet lick. We started over the viaduct that spanned the railroad tracks.

"Are you having trouble getting started?" I asked.

"I'm just trying to get this right," he said, biting his lower lip.

"Take your time."

My first instinct in a pinch was action, preferably in the opposite direction. I couldn't see where God would mind an earnest supplication from a safe place—say, my bed. Scott, however, had always prayed at the first hint of trouble. He had always been there to remind me to stop, drop, and pray—sort of a fireman's approach to prayer. When the phone call came from Ky's first grade teacher that he hadn't returned to class after recess, Scott prayed. We found our son resting on the curb a block away. He was tired, he told us, and he wanted to go home for a nap. When the savings and loan Scott worked for filed for bankruptcy, Scott prayed and continued to pray until he found a night stocking job at a discount store. The job had paid the bills, barely, until the local economy had recuperated. Now Ky was the first to pray under duress, whether it was a missing hamster or a sick friend.

We stopped beside one of those testosterone-powered trucks at a red light. Its idle rumbled, and despite my better judgment, I looked over. The three men in the cab seemed amused by the Daisy Mobile. *Just jealous.* To avoid their gaze, I turned to check on Ky. Blink thought I was getting romantic and spread a wet kiss over most of my face. The light turned green, and the big truck's idle quickened to accelerate. I hung back a bit.

"We're almost there," I said to coax Ky.

"Lord, help us find Andrea. Keep her safe and warm."

I turned onto the road that led to the state park. We passed warehouses and a gravel pit before entering a residential area.

"Lord—" He stopped. I felt him looking at me, but I didn't know how to help him. "Lord, help us do the right thing. Amen."

"Amen."

I rolled up my window as we entered the unfamiliar neighborhood and prayed against the worst-case scenario. *Please don't let us become food for the fishes, Lord.*

The truck's headlights illuminated a white horse, rows of rusted mailboxes, and a parade of abandoned farm equipment. The road wound through the dark neighborhood, where porch lights glowed dimly at the ends of long driveways. I drove slowly as Ky checked stands of trees for Andrea's car. We stopped at the state park's information hut to read a sign. It said the gate was locked at ten and reopened at six the next morning.

"What gate?" asked Ky.

There wasn't one. A locked gate would have given me the out I needed. In an uncharacteristic show of rebellion, I didn't pay the four-dollar admission. That was what they got for false advertising.

The asphalt ended and the truck's tires crunched over the gravel road. I slowed, hoping to quiet the noise. To Blink's delight, Ky lowered his window as far as it would go. Before I could complain, Blink's tail was pounding my face.

"Ky, close the window!"

"The flashlight reflects off the glass."

The park had no streetlights. Lights from the warehouses across the river gave the treetops a smoky appearance but did little to illuminate the ground.

"Be ready to roll up your window if I tell you," I said.

Ky held the flashlight with one hand and the window crank in the other. He swept the trees with the beam of his flashlight as we drove along. On the west side of the road, black pools of water multiplied the spots of light on its surface. Every so often, worn tire tracks led off into the trees and to the top of the levy that separated us from the river. If someone didn't want to be seen, it would be a good place to park a car. But Andrea wasn't there.

We drove through the parking lots for the boat ramp and a picnic area. The sweep of the headlights revealed nothing. Blink did his song and dance that meant *Put the leash on me right this second and let me smell*. I slapped his rump down to the seat. He gave me a look over his shoulder to let me know he was in agony.

The road ended in a loop that corralled a picnic ground. To tell the truth, I was relieved to find the park empty.

"Ky," I said, pressing the gearshift into reverse, "Andrea could be a million miles from here. Let's go home."

"There's a gate!"

Off the far edge of the loop, a green metal gate was closed and bolted. An oversized padlock hung from the hasp. The gate stood alone with only a couple of well-placed boulders to keep drivers from ignoring it.

"Maybe this is the gate they lock," he said. "Andrea could have parked down there before they locked it. She's probably sleeping down there right now." He pulled up on the door handle.

"Wait a minute," I said, reaching across him and pulling the door closed. "I'm sure they check the road before they lock the gate." The truck's lights shone down the road that led into a row of cottonwoods and to the river.

"The park isn't even open for summer yet," Ky said, his eyes flashing with hope. "Maybe they don't have enough people to check all the roads. She could be down there."

I gave him a one-word plea for reasonableness. "Ky."

"Mom, she's my sister."

This is the other exasperating thing about adolescents. They know which buttons to push. I wouldn't have been surprised to find a schematic of my buttons on a blueprint under Ky's bed.

Blink stayed in the truck with Ky. I told him to honk the horn if he saw anyone and made him promise to remain in the locked truck, no matter what. I didn't trust the truck's battery to start the engine if I left the lights on, so Ky sat in the dark. I commandeered the flashlight, too.

Before I'd gone twenty yards, my nose was running from the cold. My pockets were empty, so I blotted my nose on my sleeve.

The night sky bulged toward earth with its weight of stars. I found their nearness a welcome distraction but not the comfort I needed.

The flashlight's beam provided only a small circle of light in which to walk. Leaves blackened with mold paved the hard-packed tire tracks, and some early grasses grew between the ruts. Every few steps, I twisted without stopping to see if Ky had turned on the headlights. The road curved into the trees, so the truck was out of sight. I walked faster. Just as I had convinced myself I wouldn't find Andrea, my flashlight reflected off the license plates of a car. They weren't California plates. I snapped off the flashlight.

A male voice asked, "Who's there?" The voice was closer than the car. Off to the right. In the trees. Not happy about a visitor.

This wasn't a good time to make new friends, so I turned and ran. My Birkenstocks caught on something, and I landed hard on my knees. Leaves crunched under heavy footsteps behind me. I scrambled to my feet.

"Git!"

The rock hit below my left shoulder blade. I was down on the ground again but not for long. I'd lost the flashlight. Just as well. I didn't want to give the man a spotlighted target. He was doing fine in the dark.

I sprinted back toward the truck. Its lights came on, throwing long shadows through the trees. My heart did a figure eight in my chest. I ran faster but stopped abruptly when the truck came into view. The lights silhouetted two figures, not one, and a dog.

"Mom!"

"Ky?"

"I found her! I found Andrea!"

MAY

9

Wind, wind, and more wind! Watched elm seeds gather on path again. Ugh! Brighter note—Eastern Star tulips are open. Five petals open to a star shape in the afternoon sun. Base of petals bright yellow. They close to a more traditional shape as the sun sets. Need more of those for next year. Fritillaria Meleagris are a little bizarre but fun—checkered paper lanterns on a thready stock. Watching for other new bulbs in rock garden. Still cool.

A dream about a blazing meteor hitting the house woke me. Nothing like a dose of impending doom to start the day. It was all the excuse I'd needed to dress without showering and to reach for a baseball cap. Before I pulled the cap over my head, I ran my fingers through my hair. The result wasn't that bad. I put the cap back on the dresser.

God bless Virginia.

The door to the guest bedroom where Andrea slept was closed when I walked by. I stopped briefly to listen at the door. No radio or snoring. I assumed Andrea was still in there but wasn't about to check. Ky's bed was empty, the comforter pulled haphazardly into place. He was way ahead of me, in more ways than one.

He'd seen Andrea's appearance as something wondrous and magical. He'd lost a father but gained a sister. I asked myself if I should feel shame or resentment. It was hard to decide. Shame because just a small amount of thinking would have told me Andrea was living in her car. Crumpled clothing. A car packed with all her belongings. My self-absorption had put the girl in a dangerous position. But I repackaged the shame into resentment with short yet convincing arguments. Andrea hadn't planned for her own safety. She assumed she'd be taken care of. She was supposed to be an adult. How naïve. I was off the hook.

Ky was loading his book bag with the last of the Oreo cookies when I came into the kitchen. His hair was wet at the crown, where he had tried to drown a cowlick into submission.

"Is that your lunch?" I asked.

"No," he said, snapping his pack closed. "Breakfast."

"Ky—"

"We're out of milk." And in a boy's mind that is enough reason to abandon all of the food groups. "Is Andrea awake?"

"I don't know."

He stopped at the door to give me marching orders. "You should probably go to the store to get some milk and some things Andrea would like. She's a vegetarian."

I put my hand on his head and prayed, "Keep Ky in your watchful care. Shelter him in your everlasting arms."

"Amen," he said, turning to go. He stopped to remind me, "Don't forget. She doesn't eat meat," and slid a quick kiss over my cheek.

He was right. The least I could do was send Andrea on her way with a hearty breakfast, so I headed for the grocery store. I loaded my cart with things I thought someone with multiple piercings and an aversion to meat products might like—granola, organic pear nectar, and tofu. The early morning checkout lanes were all but empty, so I was out the door in no time. I rummaged through my purse for the keys. Once. Twice.

When I saw the keys hanging in the ignition of the locked Daisy Mobile, I put my head on the cab to cry. And not one of those posed movie star cries, either. My shoulders pumped. My lips curled. My chin quivered, and without looking in a mirror, I knew red blotches encircled my eyes. A puddle of mucous and salty tears collected on the cab. Even I was astounded by how quickly I'd shifted from capable to inept. Still, the release felt marvelous.

"Mibby?"

Without looking up, I recognized the voice. It was Ben. I rubbed the snot from my nose with my sleeve, but I could feel its stickiness spread across my cheek. I lowered my head for another swipe.

He wore a paint-spattered flannel shirt tucked into his jeans and ragged hiking boots. He held a bakery bag spotted with grease and a cup of coffee. His face was a map of concern. He dug deep into his pocket for a hanky and pressed it into my hand. I buried my face into the soft cotton, breathing deeply to regain control. If my prayers had been answered, Ben would have remembered his Danish and followed his stomach home.

"Got a problem?" he asked.

"Locked my keys in the truck."

"Do you have a key at home?"

"Louise will bring it."

Ben scanned the parking lot. "Is she on her way?"

I refolded the hanky and deliberated giving it back to him. Instead, I tucked it into my pocket. "I was just going to call her."

"Don't bother."

Ben added his bag to my cart and pushed it to his truck. It was an older model with the chrome and edges I remembered from the sixties—bright red with a white insert. It looked as new as my memories. Ben saw me studying it.

"It was my grandfather's," he said. "We restored it together after my senior year in high school. He left it to me." Ben turned the key and the engine responded with a rumble. He smiled at me. "Which way?"

As I told him where to turn, I waited for the lecture on responsibility and the value of organization. It didn't come. Instead, he asked me the typical get-to-know-you questions and offered me half a bear claw. I didn't want to deprive him of his breakfast, so I declined.

"How long have you lived in Orchard City?"

"Fifteen years." I kept my answers short so I could plan a way to avoid introducing Andrea when we got to my house. I cracked the window when I remembered I'd skipped a shower.

"And how long have you had your business?"

"Two years." Short of a feigned fit of hysteria, I didn't see how I could keep Ben from helping me into the house with the groceries. Introductions would have to be kept simple.

Ben, this is Andrea. Andrea, this is Ben.

Having settled that, I watched his profile as he talked about his move to the valley and decided he definitely qualified as handsome. His nose was a little big but classical in its straightness. His bottom lip was a plump cushion of flesh. I was blushing with that thought when he turned his dark eyes on me and asked, "Do you have any children?" I faked a cough to give my pulse a chance to restart before I answered.

"Yes, I have a son."

"How old?"

"Thirteen. He hit his first home run last night."

"That's great!" Then he added, "It's too bad . . ."

"Yeah, Scott would have loved that."

Ben changed the subject. "I'll finish painting the house today. Got a blue-gray color for the trim and shutters. Looks nice if I do say so myself. I'm ripping the deck off tomorrow. Maybe it won't look so much like a tugboat."

I had Ben avoid the intersection where Scott was hit, hoping he wouldn't notice.

"We went in a circle there, didn't we?" he asked.

"Just wanted you to avoid a long light."

The first floor of the house was empty when we carried the groceries through the back door. Droop was late and Andrea apparently still slept. Blink, however, tried his best to wake her with his twenty-one bark salute aimed at Ben.

Ben loaded groceries into the refrigerator, which was now on the back porch. I was glad I'd thrown away—container and all—the putrefying remains of a broccoli casserole the day before. I sorted packages of just-add-water mixes into boxes in the dining room.

He asked for a tour of the construction site, so I showed him around and told him a brief history of what we'd done to the house. I listened for movement upstairs, but the house remained quiet. When I showed Ben the entryway, he ran his hand along the railing of the staircase and smiled broadly.

"I learned to fly on one of these."

I pointed to the thin scar along his jaw. "Is that how you got your scar?"

He touched the scar with his finger and talked through a lopsided smile I hadn't seen yet. My heart thumped in my chest, and my cheeks got warm.

"No, I earned that one fair and square from my sister Pam. Something about a photograph and a frying pan."

The back door slammed, and Droop walked into the entry with a True Value bag tucked under his arm. He stopped in his tracks when he saw Ben. The two men looked each other up and down and locked their gazes. *High noon?* Droop spoke first.

"And who might you be?" he said, extending his hand.

Ben clutched Droop's hand and answered, "I'm Mibby's client and friend Ben Martin. And you?"

"Robert Ingram, contractor and watchdog."

Robert?

Droop looked at Ben over his glasses. "If you know what I mean."

Ben smiled. "Glad you're on the job." And released his hand. Droop seemed satisfied that Ben knew his place, so he started unloading his bag.

The trip back to the grocery store's parking lot was much quieter. We weren't just client and designer anymore. Droop had brought the sex difference right out there in the open. The silence grew awkward. I wanted to reassure Ben my interest in him was purely professional before he had to explain his aversion to pear-shaped women.

"Don't pay any attention to . . . ah . . . Robert. He has an overactive imagination."

"No, he's right. Pretty ladies need protection from the wolves." He said this completely deadpan.

Scott had told me I looked pretty when I wore a new outfit or finally mastered a new hairstyle. I figured he appreciated the illusion I'd created. There was no pretense at illusion that day with Ben. All I had to offer was a clean T-shirt and a day-old hairdo, not even any Nudie-Cutie lip gloss. More than likely, he was just fishing for a discount on his design.

"I like your hair," he said.

"You do?"

The Rock of Gibraltar had softened into the wispy bangs Virginia had promised. In my book, his compliment earned him a ten percent discount.

"It . . ." He looked at me. "It . . ." The crooked smile again. "It suits you. Frames your face real nice."

"Thanks." Okay, he deserved twenty percent, but that was all.

We didn't talk again until he parked beside my truck. I told him I would finish his plan that night, and he seemed pleased.

"I'm ready," he said.

Driving back to the house, I scolded myself for letting Ben's compliment addle me so. He was just being nice. He'd seen what a rough morning I'd had and wanted to make me feel better. But the thought of his tenderness warmed my chest again. For heaven's sake, Scott hadn't even been gone a year.

I whispered, "I'm sorry, honey," and set the parking brake.

Droop reminded me to retrieve my messages as I walked through the kitchen door. "There's only two. One's important. The other's not."

Before pushing the play button, I looked for Andrea. Still not up yet, but I wasn't surprised. She'd told me the night before that she hadn't slept much in the car.

Beep. "Mrs. Garrett. This is Mrs. Friedlander. We seem to be missing each other."

That was generous of her.

"I'll wait for you in my room until five." The tape recorded static for a few seconds. "It's very important that we talk about Ky's grades today."

My cheeks flushed hot, and I looked over my shoulder to see if Droop was giving me the evil eye. I made a silent promise to myself to be at the school when the dismissal bell rang.

Beep. "Mibby. Margot. Waiting to hear from you. Assume you're still alive. Had lunch with Mom. Watch for detoxifying tea in the mail. Tastes vile. It might help you." The metallic voice of the answering machine added the date and time. Sis had gotten an early start fulfilling her familial obligations.

Droop looked around the corner. "I wouldn't turn my back on that one."

Good advice.

I headed for my drafting table to fulfill my promise to Ben. Until Droop was finished downstairs, I had my work area set up in the corner of the bedroom. The light was pretty good, but it was isolating to be tucked away upstairs.

Blink nudged me out of my thinking when he squeezed his way between my feet to lie under my drafting table. I complained, but he only worked his jowls lazily and closed his eyes. I put my feet on his back. He rolled over and pawed my foot to start a belly massage.

"Blink, I really don't have time for this."

He answered with a squeaky toot and a wafting of foul gas.

"Blink! Get out of here."

As slowly as a dog can move, Blink hefted himself from under the table and walked away, stopping at the door to look back at me.

"Go on. I don't feel one bit sorry for you."

He didn't take his gas with him, so I opened the window to the cool morning. A breeze cajoled the treetops into a lively dance, and Mr. Robin whistled a song of pride over his new home from his perch in the hawthorn tree. His song worked like a starting gun for me. I sharpened my pencil and sat down to work.

I'd gotten a good start on the design the day before. The property lines were in place and the house drawn in with the windows marked. Light pencil marks showed the new line of the lawn and flowerbed. A graceful arc set the lawn in the middle of the yard like a green pond. I worked around the deep shade, keeping the flowerbed exposed to the sun. Ben had agreed to a benched arbor, so I drew it in at an angle facing the back of the house. Now for the fun part.

I marked each rose from Jenny's scrapbook in my *Jackson & Perkins* catalog with a Post-it note. Size, color, and growth pattern determined where I'd place the roses. Normally, I would design around a preferred style of rose. People who wanted vases of cut flowers chose the long stems and sculptured blossoms of a hybrid tea. Floribundas were a shrublike rose that set blossoms all season long on a tight, compact shrub. People who chose floribundas wanted their roses to be team players in the garden, not prima donnas. Climbers were all romance, the bodice-ripper kind. Their growth patterns were aggressive and passionate. Gardeners looking for a no-fuss nostalgic rose asked for a rugosa hybrid, only one step away from the wild rose found on sunny slopes. Jenny had them all.

The only common thread among the roses was their scent. They were all rated as highly fragrant. Ben had mentioned she liked the smell of roses under her bedroom window. It was my job to arrange these varied beauties into a design visually appealing with the bonus of pleasing the nose.

The climbers were easy. I drew a circle to the left of the arbor to represent the Cécile Brünner. Its profusion of pink blossoms could hold its own with the deep pink America I planned for the right side. White Lightnin' and Sheer Bliss served as my light contrast elements. I put one on each side of the arbor. Then I added color. Mister Lincoln was my misfit. His deep red didn't fit well with the pinks or the lavenders Jenny seemed to prefer, so I set him behind the screaming yellow of Sunsprite and beside the calming influence of a white. The result was intense yet balanced, a little on the hot side.

On the other side of the arbor, with the deep pink America, I cozied in the lavender pink of Angel Face. I shifted the barely pink

Sheer Bliss to the front, where she wouldn't have to compete for attention. There she could reflect the colors of the sunset on her pale petals. Magenta Buffalo Gal was placed to provide a strong bookend for the design. She was the only rugosa hybrid of the group. The end would give her the showcase she deserved and provide a transition for the rest of the landscape. Behind the arbor, I penciled in a row of Chinese lilacs. They would screen the view of the sheds and provide a green backdrop for the roses for most of the season as well as add a wonderful scent in early spring before the roses opened.

"Done."

"Good morning."

I turned to see Andrea standing in the doorway, her hair mussed with sleep. But my attention was drawn to what she was wearing—Scott's seersucker robe over a powder blue oxford shirt. We had stored our off-season clothes in the guest bedroom closet, so the robe and shirt had been moved from Scott's closet last October as the weather started to turn. Now Andrea was wearing them.

She came to the table. "This looks interesting. What are you doing?"

I'd made the robe for Scott a couple summers ago when he went on a golfing trip with some co-workers. I wanted it to be a surprise, so I didn't measure where the loops for the belt should go. He was longer in the waist than I'd thought. When he tried it on, he said, "A nerd robe—suits me perfectly." Then he'd thanked me as only a lover can, nerd or not.

"You have to take that off," I said to Andrea, my voice pressed out like the last bit of paint in the tube.

She took a couple steps back. "I will."

"Now."

She took another step back toward the door. "I will, Mrs. Gar—"

"Do it now."

I followed Andrea down the hall. She turned abruptly.

"You're nuts! It's just a robe and a shirt, not holy artifacts."

"Take it off, now, and get out of my house before I—"

"What? Hit me?"

Beyond her, Droop stood at the top of the stairs with a question etched in his face. I wasn't in the mood to be answering questions.

"Maybe you should go, too, Droop. I need some time."

I didn't wait for the hall to empty. I slammed the bedroom door behind me and had my second blubberfest of the day. By the time my sobs had transitioned to pitiful gasps, I heard Andrea tramp down the stairs and slam the front door. It took several tries to get her engine to turn over, but she finally pulled away from the curb and toward California. I surprised myself by calling, "I'm sorry" after her. That made me cry all the harder. Blink scratched at the door. Even in a fit of self-loathing, I wasn't about to let the woodwork be ruined, so I let him in. He followed me onto the bed and laid his head across my back. I woke up two hours later to the ringing phone.

"Mibby?" It was Louise.

"I think so."

"Good. Hon, I need your help right away. I've got an old guy in the Lilac Room. The water's been runnin' for an awful long time. Go to Ky's room and see if the shade is open."

It was.

"Could you get your binoculars to see what Mr. Evans is doing? I knocked on the door twice, but he didn't answer. I don't want to go in there if he isn't decent."

"Louise!" I complained.

"I wouldn't ask if it wasn't important. He might be, well, sleeping or something. He'd be so embarrassed if his nap destroyed my mother's Persian rug. Ple*ease*, Mibby."

"I think this is illegal, Louise."

"Don't worry, hon. I'll bring a scone to your cell with a file baked right in it."

I put down the phone and dug in the closet for the binoculars and then wedged the phone between my ear and shoulder and raised the binoculars to the Lilac Room's window. Most of the room was hidden behind a curve of lace curtain. But I could see the corner of the bed and Mr. Evans' white legs draped over the edge. Thankfully, the view stopped at his thighs.

"Mr. Evans is lying on the bed with his feet on the floor. I can't see any clothing."

Louise let out a small groan. "Is the bathroom door open? Can you see the tub?"

When I told Louise water was spilling over the edge of the tub, the line went dead.

Louise was credited by the paramedics with saving Mr. Evans' life. He'd gone into a diabetic coma and would have died without medical attention. I helped her mop up the water and change the linens on the bed.

"You know," she said as I wrung the last towel into the sink, "there really wasn't much to see after I got into the room. I used one of those little ol' pillows to cover him up until the paramedics got here."

Two in the afternoon. Too late to do my maintenance clients before Ky got home from school but just enough time to do some gourmet Crockpot cooking. I threw some frozen chicken breasts into the pot with some cream of mushroom soup and cranked it up to high. Then I called my Wednesday clients to let them know I wasn't going to make it. I blamed it on car trouble, which was at least a small part of the truth. That left me with a good hour to work on Ben's plan.

First, I wanted to erase any signs that Andrea had been here. I hung the Oxford shirt and returned the robe to its hook. Then I made the bed and swept the tiny maple leaves off the dresser where Andrea had put her bonsai tree.

There.

I returned to my room and picked some dirty clothes off the floor. A bulge in the dust ruffle caught my eye. It was the Campbell's Chicken Soup box filled with Andrea's letters. Another swell of shame rose and rolled in my chest as I remembered Andrea's abrupt departure. But the box held a piece of Scott's life I didn't know about.

Shouldn't I? Shouldn't I know all the things he did and what he cared about?

Had Scott known everything I'd done and cared about? He hadn't known I'd smoked hand-rolled cigarettes with tobacco ferreted from Uncle Roy's humidor when I was eleven. He hadn't known about a college boyfriend I was too embarrassed to take home but too lonely to refuse. And he hadn't known I really liked fried Spam sandwiches.

More because I wanted to be close to Scott than know his secret pre-Mibby life, I closed the door and sat on the bed with the box. The contents reminded me of my own Neverland box, the box I kept on top of the refrigerator for unopened sympathy cards. It was a place to put things I felt too disloyal to throw away but too tired to open. These letters had been opened.

I dumped the contents onto the bed and started sorting the envelopes by date. A few loose letters had to be matched with their envelopes, but there were no missing pieces. I stopped counting at one hundred. The first one was dated October 12, 1982. The last, August 7, 2003. All but ten of them were postmarked on the seventh of the month.

The envelope on top was postmarked from La Mesa, California.

Scott was working in a bank there when I'd first met him. The typewritten envelopes were addressed to Miss Andrea Marie Garrett, P.O. Box 4277, Grayson, California. I'd have to find that on the map, but I knew California well enough to know the state was dotted with small towns incongruent with the state's popular image of glitz and glamour. Grayson sounded like such a town. The return address was Scott's post office box. Inside were two sheets of pastel blue paper folded once. One was for Andrea; the other for someone named Victoria.

October 12, 1982
My dearest Andrea Marie:

It will be a long time before you read this. You will be older and you will know that our dreams don't always come true. Your mother and I thought we could become a family where you would feel safe and loved. I dreamed I would be with you forever, but the best place for you is with your grandmother.

I want you to know that I will always be here for you. If you need help or you want to meet me, I will come to you.

Love,
Daddy

At that moment I knew how wives felt when they caught their husbands with another woman. My heart pounded out an alarm, and my arms and legs turned leaden. But I didn't cry, because the picture didn't make sense. What would I be crying about? The other woman was a baby, loved long before I was around. I had slipped into some kind of twilight zone where odd happenings were a way of life. Perhaps little green men would land on my roof. Anything was possible. To prove it I read the letter to Victoria. Maybe she was the other woman.

Dear Victoria,

Thank you for writing. Although I knew Andrea was with you, I couldn't help worrying. I'm sorry it's taken me so long to write back. I feel responsible for Andrea, so I wasn't sure I could do as you asked. I've vacillated back and forth, but reluctantly, I must agree with you. Tina was over her head with motherhood. I'm sure that was why she had left Andrea with you so many times. She would never have hurt Andrea intentionally, but it's possible she would get overwhelmed again and leave her in a dangerous place. You must not beat yourself up. You've done all you can for Tina, and Andrea deserves to be protected from the cycle of high hopes and disappointments that come from depending on Tina.

Your concern touched me, but don't worry about me. The letter you sent answered so many questions. It helps to know some of Tina's history to understand why being a wife and mother was so difficult for her. I'm not nearly as noble as you think I am. I thought love would be enough to change Tina, but it wasn't. I want you to know I didn't marry her because of a sense of duty. I married Tina because I loved her. I think I still do.

Victoria, I promise to respect your wishes and stay away, although it will be difficult. I don't expect Tina to come back, but I have rented a post-office box so you can contact me without worrying that she will intercept your letters. Please feel free to contact me at any time for anything.

Even though you haven't asked for help, I'm enclosing a check and will continue to send them monthly until Andrea is 21. I have also enclosed a letter to Andrea. She will see my name on her birth certificate someday, so I signed it Daddy. I hope you don't think that is too presumptuous of me. I leave it up to you to give it to her or not. When she is older, maybe it will be important to her that there was a man who helped to provide for her needs and took the time to write.

Sincerely,
Scott

Oh my.

My mother came back to us—my father, Margot, and me—on a Greyhound bus. Spring was fanning itself into a torrid summer. The dry hills around San Diego had already turned from green to khaki, and my father scanned them often looking for signs of fire. My parents talked in soft, cautious voices Margot and I strained to hear.

Margot rushed into our room where I was reading during the heat of the afternoon. With all the urgency of an Indian scout returning to the cavalry with news of reinforcements, she made her report.

"Mibby, I heard them talking. They're going to remodel the bathroom. Dad promised Mom a new tub, toilet, and sink. Mom says she'll use tiny tiles to create a blazing sun on the floor." In case I hadn't caught the significance of her information, she added, "It will take them all summer."

Every domestic duty our mother performed gave us hope she would stay. We ticked them off on our fingers: baked cookies in the shape of hearts, prepared stroganoff for dinner, hung the sheets on the line to dry, and now, planned a blazing sun for the bathroom floor. No wonder Margot was dizzy with hope.

True to his word, my father removed everything down to the lath in the bathroom before going off for his shift at the firehouse. We had to take our baths in our wading pool and pee in the bushes until he returned.

On Friday nights we stood at the bathroom sink with our mother and counted the strokes of her hairbrush. When we got to a hundred, she tied a ribbon in her hair just the way Dad liked it. Margot and I walked to Grandma's house for a night of crazy eights and root beer floats so our parents could go to the movies or to a party with their friends or eat abalone at the beach or "just sit around the house like a couple of sane adults," as Mother would say.

I reclaimed the silver thread that held us together. I tried to keep my grip loose so she wouldn't notice its weight against her movement. But she was so beautiful and her bedtime stories so entrancing, I could not resist wrapping the thread around my wrist like the string of a balloon on a windy day.

My sister and I walked around the house on tiptoe and whispered even when we fought. But the magic of my mother's presence didn't hold. Just as Dad was installing the new bathtub, she started reading books on meditation and the mystical ways of the god within us. The living room light glowed under our bedroom door as she read into the early morning hours. She grew restless, and we ate grilled cheese sandwiches more often.

One night Margot and I knocked softly on her bedroom door.

"Mother, can you brush my hair now?" Margot asked.

Mother focused on a faraway place as she brushed my sister's long hair, carefully pulling out the tangles with her fingers whenever the bristles of the brush caught them. When all of the tangles were out, Margot softly counted each stroke as Mother read passages she'd underlined in her books. "God is a European myth used to control women and justify barbarous behavior."

Stroke, stroke, stroke.

"God is in us—is us—the creative energy of our souls." She stopped brushing to turn the page. "This part is for your grandmother," she said. "We are not sinners. We are god, and we must follow faithfully our own commandments of love and happiness."

At that moment I said something incredibly stupid. "Grandma says Jesus wept in a garden."

My mother shook the brush at me. "Don't listen to that hateful old woman. She'll poison your heart with paternalistic dogma."

I wondered if it was paternalistic dogma that had made

Grandma's bread pudding taste funny.

Mother pressed the brush into Margot's scalp and pulled the bristles through her hair with long, deep strokes. I could tell it hurt my sister, but she didn't say anything. I stopped breathing. Maybe Mother would forget what I'd said.

She didn't.

Mother threw the brush at the dresser mirror. A silvery crack split the reflection of the room. When my mother left the room, my sister picked up the brush and threw it at my head. I cowered just in time, so she kicked me hard in my ribs instead.

"You are so stupid," she said. "Now she'll leave forever."

Each day my parents spent more time yelling behind the closed doors of their bedroom, and progress on the bathroom stopped. My sister and I moved in with my grandmother until Dad got around to fixing the plumbing. He never did.

A couple days later, our mother came to see us. She told us she was going to Oregon to learn meditation from a man named Marshall Reeshy, or something like that. When she'd settled there, she wrote us a letter to say she had changed her name to Zudora and was discovering the true nature of god.

I took my diary into the bathroom and locked the door. With a stubby pencil, I added Zudora to the list of names my mother had adopted and then outgrown. The list had gotten impressively long. She'd started with the name her mother gave her, Martha. Even I had to admit that my mother was never a Martha. Too ordinary. Mother told us she had changed her name to Debbie when she moved to a new town with her parents and brother. She wanted her classmates to think she was thoroughly modern, perky, and optimistic. Margot was born during Mother's French period, which goes a long way in explaining Margot's attitude. During that time, my mother called herself Colette and baked bread in a stone oven my father had built. She was in her flower-child phase when

I was born, living simply and mastering organic gardening. Margot and I had to call her Jasmine, because *Mother* was a title of matriarchal authoritarianism. She wanted us to be friends. Grandmother called her Looney Moony, but not to her face.

Jasmine was the incarnation that best suited my mother; she stayed with it the longest. The kitchen window became a greenhouse for herbs and sprouts. Nothing conventional touched our lips. Cows became our mortal enemies. Jasmine tried to get Dad to move into a commune. When he said no and really meant it, she went without us. My father became a smoke jumper. He left us with Grandma for long periods of time. My mother kept her Jasmine name until she needed a power name to wear to Washington. She came up with Diana. The name of the conflicted Greek goddess suited her—she was the protector of the young but not unwilling to demand a maiden sacrifice. When we got the letter from Zudora, Dad had joined us at Grandma's house. It was just easier that way.

"Mom? Andrea?" Ky called as he ran up the stairs.

I gathered the letters into the box and pushed it under the bed.

Breathless and flushed, he dropped his bag and slumped into the damask chair. I think he was wearing the same shirt he had worn the day before.

"Where's Andrea? Salvador wants to meet her."

"Ky," I said, "I'm really sorry I didn't meet you at school. I got a little distracted."

He shrugged and asked for Andrea again.

"Ky, I did a terrible thing."

He stood up. "You didn't hit her again, did you?"

"Let's get something to drink," I said, moving toward the door. "You look hot."

He stood his ground. "Mom?"

"No, I didn't hit her." It was worse than that. "I asked her to leave." Could he ever understand why I considered Andrea's presence so offensive?

"Why?"

He didn't stick around for an answer. He stormed to his room and slammed the door hard. Feeling too weak and foolish to breach so great a divide between mother and son, I went downstairs to call Mrs. Friedlander to apologize and talk about Ky. If there was bad news from school, today seemed like the day to hear it.

Louise found me hugging my garden journal to my chest and fully engaged in the long-delayed blubberfest number three. The elm seeds raining down around me only fueled my tears.

She put a plate of scones on the bench and wrapped her arms around me. After a while, she asked, "What happened, sugar?"

Where to begin?

"Ky hasn't turned in any of his homework and may not move on to the eighth grade next year. I haven't been paying attention, Louise. I assumed he was taking care of his schoolwork. This never would have happened—"

"This never would have happened if what?" she said, interrupting my misery. "If Scott was here? If middle school students had coherent thoughts? If the moon was made of cheese? Do you think you're the only mother of a seventh grade boy who considers handing in math homework beneath his station in life?"

This was bad. Even Louise was exasperated with me.

I finally took a good look at her. She wore a turquoise linen suit with a silk blouse splashed with color like a Monet painting. Her shoes were made out of the same silk as her blouse. A French twist had replaced her flip, and pearls the size of cannonballs dangled from golden hoops in her ears. Louise wasn't cleaning toilets that afternoon.

"Louise, are you going somewhere?"

"No, sugar baby, the channel two news team is coming out for a live interview at five o'clock." I must have had a question on my face, because she answered it. "Because I contributed to the safety of the community by saving that old man. That's why."

Louise can be so distracting, so I returned to the topic at hand. "Ky hates me."

"Of course he does," she said, shooing my complaint with a flip of her wrist. "You're his mother. If he didn't hate you, he'd have to hate himself. Well, no middle school boy can handle that kind of angst." Louise pulled a starched hanky out of her sleeve and handed it to me.

Like most things Louise told me, I was sure this would make more sense a day or two later. Until then, sharing a lemon scone seemed like the only rational response to the day's events.

I drew a breath to tell Louise about Andrea and Scott, but what was the point? They were both gone.

"Are you all right?" she asked, handing me a lemon scone on a gingham napkin.

Now there was a question I was afraid to answer truthfully. When she saw I had no intention of answering it, she started a general purpose exhortation speech.

"Mibby girl, you're just goin' to have to get on that ol' horse of life and ride. Dig in your spurs and snap the whip. Ky wants to know who's going to be the parent, you or him. It seems a little unfair to ask him to be the parent, don't you think? He has so little experience to draw on."

Snap the whip? Who me?

Louise held my hands tightly in hers. "I better pray for you." She lowered her head, and I pushed a bobby pin back into her twist. "Are you ready now?" she asked.

"Yes."

"Dear Jesus, you have given Mibby every gift to be a good parent to Ky. Help her to trust you to provide the strength. And Lord, I ask for your intervention, too. Please don't let channel two send that little ol' anorexic newsgirl for the interview. You know, the one with the teeny tiny butt and hipbones I could hang my sunbonnet on. I'd appreciate it."

On her amen the phone rang. "You better go get that. It might be Ben."

I promised myself to ask Louise to cool it about Ben. Her comments only made it more difficult to keep him at a professional distance.

It wasn't Ben; it was Andrea. I figured she had remembered her box of letters. Her voice, pinched and cautious, came over a static-filled line. "Mrs. Garrett? This is Andrea. I know I didn't leave on the best note, but I really need your help. I don't have any money, and my credit card is maxed out." The line emptied of static and Andrea's voice. Then I heard her say, ". . . car died."

That was plain enough. "Where are you?"

Andrea's shoulders slumped as she listened to the mechanic outside the waiting room where I sat. I returned the magazine I'd been reading to the rack to watch the drama unfold. Although I couldn't hear what they were saying, I could tell the news wasn't good. Andrea gestured with open palms as she spoke, but the mechanic shook his head and returned to the garage. Andrea sat on the curb and buried her face in her hands.

If I walked out the door to extend the sympathy she deserved, I knew she'd expect help. The best I could do for all of us was to pay for the car to be repaired, so she could return to her life in California. It meant dipping into the emergency fund yet again, but if this wasn't an emergency, I didn't know what was.

Her shoulders stopped shaking, and she stood abruptly, wiped her eyes on the hem of her top, and turned toward the office. Once inside, she stood over me. Her cheeks glistened with tears.

"I cannot express how much I truly hate having to ask you for help, but I'm a little hung out here, so just keep that in mind. Okay?"

"How much do you need?" I asked.

"I don't want your money."

That couldn't be true. "How much will it cost to fix your car and give you enough money to get back to California?"

"I need a new engine."

My emergency fund would have paid for a new hose or two and a pine air freshener, not a new engine. "How about a bus ticket?"

"I thought about that. But I've decided it's better to have a broken car that needs to be fixed than no car at all. I have to get it fixed."

"I can't—"

Andrea's face reddened and her voice got louder. "I don't expect you to. I'm not going to take your money, so don't worry. I just need a place to—"

"Are you crazy?"

"No, I'm desperate. I need a place to stash my stuff until I can find a waitressing job and pick up some gigs, make some connections. It'll take a couple of days, that's all."

It took me a minute to realize what she was proposing. "And where will you be?"

"Back to the park, where else? But I can't leave my cello and my bonsai in the open. They'll be ruined. Will you keep them for me or not?"

Andrea bit her lip while she waited for my reply. The thought of her sleeping with the transients by the river again chilled me.

"I have a friend with a bed-and-breakfast. You can probably stay there."

"I can't pay her."

"That shouldn't be a problem."

Louise was one of those people who could smile sweetly and tell you that your hair was on fire. She looked from me to Andrea and back again. "I'm so sorry, but I'm filled to the tippy top with guests till the end of the month."

"I thought maybe Mr. Evans' room would be available," I said.

"I'm terribly sorry, darlin'. I had a couple as sweet as God's own angels come to the door looking for a room this afternoon. They've booked it clear up until my next guests arrive."

Andrea asked, pleaded really, "Do you have a basement? I could sleep there. I promise you'll never know I'm here."

"Oh, sugar," said Louise, drawing Andrea into her arms. "Nobody's going to put you in the basement. God has a perfect place for you. Don't you worry. You ladies sit yourselves down while I go pour some lemonade. There's nothing like a tall drink of lemonade to get my synapses a-snappin' toward a solution."

Andrea sat silently on the sofa folding and unfolding the hem of her shorts. I followed Louise into the kitchen.

"Louise," I said, and I was the one who pleaded now. "Your basement is really nice. You have to let her stay."

She stirred the lemonade lazily. "Hon, even my Aunt Pansy would know my basement is not the best place for Andrea, and she's the definition of fruitcake."

It was time to bring Louise in on the Garretts' dark secret. "You don't understand, Louise," I whispered. "That girl is Scott's daughter."

"Ky told me all about it."

"He did?"

Louise sat at the kitchen table and patted the seat beside her. "Sit down with me a spell. I can't even imagine what kind of consternation is buzzing in your head right now. Most assuredly, it's beyond my reckonin'. Help me out. What are you afraid of, sugar?"

That was easy. "Everything."

"Can you be a little more specific?"

Where should I start? "I'm afraid Ky will hate his father."

"The boy I talked to this afternoon had more concerns about his mother."

"See. That's another thing. She could come between me and Ky. I can't let that happen."

She took my hands. "I believe you, Mibby. I believe you're as scared as a mouse on a ship full of hungry cats, but none of those things has happened yet. I wonder . . ."

Uh-oh.

She pushed away from the table and poured three glasses of lemonade. She put a frosty glass in front of me. "It's funny how competitive boys can be. Why, if there's more than one person in a room, they'll find a reason to battle. And their weapons aren't anything you'd want them brandishing in public, either. I'll never forget the time my brothers, William and Pink, ate a whole pot of Mammy's beans—"

"Louise?"

She blinked. "Sorry about that. Where was I? Oh yes, I was wondering, wasn't I?" The creases between her brows deepened, and her eyes narrowed. "Do you suppose Ky feels like he has to choose the winning side between you and Andrea? We both know how ridiculous that is, but we can't expect him to be anything but the male God made him, as handicapping as that might be." Louise walked to the door and stopped. "I wonder what it would take to be the winner in Ky's eyes?" Then she left for the living room.

Louise was on to something, because I certainly felt like a loser. I was trailing Andrea by a large margin and losing ground rapidly. Going for a knockout hadn't helped; neither had cutting Andrea from the team. My only hope was to forfeit the game. I paced the length of the kitchen, hoping to figure out a way to get Andrea's car fixed and her back on her way to California as soon as possible. Since I had absolutely no idea how that was going to happen, I decided to ask for help.

"Lord," I prayed, "how can I get her out of here?" I thought I had my answer before I said amen.

As I walked to the living room, I calculated how long it would take to repay Ky's college fund. I stopped cold when I saw Louise and Andrea sitting on the sofa knee to knee with their heads bowed. Louise held one of Andrea's hands. In the other, Andrea used a tissue to dry her eyes. When I cleared my throat, they looked up and Louise said amen.

I meant to tell Andrea she would be getting her car fixed the next day and that was that, end of story. Instead, I asked her, "How long will it take you to earn enough money to fix your car?"

"A month, six weeks at the most," she answered, her voice thickly padded from crying. "Getting a job won't be a problem. It never has been. Believe me; I want to get out of here as much as you want me gone. I've got things to do."

"You can stay with Ky and me."

MAY

11

What month is this, really? Hit a record low of 29°. For crying out loud! And the wind—it keeps blowing and elm seeds keep falling.

The police officer's eyebrows creased together with concern. He flipped his notepad open and took out his pen. "How long has your son been missing?" he asked, looking around the living room.

"He's usually home by two-fifty," I said.

The officer, Michael Ortiz according to his nametag, looked at his watch. "That would make him twenty minutes late." He clicked his pen to retract the point. "How old is your son, Mrs. Garrett?"

"He's thirteen," said Droop, leaning in the doorway.

Ortiz flipped his notepad closed.

"But he's a young thirteen, not one of those rebel-without-a-cause types." I swallowed down the panic. "Listen, I was a few minutes late getting home. When I got here, he wasn't home."

"Ma'am, has he ever been late before?"

I almost told him about Andrea, how I didn't know her all that well and wasn't absolutely sure she wouldn't take Ky somewhere or do something crazy. But I saw how this looked to Officer Ortiz. He didn't know Ky or what a great kid he was. My son didn't ignore family rules.

"Never. In fact, he really just started walking by himself this week."

Droop mumbled something under his breath about mothers and returned to the kitchen.

The officer sighed. "Sometimes boys your son's age get distracted by friends or their stomachs." He stood to leave.

"Aren't you going to look for him?" I followed him to the door. An involuntary vision of me in the black suit I'd worn at Scott's funeral flashed through my head. I slid between the officer and the door. "Listen. You don't understand. Ky's not that kind of kid. He always comes straight home. Something has to be wrong."

To the officer's credit, he didn't plow through me. Instead, he lowered his voice and talked to me like he might talk to a lost child or a grandma with a cat up a tree. "Did you call the school to see if he had to stay late for any reason?"

I'd already collected a stack of books and assignments from Mrs. Friedlander. "He wouldn't be at school."

"Are you sure?"

"Of course I'm sure. You're wasting valuable time, Officer. He could be anywhere."

"It's too soon to put out an official alert. Why don't you phone a couple of his friends while I call in the description you gave me? Maybe an officer will see him and send him home."

I called Salvador. Janine answered the phone. "Is there something wrong?" she asked.

"No," I said, not wanting to take the time to explain. "If you see Ky, please send him home."

Then I called the shortstop, the catcher, and his outfield buddy.

Nobody had seen him after school.

The officer was back at the front door. "Find him?" When I shook my head, Ortiz suggested I check the school anyway, all the neighbors, and local stores. "Let me know if you haven't found him by dinnertime."

"Dinnertime! He could be—"

He stopped me with a raised hand. "Trust me. I've seen this a million times. He'll be home, and he won't even realize he'd been gone so long." With that, the officer strode down the front walk and to his car.

I grabbed the keys to the Daisy Mobile but remembered it was short of gas, so I went out to the garage for Scott's SUV. The garage was empty. Ky wouldn't have taken it, but Andrea might have.

She had only been with us for two days. The atmosphere was strained with the usual awkwardness of having a guest you don't know well. Should I say hi every time I pass her in the hall? Should I sit on the bed and talk to her while she unpacks or stay away until she gets her underwear in the drawer? Would cleaning out a drawer in the bathroom for her toothpaste and deodorant encourage her to stay too long? I had asked myself all of these questions and more, because Andrea brought a whole bag of troubles with her. But she seemed to be making an effort to fulfill her promise.

She'd already found a job at the Pampered Cow, a funky vegetarian place on Main Street. She said she would have the money to get her car fixed in a month, maybe less. Then she would be on her way. Ky loved having her. She knew just the questions to ask to get him talking about his day. And to my utter amazement, she was a Rockies fan. That had bonded them immediately.

So why would she have left so suddenly? Maybe she had hated the tension in the house. Maybe the reality of the time needed to save that much money had settled on her. Maybe she had thought it would be easier to take the Yukon and head for points unknown.

Maybe—and this was the scariest maybe of all—it had all been an elaborate lie—the letters, the picture, the documents.

Oh Lord, help me find Ky.

If they had headed out of town, there would be no way to stop them.

How could I have been so stupid? So trusting?

I called the school to make sure he'd attended all day. He had. That was good. But would Andrea head west to California or east to Denver and beyond? I considered calling Officer Ortiz to report real crimes—auto theft and kidnapping. I decided to drive around the neighborhood first. That was what a reasonable woman would do. And I desperately wanted to be reasonable and for all of this to be a simple misunderstanding. I told Droop to make Ky stay home if he showed up.

The gas indicator in the Daisy Mobile trembled above the *E*, but just barely. I decided to drive along Ky's route from home to school.

The halls of the middle school were empty. I paced around the small reception area for a few minutes waiting, but Ky didn't answer the page the secretary put out over the school's public address system. The school nurse came out.

"Is there something I can help you with?" she asked.

"If you see Ky Garrett, please send him home."

"Sky Garrett?"

Oh brother.

I checked the basketball hoops and the soccer field. I drove slowly back along our route to home and the alley that bisects the city blocks. I found the cell phone under the seat but had to dust it off to see the flashing "batteries low" message on its screen. I plugged it into the lighter to call home. I asked Droop to check the house and the shed one more time.

"Maybe you should put a bell on him," he said.

"Droop, are you going to look or not?"

When he agreed, I asked him to sweep through the neighborhood. "And call me back, Droop."

He made a sound of exasperation and hung up.

I called Janine again, whose politeness seemed forced, and she promised again to have Ky call if he dropped by. I didn't know any other numbers for his friends, so I threw the phone to the floor. I decided if I found the Yukon, I would find my son.

Lord, Lord, Lord, Lord, Lord. Amen.

I drove back to the house and ran up the stairs to check Andrea's closet. Her suitcase was still tucked in the back. More importantly, her bonsai maple still stood in the lacy shade of the hawthorn tree. I allowed myself to breathe. But only a little. Back to the truck. The engine percolated before it started in earnest.

Lord?

Only a couple of blocks from Ky's school, a main street known locally as "junk food boulevard" ran north to south, so I started at First Street and snaked my way through the stop-and-go traffic to Seventh. It was middle school heaven—pizza, tacos, hamburgers, and ice cream. I spotted the Yukon at the Dairy Queen. I should have known.

I pushed the restaurant's entrance door open hard enough for it to hit its apex and bounce back on its own, nearly hitting me while I scanned the shop's customers. The booths were full of high school and middle school kids celebrating the end of the school day. Ky and Andrea sat in a booth by the window, talking and dipping fries in a puddle of ketchup. Their heads nearly touched as they bent over their snack. Seeing them in an intimate circle of conversation, oblivious to the world around them, made me even more angry.

Ky saw me first. "What's wrong?" he asked.

"What were you thinking?" I said without trying to hide my anger.

They both tried to respond, but really, there wasn't anything I wanted to know, so I continued, only louder. "Who said you could use the car, Andrea? I've been crazy with worry." Customers turned to watch, so I lowered my voice. "You had no right."

I jumped when someone tapped me on the shoulder. It was a middle-aged man wearing a paper hat and a striped Dairy Queen shirt that barely fit over his belly. He wasn't smiling.

"Is there a problem here?"

The man's face was doughy, almost translucent, with sympathetic eyes. He reminded me of my grandmother. Before I could stop myself, I poured out my heart to the man.

"My son was late getting home. He's only thirteen, and he's never been late before. I looked everywhere."

By then I was crying, and the man gave me his hanky. It smelled like chocolate. I told him how hard things had been since my husband had died, and how a girl had showed up claiming to be his daughter, and how she had been staying with us but I wasn't at all sure I could trust her.

"Mom!" Ky's face glowed red. "For crying out loud, Andrea's right here. How do you think you're making her feel?"

Ky's question pierced my stupor. I thanked the guy for listening and gave him his hanky back. "Let's go."

I was pretty surprised—and relieved—when Ky and Andrea gathered their fries and followed me out the door.

"Ky, you come with me," I said, heading for the Daisy Mobile.

"I'm going with Andrea."

Be the parent.

"Ky, I mean it. Come with me."

But he walked behind Andrea to the SUV. Neither one of them looked back. I watched them pull out of the parking lot, wondering why I had rescued Andrea in the first place. It was clear I would have to ask her to leave again.

You're just jealous.

Before I knew it, I was arguing with myself. *No, it's more than that. She's dangerous.*

The Daisy Mobile's engine percolated again, but this time it slowed and died. Out of gas.

The walk home did nothing to cool me off. Andrea had been nothing but trouble since she started stalking me. All the things I counted on, like being married and having a good relationship with my son, were filed under uncertainty now. I longed for the simpler days of being reduced to goo from the grieving process. I'd gotten good at it, and it suited me just fine.

Andrea and Ky were sitting on the sofa in the living room when I came in. Some bug-eyed cartoon characters moved across the TV screen.

I snapped it off and turned to Andrea. "Let's get this straight. You're a visitor in my home."

Andrea sat up straighter and shot a glance at Ky. He slouched deeper into the sofa, crossing his arms over his chest.

I put my hands in my pockets to avoid pointing my finger at her. With each pronouncement my body tightened in on itself. "You are not to take the car. You are not to take Ky places."

I turned to Ky. "You are not to watch that garbage on TV."

Andrea stood up and excused herself. Her voice was calm and pleasant. "I'm really sorry, Mrs. Garrett. It won't happen again."

Her demeanor disappointed me. I had nowhere to go with my anger except Ky. "Kyle, I am so disappointed in you. Go upstairs now and get to work on your homework. We'll talk about this later."

"I'll do it after practice," he said, using the remote to turn the TV back on.

Whether I deserved it or not, nothing cut deeper than being treated with contempt by the son I'd almost died birthing. It made me more diabolical in my discipline than usual.

"There will be no baseball until you're caught up with your schoolwork and you're on your way to the eighth grade." That got his attention.

"Coach won't let me play if I don't go to practice."

"So be it."

His face and neck darkened to red. I needed to stand firm, but I felt my resolve caving. As I was about to offer him an olive branch and strike a compromise, his anger lashed out.

Under his breath, Ky muttered the dreaded epithet. A wave of shame shadowed his face as he turned and walked slowly up the stairs. I should've said something, but what? The word referred to a contemptible woman. It seemed to fit pretty well. I headed for Louise's back door for some love, and more importantly, something buttery.

"Have you tried to see this from Andrea's point of view?"

Louise passed the ice cream carton back to me. I shaved a thick curl of rocky road onto my spoon, aiming for a marshmallow. It wasn't a scone, but it would have to do.

"Should I?" I said around a mouthful of ice cream.

"Mibby," Louise said as if speaking to a recalcitrant child. I sat up straighter. "Jesus suffered so He could understand us better. Don't you think it would please Him if you let all the sorrow of these last months help you to understand others?"

She let me think about that as she jabbed at the hard ice cream with her spoon. To let her know I wasn't beyond redemption, I asked, "You mean Andrea?"

She sighed and handed back the ice cream without loading her spoon. It wasn't like Louise to short herself on chocolate.

"Let me help you," she said. "Andrea has quite a story for those willing to listen."

Ouch.

"She was raised by a loving mother—or so she thought—in a tiny button of a town by the sea. She thrived under the dotin' attention of her mother, for that is who Victoria will always be to Andrea. The girl had lots of friends—she played her cello at weddings and anniversaries. Life was good. Her future was nothing but bright. But then Victoria became very ill. Andrea watched her mother wince with pain every time she moved and heard her stifled moans all through the dark night. Andrea begged her to go to the doctor, but Victoria convinced her she was just going through a hard time. Things would get better."

Louise touched my arm. "Young girls are vulnerable to hope and bright tomorrows, you know."

"How do you know all of this?" I asked, offering her the ice cream, but she refused it.

"I talked to her while you were working. Now don't interrupt."

I put the top on the ice cream and sunk into Louise's overstuffed chintz sofa.

"That sweet child found her mother dead in the bathtub. Can you imagine?" Louise's eyes pooled with tears. "Then the crusty ol' medical examiner told Andrea, like he was reporting the weather, that Victoria had died from ovarian cancer that had spread to her lungs and liver. He asked Andrea if she'd noticed her mother's eyes yellowing. Why, that ol' goat insinuated she was responsible for Victoria's death."

Louise shifted her weight and drew in a deep breath to compose herself.

"In spite of her loss," she continued, "Andrea returned to college and graduated on time with a degree in music education. When she finally had the time to sort through her mother's belongings, she found the letters between her grandmother Victoria and Scott. The letters restored her hope that she wasn't alone in this world. That's when she started looking for Tina and Scott but found you and Ky."

She was clearly depending on Andrea's point of view, but there was more to the story. "Louise, the letters I read made it sound like there was doubt about Scott being Andrea's father."

"What would it matter?" she said, her voice stepping up an octave. "Scott was the closest thing to a father Andrea had. It's what he'd considered himself. What would it really matter if it was his little ol' sperm or someone else's mad dasher who made Andrea?"

I usually spent time in Louise's living room—the Rose Room—trying to identify the antique rose blooms in the upholstery and wallpaper. That night, I was too busy sorting out my contrary feelings for Andrea. On one hand, I had to admire the girl. She needed a family, so she went looking for one. On the other hand, I just had to hate her, vehemently most likely. Every time I looked at her, I was reminded that Scott had secrets. Not the smoking-behind-the-barn kind of secrets, but secrets that showed a side of Scott I'd never known. How many other secrets did he keep after we were married? Were there other children out there waiting to claim a stake on his legacy?

"Mibby?" Louise looked at me like my ninth grade English teacher did the day she had asked me who represented good and evil in *Moby Dick*. My answer to Louise would be the same.

"I don't know."

Manley cleared his throat in the other room. Louise smiled slightly and said, "Mibby, maybe we should talk about this tomorrow. It'll give you a chance to sleep on it."

I put the ice cream back in Louise's freezer. "I need to get home anyway. Ky might need some help with his homework."

Like he would ask me.

She followed me to the back door. I'd reached the garden gate before she called out. "Mibby, I wonder . . ."

Uh-oh.

"I wonder if Jesus was crying at Lazarus's tomb because He missed His friend or because He felt the sorrow of the mourners?"

Ky and Andrea were huddled over his schoolwork on the dining room table when I walked in. Andrea raised her head. Ky didn't.

"Hi," she said. "I just finished explaining reciprocals to Ky. He picked it up really fast. He has a problem-solving page to do, and then we'll get to a reading assignment. That was our goal for the day."

"Goal for the day?" I asked, because I couldn't think of one smart thing to say about reciprocals.

Andrea explained how they had divided Ky's work into daily goals. "He'll be done in time for the playoffs."

"That's great," I said. He copied another math problem onto the paper. I made an appeal to his stomach. "How about some dinner? I have some pizzas in the freezer."

"We already ate. I found some macaroni and cheese in a box." Andrea sucked in a breath, like she'd suddenly remembered something important. "I hope it's okay that I did that. Ky was hungry."

"Sure," I said. *It's okay for you to feed my son while I grease my guilt with rocky road ice cream.*

Ky finally looked up, his brows folded into a crease of worry. Was he afraid I'd wash his mouth out with soap? Ground him until he'd registered for the draft? Make him pick up the elm seeds with a pair of tweezers? I wanted to let him off the hook, but I was worried, too. I looked into the future and saw a lonely place, a wizened woman and her gray-muzzled dog eating scones in bed in a cold and empty house. The worry pulled all of the air out of my lungs, leaving me no breath to speak. Ky returned to his math assignment.

I invited Blink up to my room for a little TV, but he laid his head on Andrea's feet. I wouldn't beg.

I took a long hot shower and climbed into bed with the remote. I heard Ky and Andrea come upstairs just as my favorite doctor show started at ten. I turned down the volume, anticipating a good-night kiss from Ky. Instead, I heard Andrea say, "Good night, Ky. Sleep tight."

"G'night," he said.

When our local TV station signed off with "The Star-Spangled Banner," I turned off the TV.

"Weep for me, Jesus."

MAY
12

Here is a minor mystery. One of the plumbagos I planted last spring is almost a foot tall. The other one is two inches tall! Same watering schedule, same light, same soil. Just goes to show that plants are individual living things. The fact that we have twisted and pulled on their genetic codes and put them in our gardens doesn't mean they have to be nice. Sort of like teenagers.

Judith plunged her shovel into the mountainous pile of manure and offered it for my inspection. The manure sifted easily through my fingers. It smelled rich with life, not fetid, with just a faint odor of decomposing wood and the slightest hint of sharpness, which meant she had aged it for at least a year.

"This is good stuff," I said.

Judith smiled broadly. "I got it from the dairy farmer on Tundle Road. I think he feeds his cows Cobb salad. It's the best." When I returned a smile of agreement, she added, "Your friend Ben was in yesterday. He bought three yards of this stuff for his rose garden." She leaned toward me. "He told me he liked working with you."

My heart fluttered. *Get a grip.*

"Have you finished his plan?" she asked.

I brushed the manure from my hands, making sure I returned it to the pile. "Almost."

Judith frowned and flashed me the evil eye.

"I had a lot of interruptions this week," I said. "That's why I'm working on Saturday."

"I really would have thought you'd be at the ballpark today."

"Ky's taking a break from baseball to catch up on some schoolwork."

Judith's frown deepened. After all, she had been the one who had convinced me years ago T-ball wouldn't turn Ky into a competitive maniac. "Boys need to be out in the sunshine. They need to tire out their muscles so they can think," she said.

"Really, Judith, he's done far too much playing in the sunshine and not enough thinking lately." She was unmoved, so I lowered my voice as if beckoning her into a confidence. "He's home with a tutor."

He was, too. Louise had convinced me to leave Ky with her so I could get caught up with my clients. She was probably tutoring him this very minute on accessorizing according to theme. "Enjoy your freedom," she had said. "Go see Ben." I was surprised by how inviting the idea had sounded.

Judith turned on her heels and brushed off my reply with a swish of her hands. "Whatever."

I watched her stride off with one pant leg tucked in her boot, the other out. She stopped by a pile of aspen mulch to look at me again. I was surprised by how much I needed her approval, anyone's approval.

"Have you contacted that client I referred to you the other day?" she asked.

Somehow I didn't think she wanted to hear my excuses, so I shook my head.

"Mibby, this is business. Are you ready for clients?"

"I am," I said, and again so I would believe it, "I really, really am."

Judith's front-end loader was out for repairs, so I shoveled the bed of the Daisy Mobile full of Judith's crème de la crème soil mix. It was the perfect blend of sandy soil, peat moss, and composted bark to buff up Margaret's vegetable garden.

On my last visit with Margaret, she'd pointed out the narrowing of the swan's neck, a field of snow at the rim of the Grand Mesa shaped like its namesake. When the snow melted enough to reveal the ground and make the swan's neck appear broken, farmers and gardeners in the valley planted their tomatoes and peppers. Margaret wanted to be ready for that day.

A slight breeze powdered me with a fine layer of the stuff as I shoveled. I turned to call Blink before I remembered he'd stayed home with Ky and Louise. He knew where the food was.

A crosshatching of contrails scarred an otherwise clear sky, and yet the cool air raised goose bumps on my legs. Margaret greeted me at the end of her walk wearing a red wool coat buttoned to her neck. On her arm she carried a purse the size of a feed bag. When she shook her finger at me, her keys jangled in her hand.

"For goodness' sake, Mibby, I thought you'd forgotten about me."

"I'm sorry. I had some unexpected company." *And how*.

Margaret's eyebrows lifted, but I didn't quite know how to explain Andrea.

"I should have the garden ready for planting in a jiffy," I said, dodging her unspoken question.

She rifled through her purse, probably looking for a list of jobs for me to do. She handed me a fat wallet and her checkbook.

"Louise called," she said, shaking the contents of her purse to one end. "She told me she's planning a stakeout for the next new moon. Said she'd do some baking. Asked me what I liked." She stopped looking through her purse to think about it and turned her eyes to me. "What do you think would be good for a stakeout?"

"Louise is planning a stakeout?"

Margaret returned to her purse. She handed me two bottles of nail polish, a wad of coupons, and a stained toothbrush with splayed bristles.

"She thinks she's going to catch the person poisoning my roses. But you know, I think Walter is right. It had to be them boys. I sit on the porch every morning and afternoon until they walk by. They wouldn't dare hurt my roses while I'm watching." She added a fistful of pens to my hands. "Hold these."

I pictured the diminutive Margaret sitting on the porch, her cotton housedress pulled tightly over her knees. "Do you think that's such a good idea?"

"They don't pay me no mind." She showed me the keys in her hand. "Here they are!" She opened her purse for me to return her belongings. "I hope you'll be here on schedule next time, and please leave the yard nice and neat."

With that, Margaret ambled off to her Impala, the only car I know of with an eight-track that still works. She stopped at the end of the driveway and rolled down her window. "Tell Louise I'm too old for a stakeout, but I'll bake some brownies for you girls."

Before I started my work in Margaret's vegetable garden, I checked Don Juan number three for signs of abuse. The immature burgundy leaves of last week had been replaced with the broad green leaves of summer. Joining them were clusters of passionate red blooms. Don Juan's charms still beckoned unwitting señoritas, at least for a sniff. He looked healthy to me.

I used a rake to spread an even layer of soil mix over the garden plot. Then I turned the soil over with a shovel to mix the old with the new and raked it again for a smooth finish. Out came clods and rocks, and depressions were leveled. The result was a nutrient-rich spongy bed for Margaret's vegetables, a plot of hope right there on Cottonwood Lane.

With my muscles all rubbery from the effort, I stood back to admire my work. I was as satisfied as I'd been as a child building a city of sand houses and banked highways in my sandbox. Dirt-packed fingernails had a way of rekindling my memories of aimless summer days and building anticipation for candy-sweet tomatoes, but I didn't have time to indulge them. I wanted to get home to Ky.

Ky had taped a note to the screen door: "dear mom Louise says not to worry about dinner she is making plenty for everybody love Ky". Weren't they teaching him punctuation in school? An arrow pointed to the corner of the paper. Ky had written "I'M SORRY!" in all caps on the back.

I was blowing my nose for the third time when I checked my phone messages.

Beep. "Hey, Mibby, this is Ben."

I punched the pause button to have a little talk with myself. *You can't be doing this, girl. You're too fragile, too vulnerable, too—what? Too raw to be getting flustered over a man, that's what. Take a deep cleansing breath.*

I twisted my wedding ring while I listened to the rest of Ben's message.

"I borrowed my neighbor's tiller and got the manure worked into the rose bed. I have the final grading to do. Then I'll be ready to plant. Is the plan done? Call as soon as you can."

I took a breakfast bar and a jar of peanut butter up to my drawing table.

A piece of paper with swirls and botanical names didn't mean much to most homeowners. They needed to see the colors and shapes of the plants to appreciate the disposition of a garden design. That was why I transferred Ben's design to watercolor paper. I mixed and remixed the green, black, yellow, and blue from my watercolor paint box until I stumbled upon the colors of the foliage and the lawn. Then I loaded my brush with shades of pink, red, and lavender to dot in the blooms. To add texture and detail, I used a fine-tipped black pen to outline the shapes. I'd already painted a rendering, the garden as it would be in three years, for the design package cover. Several of my clients had framed their renderings and forgotten about putting in their gardens. I suppose they didn't like dirt under their fingernails. Pity.

I dialed Ben's number and watched Louise, Andrea, and Ky from Ky's bedroom window. Louise's black-and-white-checkerboard smock vibrated in the afternoon sun but couldn't keep her awake. She dozed on a chaise longue while Ky read a textbook and Andrea played her cello. Blink watched a plate of Louise's muffins rise and fall on her belly.

Andrea swayed with each stroke of her bow. I opened the window to listen. She played with her eyes closed and her face pinched with concentration. The sonorous melody of Andrea's cello reminded me of cake batter being poured into a pan, a heavy stream poured out until it stretched to a thin thread winding around its own sweetness. It made me wonder who was going to get to lick the beaters.

Even from that distance, it was clear Louise's coreopsis needed some tidying. Just as I was about to hang up and join them, Ben came on the line. I turned my back on the tableau to talk to him.

"Can you bring the plan out now?" he asked.

I looked down at myself. I still wore a heavy coat of potting mix on my arms and legs—and probably my face.

"There are a couple of things I need to do first." Take a shower and maybe shave my legs.

"When can you get here?"

I assured him it wouldn't be long.

"Come as soon as you can." He hung up.

I headed for the shower.

Ben was pulling a T-shirt over his head when I came around the corner of his house to the backyard. He emerged through the neck hole smiling, the creases around his eyes fanning out with the smile's warmth. The little bit of stomach I saw was rosy brown.

After I marked the placement for each rose and the arbor, Ben came from the house with two bottles of orange crème soda.

We rested on the concrete stoop at the back door. A stand of coppery hair on my right knee glinted in the sunlight, so I crossed my legs.

In May, the sun kept a friendly distance, not too close or too far. It was the last chance in the valley to enjoy such a cordial relationship. By the end of the month, temperatures would rise quickly to the midnineties and stay there until the sun dipped below the Colorado Plateau. This was the high desert after all. Until October, people would save outside jobs for early morning or twilight whenever possible. We lived for summer nights when temperatures dropped thirty degrees. Windows were opened to the night sounds of crickets and owls to let the cool air slide over us like a lover's first tentative touch.

We sat in silence. Somewhere a farmer had cut his first crop of alfalfa and left it to dry in his field. The cooling earth swept the aroma toward us. I admired Ben's work with the rake. He had created a level bed of loamy earth ready to plant. Did his back ache as much as mine?

"Jenny was legally blind, retinitis pigmentosa," he said, answering a question I hadn't asked. He focused on a place beyond the barn and storage sheds. I watched for his eyes to glisten with tears. "Her field of vision had gotten so narrow.

"The roses reminded her of her mother's garden. She didn't have to see them to enjoy them." He talked faster; his eyes remained dry. "I found her sitting by the roses a lot, especially when I got home from a mission."

"Mission?"

"I flew refueling missions over the Gulf. We moved a lot, too. That's why Jenny kept a scrapbook. She wanted to show our kids all the places we'd lived someday. It was a stressful time for all the wives, but especially so for Jenny."

Ben finished his soda and worked at loosening the edge of the label. "It was hard for Jenny to make friends and find her way around. She stayed home most of the time. It was lonely for her, but she didn't complain."

He looked at me and back to the field. "I was late that day."

He didn't have to explain. The day your spouse dies is always *that day*.

"I was back stateside running training exercises. We had to make an emergency landing to check a faulty indicator light." He rolled the amber bottle between his hands and frowned against the memory. "I don't know where she was going, but she stepped out in front of a car. The ER doc said she died instantly."

Ben turned to me, his face relaxed, free from shadows. It wasn't what I'd expected.

"How can you do that?" I asked, my voice more accusing than I'd planned.

He ran his fingers through his hair and sighed. "You're right. I should have separated from the Air Force earlier. It would have made things easier for her. I know that now." The muscles of his jaw knotted and released. "I agree; it wasn't fair to her."

He'd misunderstood me. But knowing he carried regret with his grief only added urgency to my question. "No, I mean, tell the story."

Ben threw his bottle into a trash can by the gate. "It wasn't so bad."

That was exactly what Louise had said about getting her legs waxed. She had been wrong about that, too.

"It doesn't change anything. I still miss her." He leaned his shoulder into me, coaxing me to jump into the conversation. "You should try it."

I've always been a sucker for the sincere salesman. I had ordered an outrageously expensive vacuum cleaner when the man at the door claimed it healed his wife's allergies. Even Margot, genuine as Naugahyde, had enticed me into a freezing lake, saying, "It's a lot warmer than last year, Mibby." I'd cannonballed right in. The cold water crushed me like a pop can. And there was Ben, just returned from his own dangerous waters, beckoning me to join him. He leaned against the railing and waited for me to speak.

"I don't want to talk about the accident," I said.

"It was an accident?"

"Yes."

"Tell me something funny about . . ."

"Scott."

I reached back to the early days of Scott's and my story, hoping the distance of time and geography would make it seem like I was talking about someone else. "Scott proposed to me with a mug of coffee."

I would have been happy to stop with that, but Ben gave me an encouraging smile. I would know soon enough if that smile was enough to keep me tiptoeing around referring to Scott as *was*. Scott *was* good. Scott *was* smart. Scott *was* alive. That was my whole problem—Scott *was*.

"He had woken me up by throwing rocks at my bedroom window. He wanted to take me out to breakfast. That should have told me something was up. Scott never ate breakfast."

Ben watched me with cottony permissive eyes, telling me to take my time. The memory caught me like a kite on a gusty wind pulling greedily for more string.

"He took me to a restaurant in La Jolla that overlooked the ocean. It was a pretty nice place. I was embarrassed that I hadn't dressed nicer, but he treated me like a princess.

"The hostess took us to a table right by the window. There was a bouquet of montbretia on the table. Scott said, 'You must be special.' I told him I wouldn't be special until I'd had my coffee."

Ben laughed. "Never come between a woman and her caffeine."

"That's right. I thought at first the waiter understood that. After all, he brought two cups of coffee without even taking our order. It was good, too. Definitely French roast. I sipped away and watched the waiter pour refills for the people around us, even Scott, but he ignored me. I asked Scott to get the waiter's attention.

"He told me we weren't in a hurry, that the waiter would be back with a fresh pot soon. I was miffed at Scott, told him the service was terrible. Well, when I finished the coffee, there was a message written inside on the bottom of the mug—'Mibby, will you please marry me?' Of course, I said yes. Scott . . ."

"was . . ." Ben offered.

". . . pretty romantic." I'd walked to the precipice and teetered precariously but didn't fall.

"How about another soda, or would you prefer a cup of coffee?"

"I'll stick with the soda."

Ben shared his dreams for his property. He planned on subleasing his pastures to a farmer and digging a fishing pond.

When I threw my empty bottle away, I saw that the can was nearly full of amber and green bottles. My heart sank. Not all of them were pop bottles. They were mostly Coors and some Budweiser. If Scott had been standing there, he would have harangued Ben for drinking too much, even if he'd only just met him. Scott had lost his childhood to his parents' alcoholism, so as surely as if he'd been commissioned by Alcoholics Anonymous, the loss had given him the moral authority to warn off unsuspecting imbibers. He took his responsibility seriously. Who could've blamed him?

"Kids drive by here on their way to the desert for drinking parties," Ben said. "I must pick up a dozen beer bottles, and even more cans, every Sunday. I'm thinking about building a bottle house like that guy out in the Mojave Desert."

In my heart I scolded Scott for jumping to conclusions.

Ky adjusted his bedside lamp to light his book. If I'd been paying attention, I would have known our good-night visit was over. I didn't want to leave. I wanted to sit on the edge of his bed until his breathing deepened and his hair dampened from sweat, until he slipped into the deep crease of sleep where I could lean into his face and feel his breath on my face. Ky turned the page and sighed.

I shuffled through the dragon portraits on his desk. A bespectacled middle-aged woman had replaced unidentifiable carcasses in his pictures.

"Ky, is this Mrs. Fudlinder?"

"Friedlander, Mom."

"Is it?"

He held my gaze.

"Ky!"

"Andrea likes it."

Of course she would. It was dark in an artsy sort of way. "I'm concerned about the gore, Ky. You didn't draw blood and guts before."

He shrugged his shoulders. "Don't worry, I'm not going to eat Mrs. Friedlander."

But worrying was what I was all about. If I gave it up, I might fade away. "Just promise me that you won't take them to school. I don't want to see you on the five-o'clock news."

"Five-thirty," he corrected.

It was so convenient that he was getting snotty right when I was afraid of losing him forever. It took the sting right out of saying good-night and closing the door.

MAY

13

Spent a refreshing (cold) day hiking and fishing on the Grand Mesa. Patches of snow still lay in the shadows of the spruce groves. The aspens wore their new leaves timidly, like a summer dress brought out a week too early. Nothing going on in the wild flower department—too early. For better or worse, Graham Lake kept all its fish. The good news: no mosquitoes yet!

The click of my bedroom door opening woke me.

"Happy Mother's Day," sang the cheerful duet.

Mother's Day?

Ky rubbed my shoulder with slow circles. "Happy Mother's Day," he said warmly into my ear. "We made breakfast for you. Well, Andrea did most of it. It was her idea."

Blink had his front paws on the bed, so I backed him down with a look.

Andrea stood at the foot of the bed, a cautious smile waiting for the green flag. I decided to give it to her.

"Is that for me?" I asked.

An omelet bulging with mushrooms, peppers, and carrots—*carrots?*—filled the plate, leaving just enough room for a dollop of sour cream and something lumpy and purple.

"That's blueberry salsa," Andrea said. "It's really good on eggs, but I left it on the side in case you didn't like it."

A smoothie, coffee, and toast rounded out the offering. This was definitely a cut above the toaster waffles I'd usually been served. If you're going to be whammied, you might as well have a gourmet whammy.

"I made the smoothie," said Ky, sitting on the bed and inviting Blink to join him. Blink held the omelet in his hypnotic gaze. He'd be drooling in a minute. Ky smoothed the folds of the quilt so Andrea could join us.

"Where's yours?" I asked.

Ky and Andrea pulled forks out of their apron pockets.

"Andrea didn't think you could eat it all by yourself."

I agreed.

Andrea and Ky chatted easily about their culinary adventure in the makeshift kitchen.

"I didn't think we'd ever find enough extension cords for the frying pan."

"When you brought out that chunky purple stuff, I thought I'd spew."

"Blink liked it."

Andrea gave Ky a friendly shove. In return, he showed her the contents of his mouth. I felt like the new girl in the school cafeteria.

Andrea turned to me. "I'll bet you're anxious to get your kitchen done."

It was an attempt to include me in the conversation. It was nice. I told Andrea how we'd been living—camping really—with the kitchen since November. She smiled slightly and asked me about my career as a garden designer. That made Ky laugh.

"She only does it 'cause Dad was afraid he'd lose his whole lawn to flowers." He cradled Blink's jowls in his hands and shook the rubbery lips. "Dad was protecting Blink's turf."

Ky spoke about his dad without the telltale stutter of the self-conscious griever. But Andrea and I shared an awkward glance.

"Oh," she said.

"What about you, Andrea?" I said. "What do you have planned?"

"I would love to play the cello professionally, but I don't know. . . . Someday, maybe. I'm hoping to get a teaching job in the Bay area so I can play with one of the better community orchestras at least. Napa Valley would be great, such a good location, but it's hard to get on with the school district there."

While she talked, I watched for Scott to surface in her mannerisms. She certainly didn't dress like him. An organic minimalist, I'd say. No buttons or ornamentation,. just heavily textured cottons, mostly black with an occasional shock of color. New Age Amish? Her pores were invisible. When she bit her bottom lip to remember the title of her first solo, I gasped. Scott had done that. Andrea noticed.

I swallowed the clump of omelet I had in my mouth. "This is really good."

At that moment, I wondered if Andrea had always been with us, at least in Scott's secret thoughts. Maybe it had been Andrea whom Scott had gone to visit when he seemed to fade away from a moment. I'd asked him many times, "Where have you been?" and he would answer, "Just thinking," and rouse himself to join us. Or maybe she had been the source of his melancholy on Father's Day. I'd assumed he mourned his own lost father in the midst of our elaborate tributes to his high achievement as a dad. Or maybe it had been guilt, and not the heat, that made him hate the Fourth of July so. If these things were true, it all meant Scott was deeply tied to Andrea. I'm not sure what that meant about him. What kind of father would promise to stay away from a daughter, only to father a son to whom he was devoted?

Scott was a perfectionist. He styled his image as community good guy like a mason built a wall. One brick after another, tamping them skillfully into plumb. One selfless act rested next to a generous gift until his character became a landmark in our community. It made me wonder if all of Scott's philanthropy had been meant to redeem him from abandoning his daughter. Was his devotion to Ky and me the ultimate act of penance? Who was Scott, really? Devoted father and husband or guilt-ridden mutineer? It would have been easy to hate Andrea for making me ask these questions, but asking them at all was pointless without Scott to answer. The whole puzzle ruined my appetite. I surrendered the last bite to Ky.

"Mom, can we go fishing after church?"

I thought about the pile of laundry in the basement, the bills that needed to be paid, and the unusual bacteria growing in the toilets. Then I looked at Ky. He wore his expectancy like a flashing vacancy sign at the end of a long road. It beckoned me.

Before I could acquiesce, Andrea said, "Ky's doing really well with his work. He has two more short assignments in math and some reading and a book report for English." Andrea looked at him as if checking a list. "And a project for science."

Shame on me. I hadn't even thought about checking his schoolwork progress.

"Mom?"

Be merciful, just as your Father is merciful.

"Sure," I said. "Do you want to ask Salvador?"

"He's in Alamosa visiting his grandmother." Ky looked at Andrea and back to me. "Andrea would like to go."

I could see that Andrea had slipped into a safe place. Her face was a blank wall. I recognized it from my own childhood. It was the place where I'd guarded myself from my mother's indifference. It was my job to invite Andrea out into the sunshine.

I put on my best Wal-Mart greeter face and said, "Andrea, of course you can come."

Ky skipped stones on Hidden Lake while Andrea sat huddled on a tree stump, gathering heat from the sun like a lizard. Her lips had shifted from blue-gray to a shadowy pink. She was thawing out. Blink hunted for the perfect rock under the lake's surface. Ky urged him on with a familiar chant, "Get the rocky, Blink. Get the rocky." Blink obliged Ky with a frantic search, testing each candidate before dropping it back into the water.

We'd left the fishing gear back at the SUV. Two hundred of the three hundred lakes on the Grand Mesa were stocked with trout. Hidden Lake wasn't one of them. Not enough people braved the hike to ten thousand feet to justify it. The Grand Mesa's rarefied air made lungs and hearts work harder and knocked twenty degrees off the valley's temperature—in the sun. The hike from Graham Lake to Hidden Lake wound through the deep shadows of spruce groves skirted with lacy-edged patches of snow. Andrea had made the mistake of looking to Ky for the proper high elevation attire. They both wore sweatshirts with their shorts, but Ky was undaunted. I wore roomy overalls and a couple layers of shirts plus a sweatshirt and a windbreaker and a cap. I should have brought my down parka. Andrea tried to rub the goose bumps out of her flesh. I offered her my jacket, but she declined.

"So," Andrea said, "what kind of name is Mibby? Is it short for something?"

Keep it simple. But I didn't. I blamed it on the lake. Its surface, etched only by the wind's breath, lulled the secret out of its hiding place. "My sister gave it to me, but it really stuck when my best friend saw my tattoo."

That got Ky's attention. "You have a tattoo?"

"Very small. Just my initials."

"Where?"

That was the question I'd dreaded. "Someplace personal."

"Oh."

Ky resumed his search for skipping stones. Thankfully, he followed the secret code of teenage boys: know nothing about your mother's body. But Andrea watched me expectantly.

I'd already said enough, but that didn't release me fully from the lake's magic. "My initials are M.I.B." That did it. I'd found my stopping point. I zipped the windbreaker to my chin and stood, hoping to signal the end of the conversation. It must have been too subtle. Andrea didn't move.

She rubbed her legs more vigorously, as if stoking an idea. "What's your mother's maiden name, Ky?"

He picked up a rock, rejected it and picked up another, played with the weight of it in his hand, and skimmed it over the lake. *One, two, three, four . . . five!* "Brown."

Andrea stopped rubbing her legs to think. "Mary Isabelle Brown?"

"No."

"Margaret Isadora Brown?"

"No."

"May Ilene Brown?"

Blink trotted toward me dripping a trail of lake water behind him. He was looking for someone to share his shake with. I waved him off, so he planted his feet near Andrea and shook hard. That ended the name game, and I can't say I was a bit sorry. She accepted my second offer of the jacket for the hike back to Graham Lake and the fishing we'd come for.

Blink made his own trail back to the car, stopping occasionally to check our progress. He'd already forgotten about his failed rock hunt. He was so lucky that way. By the time we got back to our picnic table, our lunch bag was another of Blink's forgotten memories.

"The poop deck sure will be interesting tomorrow," said Ky.

"Mibby?" the phone message from my mother started. "I'm a little worried about not hearing from you today." Pause. "Well, maybe we can talk next week. Watch for a package. I sent a little surprise for you."

At my mother's insistence, Margot and I had stopped giving her Mother's Day cards when she was in her Diana phase. The holiday, she told us, represented the oppression of women with menial work. That she was expecting a call from me meant her newest self had room for a feigned holiday and a sentimental phone call. My heart gave an unsolicited trill.

Young girls are vulnerable to hope and bright tomorrows, you know.

An afternoon thunderstorm, the first of the season, had sprinkled enough rain to sweeten the air and drop the temperature. Louise and I would have been inside if she wasn't trying to avoid a whining guest. For once, we'd dressed according to the same theme—warmth. Her crystal earrings looked like swaying ice cubes. We were eating the day's leftover, blueberry streusel muffins.

Louise pushed the last bite of muffin into her mouth. When she'd swallowed and brushed the crumbs from her sweatshirt, she said, "Now wasn't that better than love?" She said *love,* but I knew what she meant.

"I can't remember," I said.

"Oh, hon, you will. Then you'll call to say my blueberry streusel muffin was better."

Before I could stop myself, I thought of Ben, not Scott. "I have to go, Louise."

"Made you think of being alive, didn't I? Just a little, huh?"

"Louise!"

"Now listen, honey. There isn't anything wrong with remembering you're a woman. God made you that way—double X and inclined to desire a warm touch now and again."

I didn't dare surrender that point. There was no telling where Louise would go from there. "Really, Louise. I'm pretty numb still." I stood to leave.

"Why don't you take another muffin?" She smiled, eyes wide with innuendo. "It's better than nothing."

I let her wrap up two muffins to take home, saying I would give them to Ky and Andrea.

The day really hadn't been so bad until Louise reminded me I was destined to get all my pleasure out of life from baked goods. I'd eaten a delicious breakfast in bed, my time with Ky and Andrea had been surprisingly enjoyable, and I didn't have to clean any fish. Even so, crying myself to sleep seemed reasonable on my first Mother's Day without Scott, especially since I'd committed adultery in my heart.

Hadn't I?

MAY

15

Peeked under the mulch to check the monthretia. Seven spiked sprouts poked through the soil. Go, monthretia, go! Pond is gross—waiting for lilies to shade water so algae will get under control. Pretty sure the fish are still in there. First pale peach blossoms on potentilla—5 round petals fade to vanilla as they age.

While waiting for Miss Beatrice Dubois to open her door, I straightened the papers on my clipboard, pulled pigweed from the shrub bed by the door and stuffed it in my pocket, adjusted my hat, found a spelling error in my brochure, and watched tail-switching Appaloosas graze across the highway. The foal grew an inch while I watched.

The door finally opened. I was glad I'd stifled the urge to look in a nearby window. One of us surely would have thought we'd seen a ghost. Her skin was as pale and papery as phyllo dough and looked as if it had been tucked into her hairline like a badly fitted sheet. A thick layer of powder kept her wrinkles from sticking to each other so she could greet me with a polite smile. Otherwise, I was sure the exertion would have caused a tear.

"You must be the gardener," she said with a voice like a washboard road.

"Garden *designer,* Mibby Garrett." Anyone can weed. I stopped playing with the pigweed in my pocket.

Miss Dubois looked me up and down with cornflower eyes. Her hair was molded into an ink-black flip, sparse, with a good view of the scalp, round and white under the stiff coif. The center part was a half-inch wide. I estimated the hairdo to be at least forty years old. She lingered on my mud-caked Birkenstocks, and her penciled black eyebrows rose.

"You may walk through the side gate." She gestured the way with a dramatic sweep of her arm. "I will meet you in the garden momentarily."

Miss Dubois lived in one of the new town house complexes at the base of the Colorado National Monument, Santa Fe–style with flat-topped adobe roofs that suited their surroundings better than most. As with most town houses, Miss Dubois' came with a landscaped front yard of yuccas and Russian sage to honor the architecture. Her backyard consisted of a covered patio and a patch of red loamy soil, courtesy of the nearby sandstone cliffs and an ocean that had moved away a long time ago. A low stucco wall defined Miss Dubois' boundaries but didn't obstruct the view of the cliffs that rose red and commanding two thousand feet straight up to the sky.

I didn't expect Miss Dubois anytime soon, so I did something very unprofessional. I started without her. I sketched a rough outline of her small yard and added a curving sandstone retaining wall to raise the eye. I penciled in the cultivated cousins of my favorite high desert plants: gold yarrow, silver mound, and sunrose with wine-cups trailing over the low wall. Under the Gambel oak, I would plant cushions of blanket flowers as conspicuous as the sun. Before she slid the patio door open, I had the preliminary plan completed. Architecture, geology, and flora in perfect harmony.

That was easy.

"I want an alba garden," she said behind me. She held a trembling Chihuahua in the crook of her arm, a dog Blink would have considered a squeaky toy.

"An alba garden?"

"Yes, I want something romantic and elegant." She tilted her head to the side to look at the empty space. I knew she was imagining her perfect garden. I'd seen it before. Her head snapped up. "You do know what an alba garden is, don't you?"

I turned my sketch over. There had been an alba garden at one of the many botanical gardens I'd dragged Scott to during our anniversary visit to the Carolinas. The fragrance of snowy white gardenias and Spanish jasmine had floated lazily on the steamy air. It was most definitely romantic.

"Sure," I said.

Miss Dubois explained anyway. "Alba means white, you know. All the flowers in an alba garden must bloom white. Can you do it?"

"We don't have as many choices here, but there are white lupines, snowballs, peonies."

I started a list on the back of my discarded plan: white Jupiter's beard, White Dawn climbing rose, hosta, snow in summer. I wrote quickly, trying to keep up with the white blooms that popped in and out of my memory.

Miss Dubois cleared her throat.

"Sure," I said again, hoping she would believe me this time.

"I need a little lawn for Pinky, too. And don't you think a small wall to terrace the area would make it all less boring?"

I was so glad she'd said that.

I stopped by to check Ben's progress. It was easy for a novice gardener to plant a rosebush too high or too low, only to invite some unspeakable menace into the garden. As his designer it was my duty to steer him toward gardening success. Besides, it was only ten miles out of my way.

Jenny's memorial garden shimmered with color and order in the midmorning light. Each rose stood in solitude, looking a little lonely in a sea of coppery cedar mulch. They'd be more companionable when they'd had a couple of years to grow closer and their branches nestled together. Only the arbor had to be installed and the climbing roses planted for Ben to be finished.

"They'll deliver the arbor tomorrow morning," he said.

I brushed the cedar mulch away from the base of each rose to check its height. Ben had planted the roses a tad higher than the surrounding ground level, just what they needed for great drainage, the key to happy plants in the heavy clay soils of the valley.

"What are you doing for the next hour?" he asked. His hair was still wet from a shower and combed neatly away from a straight part.

I checked my watch.

"Not much."

"Let's go," he said, giving my arm a tug and turning toward the gate.

I was latching my seatbelt when I thought to ask, "Where are we going?"

Ben took his sunglasses from the visor and slipped them on. "Flying." He turned the mirrored lenses to me. I was frowning back at myself.

"Are you okay?" he asked.

I had to think about that. Flying was something I usually anticipated for months, planned for down to the number of clean pairs of underwear I needed to pack. It wasn't something I'd ever done on the spur of the moment. Jumping into a truck and heading for the airport to fly in an itty bitty plane unsettled me for a minute. As least I thought it was the flying that had rattled me.

"Sure," I said. "I've flown lots of times."

Ben released the brake and shifted into reverse. He flashed a smile that told me to hold on to my hat.

"This will be better."

The plane headed for a solid sandstone cliff. Ben's face hid any sign of alarm. Was his calm the composure of a man accepting his bleak fate or the calm of a man who planned on turning soon? He spoke through my headset.

"It seems a lot closer than it actually is."

"That's good."

Ben smiled broadly and banked the plane into a gentle turn back to the center of the valley.

"Better?"

"Much."

Flying this close to the cliffs seemed more like a dream than reality, only I didn't keep falling to the valley floor as I did in my dreams. We flew along the edges of the canyon walls with their wind-shaped ramparts of softer sandstone. Juniper and piñon trees dotted the sloping skirts of scree like so much green lint. Smooth depressions, caves almost, pocked the cliffs high above the valley floor. Below, a band of green bled into the desert on both sides of the Delores River. And in the distance, clouds gathered like rival teams over surrounding mountain ranges. Ben dipped the plane's wings.

"That's the town of Fremont."

The town stood in a loose cluster on either side of the road, about half a dozen buildings; no more.

"My grandfather had a friend with property along the river," he said. "I spent many days fishing and harassing the prairie dogs down there." Ben checked his watch. "I think we better head back."

The small plane bumped roughly and then dropped suddenly.

Ben's voice came over the headset smooth and steady, like a skilled labor nurse. "Try to think of the plane as a boat on the sea. Every once in a while a wave will hit the boat so it yaws and dips. The boat corrects itself because the keel is designed to go through the water at a certain level. A plane does the same thing with air currents." We hit another wave of air. Ben took his hands off the controls. "See, it rights itself just like a boat."

The plane rose out of the valley and over the ridge of the Colorado Plateau. The land spread sparse and immense before us. Dirt roads lead to small cabins in stands of piñons far from any neighbors. What kind of madness or brilliance would move people to settle in such an isolated and severe country? I conjured up a cross between Quasimodo and the Unabomber.

"You were telling me about your job," I reminded Ben.

"My friend Tom is starting air passenger service geared to businesspeople going to Denver for early meetings. Right now, it's nearly impossible to be on time if they fly one of the bigger carriers into DIA. The airport is too far from downtown to land, rent a car, and drive all that way in by eight. We'll fly our passengers into Jefferson County Airport. It's just east of the Tech Center and a lot closer to downtown. At the end of the day, the passengers will have time to finish up their business and head for our terminal. We have a big-screen TV and a bunch of recliners, so they can take a nap or watch the news until everyone's ready to leave. It's the next best thing to having a personal pilot."

"So you'll be in Denver all day?"

"That's the hard part, but I'm hoping to pick up some charter work out of Jefferson during the day. And I've hooked up with a charter business here, too. It would surprise you how many folks insist on being flown to their mountain retreats."

Below us, canyons scarred the plateaus as if the Creator had played in the sand and liked His work so much He let it harden.

The world slipped under us and soothed my uncertainty to sleep. From here, Andrea was only who she said she was, Ky soared effortlessly through his teenage years, and all of my surprises were teeny tiny and absolutely manageable. I could get used to looking down on life.

We flew steadily toward the rim of the plateau, where the sandstone cliffs dashed vertically into the valley. The hot air of the valley rose to buffet us, and the plane bumped along the currents. I sang to myself, "Row, row, row your boat" and marveled at the joy the song stirred in my chest.

"Maybe you could come to Denver with me sometime," Ben said.

The woman reflected back to me from his glasses was a woman I hadn't seen in a long time. Her eyes glittered with hope.

Once we were over the valley, blocks of farmland stitched together with dirt roads textured the valley like green chenille fabric. The plots grew smaller and the homes grew bigger as we got closer to the airport, until dense clusters of homes huddled together. The landscape faded into denuded slopes of Mancos shale as we made our final approach. Ben got busy pulling levers and spinning a wheel beside his seat.

"Does that smile of yours hurt?"

I covered my mouth self-consciously. "No, why?"

The nose of the plane came up slightly and the wheels touched the runway with a slight bump. Very smooth. The flight tower chattered something about taxiing. We were heading back to the hangar when Ben answered, "You should do it more often. You look beautiful."

I parked behind Droop's truck in front of the house, singing

"Sunshine, Lollipops, and Rainbows" along with the radio as I looked at my watch. *One hour and nineteen minutes?* I hadn't thought of Scott for one hour and nineteen minutes, almost twenty.

"You'll cry yourself to sleep because you didn't think about Scott for one whole hour," Margaret had warned.

Great, I'd beaten her worst expectations by a wide margin. Nineteen whole minutes. Almost twenty.

While I was surprised the tears didn't come, I knew they would, so I put the Daisy Mobile in gear and headed north. I found a barren place that fit my deflated mood perfectly. Surprisingly, the blubberfest I conjured wasn't satisfying—a bit boring, in fact, like a dish of fat-free vanilla frozen yogurt. Ho-hum. I tried to rev it up, drudge it from a deeper place, but the carton was empty. I blew my nose and drove home.

Droop spat the tea back into his mug. "What swamp did this come from?"

"My mother," I said.

Louise lowered her cup and picked lint that I couldn't see off of her pants. "It smells interestin'. What's this s'pose to do for you?"

"According to the box, it's a detoxification tea." I had to check the label again for its benefit. "It will bring synergy."

"Sneeragy won't hurt your flowers, will it?" Droop didn't wait for the answer. He carried his cup to the back porch and poured the tea into my flowerbed. "I sure ain't gonna put this toxic waste down my new drain. Let me help you with that." Always the gentleman, Droop delivered us of the noxious brew to water more of my flowers. "I think I'll go home and let Honey freshen me up with some of her sweetness."

After Droop left, I found a glass and poured an iced tea for Louise. "I'm sorry."

"For what?"

"The tea." *My mother.*

"The tea?" Louise frowned, then smiled. "You mean your mother, don't you?" The rhinestone eyes of Louise's tiger T-shirt glinted in the afternoon sun. "Your mama is lovin' you the best way she knows how. It may not be the way you want to be loved or the way you need to be loved, but this is how she's lovin' you." She paused, searching the ceiling for inspiration. "You're so far apart, and she knows you're hurting. This is her way of gathering you in her arms and lovin' that hurt away."

I don't think Louise believed that any more than I did, so she changed the subject.

"How are you and Andrea getting along?" she asked.

"It's been interesting."

I looked past Louise to the refrigerator. Yellow Post-it notes covered the freezer door, most with Andrea's handwriting, one with Ky's. Each yellow flag was a guess about my given name. Figuring out the mystery had become Andrea's mission. It was obvious she had done some research in a multicultural baby name book. *Maata Ikabela Brown? Maeiko Ishi Brown? Madonna Immaculada Brown? Myrtle Iris Brown?* One of the Post-it notes asked a question: "Am I getting close?"

Yes and no.

Ky's guess was, "M.O.M. Marvelously Outstanding Mother."

Thanks, Ky. I needed that.

Louise leaned toward me. "I really like her. She is so interesting and talented—and she is so open to the things of God."

A funny feeling stirred my chest. "Really?"

"Oh yes, she's a sincere seeker, all right." She pushed away from the table and covered the tiger's eyes with her interlaced fingers. "I'm going to ask Andrea to help me service the rooms in the afternoon. It will give me a chance to get to know her better, and quite frankly, I could use the help. Would you mind?"

The picture of Louise and Andrea fluffing pillows and sharing confidences weighted my heart. "I wish *I* could help you."

"Don't be silly," she said. "You have enough to do."

At that rebuff, ever so gently made, I knew the feeling. Jealousy.

Louise put her doughy cheek to mine to thank me for the tea and to say a prayer. "Bless Mibby for such sweet hospitality, Lord, and bless her with a deep knowing of your love."

The first summer Scott and I lived in Colorado, we'd gathered camping supplies at garage sales. Filling our basement with rugged green equipment was our way of transforming ourselves from beach bunnies to alpine campers. By mid-August, we were ready. Cookstove. Cots. Tent. Lantern. We drove to the Grand Mesa and found a level place to set the tent among the aspen trees. A clap of thunder woke us at two in the morning, and by three, a small stream ran through our tent. We packed our Honda Civic and headed down the mountain.

With the heater on high, we shivered in our damp clothes. But an unexpected source of joy came to us over the radio. We found an AM news station from Southern California, one we'd listened to while lying on the beach or driving through evening traffic to a restaurant or movie. We smiled in the green glow of the dashboard, a little less homesick, a little less cold. As the road dropped below the rim of the plateau, the signal got fuzzy with static. Scott adjusted the tuning knob to strengthen the signal. We listened until the static scrambled the familiar place names and people beyond recognition.

On the way to bed this evening, I stopped to look at Scott's picture in the family gallery and tried to remember what his stubbled cheek had felt like against my face, or what his morning kisses had tasted like, or how a day's perspiration had been both bitter and sweet—alarming, yet beckoning. It was getting harder and harder to conjure his face with depth and texture. Soon, I feared, he would only be a two-dimensional photo with a matte finish, like one of those life-sized cutouts of a movie star.

I went to bed praying for a dream of Scott. Hearing his voice again would freshen his fading image, like a fuzzy radio station cleared with a slight adjustment of the knob.

The dream I'd wanted didn't come. I got a mother dream instead. In it she chased me through a shopping mall with a teapot of her detoxifying tea.

"You didn't steep it long enough, dearest," she said.

In my dream, she was Jasmine again, the most enticing of her manifestations. I wanted to sit down and sip tea with her, but it smelled so bad, sickly sweet and hot. It made me dizzy. I knocked over a display of jelly-bean-colored radios as I was trying to get away from her. I wanted to tell the saleslady I was sorry, but I didn't—couldn't—stop running. An open elevator seemed like a good hiding place, but when I stepped in, Andrea asked, "What floor, please?" I woke up when my mother entered the elevator with the teapot and a growling French poodle.

The odor followed me out of the dream and into the darkness of my bedroom. Only a dim light from the streetlight bled around the shade to outline the room's contents. It smelled like my compost pile was on fire. But I didn't see any smoke coming from the garden. And the power light on the smoke detector beamed steadily outside Ky's door.

I heard Ky's snore before I saw him sprawled on the bed with one foot over the edge. But the odor wasn't as strong in the hall or Ky's room. I was tempted to crawl back into bed with Blink, but the odor got stronger again as I moved back toward my room.

Andrea's door stood open, her room empty. The bedside clock glowed 2:49.

Still jamming with her coffee house friends.

After checking all the second-story rooms for smoldering wastebaskets, I went downstairs. The odor was stronger. Something organic was definitely burning very close by. I headed toward the kitchen, but the sound of soft laughing on the front porch stopped me. Laughing and something sickly sweet burning? How could I have missed it? I listened at the front window.

Andrea said, "This is good."

The way she talked with a rubbery tongue confirmed she wasn't talking about one of Louise's muffins.

A male voice, plodding and low, said, "My cousin grows it in his basement."

I leaned heavily against the wall. What had happened to my ordered life, or at least the predictably dismal life I'd composed? Why was I losing my son? Why was I calling the police for help finding him? Why had my best friend abandoned me? And why did I have to start patrolling my own home for illegal activity?

Andrea.

I stepped onto the porch, glad I'd thought to slip on some sweat pants. The man and Andrea were shadows on the swing. A red glow brightened with the man's deep inhalation and then dimmed. I promised myself to stay calm so I wouldn't waken the neighbors.

I started out reasonably enough—direct, yet not demanding. "Andrea, I want you and your friend to take your . . . your cigarette . . . your pot somewhere away from my home and son." By the end of the sentence, my voice oscillated with anger.

She shifted and waved away the glowing joint the man offered her, but they didn't move.

I started again. "You need to—"

"What's the problem?" the man said, rising from the swing. "We aren't hurting nobody."

When he stepped from the shadows, he wasn't a man at all, not really. His beard was ambitious but patchy. A skateboard leaned against the railing. He was too young and too stoned to argue with, but I couldn't help myself.

"You woke me up."

"We'll be quieter, I promise," Andrea said.

"That's not the point. It's illegal. You need to get it off my property, now."

"It's time for you to go," Andrea told the boy.

"Are you sure?"

"Yeah."

"And take your pot with you," I said.

"No problem."

The boy picked up his skateboard and clumped down the stairs. I hoped he got a DWI on his skateboard. He stopped at the end of the walk and called to Andrea, "See ya at the Cow."

I didn't wait for Andrea to say anything else. I took the stairs two at a time back to my room and bed and Blink. On my fingers I counted off the days left in the month-long commitment I'd made to Andrea. There were too many, really. She didn't belong in the same home—or gene pool—as my son.

Andrea knocked softly at my door. I pretended to be asleep. I wanted to hear her say she was sorry but not until I'd made a couple of phone calls in the morning. I needed my anger to set my resolve. Her door closed with a soft click. Blink rolled out a low whimper.

I got out of bed and turned on the lamp on my drawing table. By sunrise, I'd finished Miss Dubois' plan.

MAY 18

Peonies bending to touch the ground from weight of 6" blooms or from depression over the turn in the weather. Poor things. They won't last till Memorial Day. High of 59° today. Nevertheless, the peonies need taller cages next year. Coreopsis and Bloody Cranesbill livening up the place with yellowy orange and rosy purple blooms. Intense!

I played with the broken bracelet I'd found in my pocket, pulling it in and out of a coil on my drawing board while I talked to Salvador's dad, Emilio, on the phone. Once we had exchanged amazement about the weather, he asked, "Are you calling about Ky? Have you changed your mind about letting him play?" His voice sounded breathy with hope. I hated to disappoint him.

I told him no, I hadn't changed my mind.

"Oh," he said. "Then how can I help you?"

I gave him the story I'd concocted about a friend needing to know when her ex-husband's first divorce had become final. I couldn't help feeling like Lucille Ball trying to outwit a stage manager—and failing.

Emilio didn't answer for a long time. "Can't her lawyer do that for her?"

"She's a little low on cash." I should have felt bad about asking for pro bono help under false circumstances, but all those orange slices and after-game snacks I'd provided for the team should have earned me something.

Perhaps Emilio had the same thought. He sighed heavily into the phone. "Do you know the county where they filed their divorce decree?" He drummed his fingers in the background.

Forget the orange slices. I deeply regretted calling him. "I'll just get on the Internet and see what I can find. I'm sorry I bothered you."

"It's no bother, but let me give you some Web sites where you can start so it won't take so long. Just give me a minute to think." He tapped feverishly on his keyboard.

Downstairs, Droop turned on the table saw, so I took the phone into the bathroom and sat on the edge of the bathtub to wait. Droop had finished the subfloor the day before and had started installing the oak planks to match the rest of the house.

The oak floor had been Scott's idea. It's funny what two people in eternal love will fight over. Scott and I had a barnburner of a fight over how to finish the floors. He wanted to remain true to the architecture. I wanted dog-food-colored tile to camouflage Blink's debris field. Scott won the battle when he promised to help keep the kitchen floor clean. I was left to sweep up the dog food crumbs off the floor I hadn't wanted, and it was hard to feel good about resenting my dead husband, but in a way, I did. Just a little. That had to be some sort of crazy milestone in the grieving process no one talked about.

"You—*she*—can get a copy of the original marriage dissolution record from the clerk of the Superior Court of California," Emilio said. "She just needs to know which county. Does she?"

"I'll have to ask," I lied. "Do you have another minute? She wants to know something else."

"Sure."

"Is a man's name on a birth certificate proof he's the father?"

"Legally or morally?"

Good question. If it was legally binding, Andrea would have a claim to Scott's estate, especially if Scott had never found Tina to sign the divorce papers. Morally binding? I supposed I should welcome Andrea into the family. Sadly, all I wanted to do was cut her a check and be rid of her. I brushed the bracelet off the table and into my pocket.

"Either way, your friend would have to have a DNA test to disprove parentage. That's not so difficult anymore." Emilio cleared his throat with a shallow cough. "Mibby, is there anything I can do to help *you*?"

"Oh no. Absolutely not. Everything's fine and dandy. Yep. Just great."

The lady at the San Diego Superior Court said it would take at least three weeks to get the marriage dissolution record, and it would only cost me ten dollars. All I had to do was get through the next few weeks with Andrea. I would have to get specific on house rules, like no dope on the porch, front or back, or in the house, or in the yard. That would make the point. Oh yeah, not in the car, either. And no men at the house.

I could do that. I'd been pregnant for nine months. Andrea was only going to be here for—what?—twenty-three days of a lunar month, twenty-five more days on a calendar month.

I could do that.

"What do you think of Walter?" asked Margaret.

One look at her face and I knew she didn't want to hear that I thought he was a judgmental old coot. Margaret smiled with her eyes, like someone buying a priceless antique at a garage sale for fifty cents. She tried hard not to give herself away, but she had already made her mind up about Walter. He was an undiscovered treasure.

I snipped the last of the tired blossoms off a ruffled apricot iris and stretched against the ache in my back. "He seems determined to protect your roses—and you."

"Oh yes, Walter shares my love for them roses, all right. He's here every morning and every afternoon to wait for them boys to pass by. And if they dare dawdle, he tells them to git on home."

"I'm glad he's here for you, Margaret." And I meant it.

"He's so good to me. He brings coffee and something sweet when he comes. And last Sunday, he came to church with me. He has a lovely singing voice."

Margaret recaptured a stray lock of hair with a glittery barrette. All of her nails were painted the same magenta color. Maybe Walter was good medicine for Margaret. She busied herself cultivating the soil around the irises, stopping to pick the weeds as she worked down the bed.

"He asked me to marry him," she said, snapping off a dandelion.

"Did you say yes?"

"I'm too old to be marrying. I do just fine by myself. Don't need no man messing up my house." She stopped hoeing to look at me. "He wouldn't want me to live in his house, would he? Because I can tell you I wouldn't. I'm used to this house. This is where I belong."

"Maybe you should ask him."

A flitter of panic crossed Margaret's face and was gone. Her hoeing became energized. "He told me not to answer right away. 'Take all the time you need,' he said. He wasn't going nowhere now that he'd found his sue-*preeeeem* love." Margaret laughed at her imitation of Walter's speech. "Can you imagine? He's so funny."

Walter must have saved his true self for Margaret. I suppose that's how it should be. "If you love him, he must be wonderful, Margaret."

"Who said anything about love?" Margaret leaned on her hoe. A small smile lit a spark in her eyes. "He is awfully nice."

On the way to my next client, I asked Blink, who had his head out the window and his rump in my face, "Do you save your best self for me, old pal?" The wind flipped Blink's jowls into a wind snarl.

"That's what I thought."

I spent the rest of the morning trimming Harlan Chandler's shrubs. He liked his shrub beds as orderly as a chessboard—before the game began. It was my job to keep his shrubs in their appointed places and minding their manners. No touching. The Manhattan euonymus—the most boring plant on earth—seemed to lift its branches in a cry for mercy. None was to be found in that yard.

Mr. Chandler stood over me as I worked on my hands and knees. His beloved dog, Buttons, yapped continuously from behind a picket gate. Unscathed, Mr. Chandler saw my preoccupation as a chance to tell me all about his dog's bowel habits. Evidently, Buttons was having intestinal problems. Blink tried to distract him with his own bowel habits, but Mr. Chandler ignored him, concentrating hard to describe each of Buttons' episodes in exacting detail. Unfortunately, I missed the end of the story when I turned on the industrial grade vacuum to clean up the litter I'd made. Pity.

When I came home to find the house empty and a note from Droop saying he'd be back in a week, I sat down on a carton of oak planks for a lunch of blueberry streusel muffins. Its buttery goodness cleared my head of Buttons's health problems. Blink could see that I wasn't in a sharing mood, so he sprawled at my feet and let out a pitiful groan. The phone rang.

"Mibby?"

I coughed streusel topping at the mouthpiece. "Ben?"

"I finished the rose garden. It looks great. Want to come and see it?"

"I have an appointment at one. I could drop by after that."

Miss Dubois stroked Pinky's head as I showed her the plan, carefully describing each plant and its blooming habits. I was proud of the design and had allowed myself to fantasize about entering my work into the small garden category of the Dos Rios Garden Club contest next year. By then all of the plants would have melded themselves into a respectable alba garden.

"The hostas will bloom by mid-June with trumpet-shaped flowers on a slender stock," I said. "What really makes this variety wonderful is their leaves. They're glossy bright hearts as big as dinner plates, kind of tropical looking."

I paused to push my bangs off of my sweaty forehead and to check Miss Dubois' face for approval. Her expression remained neutral, somewhere between bone-cracking boredom and indifference. The air in the house pressed on me with stealthy persistence, hot and dry. There was a clock ticking somewhere and the fan of a heater going on and off, but Miss Dubois sat motionless except for stroking Pinky's head to the beat of the clock. No beads of sweat on her lip.

"Are *all* the blooms white?" she asked.

"Yes," I said, pleased with myself.

She stopped stroking Pinky's head, so he jumped from her lap and headed for the kitchen. I heard him lapping a drink.

Lucky dog.

"They're all white? Every last one?"

"Yes. Isn't that what you wanted?" I pulled the notes out of my satchel as Exhibit A, but she didn't give me a chance to show them.

"That would be rather boring, wouldn't it?"

"Not if that was what you wanted. You know, an alba garden?"

"Alba gardens are for unimaginative and hopeless romantics. No one will ever accuse me of being unimaginative."

I tried not to think of the sleep I'd traded to get Miss Dubois' plan done. She explained to me that her life was a kaleidoscope of light and color. She liked her art, her ideas, and her passions to be hot with color. She wanted her garden to reflect her vigor.

I remembered my original ideas for her garden. "Do you want a southwestern garden?"

"Oh no," she said. "Too much of a cliché. Just stick to my original instructions this time."

Though I doubted I'd ever please her, I took out a fresh pad of paper to take notes. As I drove to Ben's, I made mental notes of plants that bloomed the energetic colors of a freshly opened box of Crayola crayons. At least I had a lot to work with.

Like oil and vinegar, a brew of guilt and glee tumbled just below my heart as I drove up Ben's driveway. Was I like Scarlett O'Hara dancing with a handsome gambler in her widow's rags? Was I too ready to join the party when I should have been at home, alone and pitiful? It had always been my credo to avoid guilt at all costs, so I had a plan by the time I skidded to a stop: take a cursory look at the rose garden, hand Ben the bill, and make a speedy exit as per my usual.

Ben sabotaged my plan. He greeted me with a mug of coffee and smelled of steam and soap—evidence of a certain anticipation of my arrival on his part. Despite my resolve, there was a break in my heart's rhythm.

Ben's benched arbor turned out to be a swing with freshly

drilled holes in the arms to serve as cupholders. I had to smile at that. The roses stood at attention for my inspection. Ben had followed the plans meticulously.

"This looks great." I handed him the bill. He started to open it, so I told him there was no hurry. "Payment is due by the thirtieth."

He folded the envelope in half and put it in his shirt pocket. I turned to leave, but he stopped me with a touch on my arm.

"Do you have time to sit and enjoy the garden with me?"

"Okay," I said, "but I can't stay long."

Ben pushed the swing into a drowsy rhythm. We were quiet for a long time. I thought I recognized his soap, Ivory, the original no-nonsense get-'em-clean soap. It suited him.

Not one cloud dangled in the sky to fix my attention on. Although I avoided looking at his face, I couldn't miss the stretch of his legs or the smooth underside of his forearm or the darkening flesh where his wedding ring had once been. I'm not sure I was breathing when he spoke.

"How are things going?"

There was no way, sitting that close, feeling the warmth of his leg next to mine, that I could answer the question simply. I poured out the whole story about Andrea and Scott, how I felt betrayed and used, and how Andrea's presence had made the past as uncertain as the future. Ben didn't scold me for my lack of charity, so I told him about Ky, too. I worried about not being a good mother and was afraid I'd lost his loyalty to Andrea, and I told him that I wasn't even sure, really, that my marriage to Scott was legal. My armpits got sticky when I said that out loud.

Ben tucked a length of my hair behind my ear. I shivered. He couldn't have missed it, but he didn't say anything. For a while, only the squeak of the swing's chain filled the silence between us.

"Let me take you out to dinner tonight," he said.

Whoa there, big fella.

We had just been talking about a stepdaughter appearing from nowhere and a recalcitrant son, topics meant to keep the conversation out in the open where it was safe. Where did that come from?

"Oh no, I couldn't," I said and got up to leave.

"It would be good for me, too," he said, matching my stride. "Mibby, please stop and talk to me."

I stopped, but all I could think was that I zigged when I should have zagged. I must say this for Ben, though. He wasn't afraid to wade into swirling waters.

"What's troubling you?" he asked.

"Just about everything." Including the way my heart and body turned mutinous whenever I was around him. But I said, "I still feel married, really married. This is just too—"

"Then it won't be a date. It'll be a business dinner, client and designer completing a business transaction."

I followed his logic, but in my real world—the one that had died with Scott—that invitation never would have happened.

Ben leaned into me ever so slightly. "I'll bring my checkbook to pay the bill."

Retreat!

Ben leaned through the window as I tried to start the Daisy Mobile. His wry smile let me know he enjoyed the effect he had on me.

"Why don't you just call me when you get hungry."

The engine caught on the third try, and I looked at Ben. Big mistake. All I saw was the dessert tray at DiAngelo's, and Ben was the tiramisu.

"Okay."

Louise plopped down on a pile of oak planks. "No . . . more . . . musicians," she said, resting her forehead on the handle of the large basket in her lap. "Even my hair is tired."

"How about some tea?" I asked.

"With honey?"

Blink noticed the basket right away. He watched Louise intently while I made the tea. By the time the teapot whistle blew, Blink had a respectable puddle of drool collecting at her feet. I handed Louise her tea and suggested we move out to the garden.

"It's awfully chilly out there."

"The fresh air will revive you."

Louise chose the chaise in the sun and closed her eyes to its warmth like a hound dog on a porch. Despite a generous application of concealer, dark circles shadowed her eyes. Even more telling, she wore all black. Louise was mourning something, probably a good night's sleep. Without opening her eyes, she filled me in on her night with musicians as houseguests.

"I promised those Auxiliary ladies I'd house the musicians they booked for their fundraiser. I didn't charge them a thing, either. Why, it was the president herself who'd told me they'd be older gentlemen, classical musicians. N*ooooo* trouble at all. They were classics all right, classically rude."

Louise pushed half a scone into her mouth. Yellow crumbs collected on the black shelf of her bosom. I followed her example with less dramatic results, but the scone melted in my mouth, so I wasn't too disappointed.

"I knew I was in trouble," she continued, "when the guitar player asked for a three-o'clock wakeup call. Mind you, he meant three in the afternoon." She brushed the crumbs from her chest, and Blink licked them off the bricks. "Do you know how musicians get better? They practice and practice and practice; up and down the scales hundreds, thousands of times, all during the hours from midnight to six. About four this morning, I dozed off and dreamed about teeny tiny toy soldiers going up and down invisible staircases. You know I need my sleep." Louise patted her dark circles tenderly. "I could carry all of Manley's plumbin' tools right here in these bags."

Louise reached under the cloth for another pair of scones and handed one to me.

"Andrea's over there right now getting the rooms ready for our next guests, who arrive on the California Zephyr." Louise put her hand to her heart and raised her eyes to the sky. "Thank the Lord it's running four hours late." She sipped her tea cautiously and settled back into the lounge. The storm was over.

She spoke with one eye closed against the sun and one on me. "Andrea's a real gift from the Lord. I don't know how I'd ever be ready without her."

I stopped chewing and Louise noticed. She watched me over the rim of her mug as she took one sip and then another before setting it down much more carefully than its value warranted. My lips stuck to my teeth waiting for Louise to gather the sermon I knew was coming. She sat up and turned to face me.

"Give me your hands and your heart for just a minute."

Louise cradled my hands in her pillowy flesh. Her eyes, soft and approving, held me warmly.

"Life has surely ripped your heart out and done a double-time polka in the hole that was left. And now there's Andrea. Don't you know your fretting over her only adds acid to your wound?"

A deep ache heated my chest and rose to burn my throat.

"Honey lamb, I'm saying this out of years of learning by trial and error, and it was mostly error. Don't waste your time worrying about what you don't know. It's so much healthier to keep yourself busy with what you do know. And you know God wants you to love as purely and as lavishly as He loves you. Besides, He's got a holy host of angels and the Holy Spirit to protect you. You and Ky are in good hands."

Louise paused to kiss the backs of my hands.

"God's love is like a swollen river in spring, Mibby girl. Its power to heal rushes in when we welcome someone new to love just like God welcomed us when we were least deserving. It's time you did that for Andrea."

Blink whimpered in his sleep and woke me up for the third and last time.

"Wake up, Blink." Light glinted off his corneas. "Go on," I demanded, putting my feet in the middle of his back and pushing hard. "Get off the bed."

He worked his chops to let me know he had considered and denied my request.

I resorted to pleading. "Go on, boy. Go sleep with Ky. He doesn't kick, and he'll give you a treat in the morning."

Blink lifted his head to see if I was telling the truth, then stretched and collapsed on his side with a grunt. He left me with no choice but to bluff.

"Blink, it's time for a bath."

He slunk off the bed and trotted to Ky's room without looking back.

There's nothing like matching wits with a dog in the middle of the night to draw attention to the things you left knocking at your door during the day. Like Andrea.

There was no doubt about it, Andrea had reintroduced ambiguity into my life, that undulating ground between black and white, between knowing what is true and total befuddlement. I thought I'd escaped that dangerous place when I'd left my mother's home. With her, I had never known who would come out of the bathroom in the morning. Diana? Zudora? Or my beloved Jasmine.

And now there was Andrea. Was she Scott's darkest secret or his most selfless act of love? My curse? My blessing? A foe? A friend? Ky's sister or the robber of his birthright?

I snapped on the bedside light and did something I hadn't done since Scott died. I reached for my Bible, the book I'd opened each morning of my married life as if I'd heard a friend calling from the garden gate.

I'm here! I'm here!

My fingers left dark swaths through the dust on the Bible's cover, which I quickly erased with the hem of the sheet. I cradled the Bible to my chest—my way of avoiding eye contact with God just a bit longer. It's not that I'd stopped believing in God or that I was angry with Him. I was just disappointed was all—terribly, terribly disappointed. This wasn't the life I'd dreamed of, and I wasn't adjusting well to the revised version, so I'd put God in the corner, nose to the wall like a naughty child, not completely out of my life yet not in the center of it, either. Now Louise wanted me to welcome Andrea into my life and gush her with abundant love. That was asking a lot.

I started to put the Bible back on the nightstand, but I heard the familiar beckoning in my heart.

I'm here! I'm here!

I turned to the Psalms. Anything God had to say through a despairing man being swallowed by miry clay would apply to me. I read my favorite passages marked with tiny inked hearts and highlighted yellow. The words reminded me over and over again of God's love, strength, and protection. As I finished reading the exuberant praises highlighted in the last psalm, I slid wearily to my pillow and turned off the light. The illuminated numbers of the clock promised me two hours of sleep before it woke me at six-thirty.

In the half-light of reality, where dreams began and even my heart was amenable to God's voice, I remembered a verse from a Bible study I'd done with Scott: *We love because He first loved us.*

"It's all about love," Scott had told me then. "It's all about love."

MAY

21

A bit warmer—70°—but the wind is kicking up a clay-colored haze and scattering leaf debris everywhere. Kind of depressing. In spite of all hardships, the pyracantha branches are thick with creamy blossoms. Hardy doesn't begin to describe this toughie. Its tenacity inspires me.

I woke to the sound of cello music coming from the basement. Six-thirty. Ky would be up soon. The voice of Andrea's cello sang a song like a walk with a friend on an October afternoon, warm and companionable. I slipped into my robe before descending the basement stairs to listen.

Andrea chewed her bottom lip in concentration as she played. From the stairs I watched and listened without her noticing my arrival.

A story unfolded in my mind, drawn from my imagination by the melody. A young girl with dark braids ran from a village of stone cottages. She wore a peasant dress with a white apron tied around her waist. She carried a parcel close to her chest. The music laid a footpath of waxing and waning hope as she entered the woods, as if the girl had been on this mission before. A thick blanket of pine needles silenced her steps. She approached a thatched cottage to knock and knock again at the heavy door. The trail beckoned her back to the village, but the door opened and the little girl handed the package to me. The music and my story ended abruptly.

Andrea's shoulders slumped. "I need more bow."

I must have sighed with her, because she looked up to find me on the stairs.

"I'm so sorry," she said, closing her music. "Did I wake you?"

"No, I came down so I could listen. I hope you don't mind."

Her liquid eyes studied me, probably wondering if she should expect a blow, physical or otherwise. A beat of sadness thumped my heart. I moved closer with my hands clasped behind my back. She leaned on her cello, eyes to the floor. "I just can't get this piece right. I should be practicing more."

I wanted to tell her about the story her music had evoked and how fun it had been to let my imagination run free. I said, "It sounded great to me."

She smiled a small thank-you, the kind you saved for well-meaning people who were completely clueless. She busied herself stowing her music stand and cello.

I stood over her like a child watching the waves wash away a sand castle. I commanded myself to say something to prevent a lost opportunity. "You don't have to stop playing."

"I have to be at the Cow earlier than usual." She polished the honeyed wood of her cello with a white cloth. "Some group is having a breakfast meeting in the Udder Room."

I put my hands in my pockets and remembered why I was there. "Andrea, I think I may have found something of yours." I held the bracelet out to her.

She clutched it over her heart. "Where did you find this?"

"I think you dropped it the first time you came to the house.

The clasp was broken, so I got a new one. It looks a little different. I hope it's okay."

She held the bracelet toward the bare light bulb on the ceiling. "It's great!" She attached the bracelet around her ankle. That explained its size. "I can't thank you enough. This was my last gift from my grandmother. I thought I'd lost it forever."

Andrea stood to give me a hug. I felt the flutter of her heart against mine. Her face mirrored my surprise at the intimacy of her gesture. She bent down to settle the cello and bow into the case.

"Well, have a good day then," I said and turned to leave.

"Mibby?"

She bit her lip again; her eyes turned earnest. "I want to tell you how sorry I am about the other night. It was careless, stupid really, of me to smoke weed on your porch like that. It won't happen again, so you don't have to worry."

"I appreciate that."

I climbed a couple steps but stopped, not wanting to interrupt the volley of goodwill we had going. "Andrea?"

She looked up from clamping her cello case closed.

Because He first loved us.

"I'm glad you found us."

Judith hefted the bale of peat moss to her shoulder, a cigarette hanging from the side of her mouth, and I followed her to the Daisy Mobile. I carried a flat of Atlantis Yellow marigolds and a coffee-stained piece of paper with an address written in Judith's bold printing. We sidestepped the throng of customers coming up the main walk. Judith seemed to be avoiding eye contact with her customers, even though several called out her name. She talked to me over her shoulder.

"Tell the Madisons this is the last time I'm replacing their marigolds. I don't care how long he farmed in Iowa; the guy's an idiot." Judith dropped the bale into the bed of my truck, narrowly missing the tomato plants I'd loaded earlier. "Grab a bag of mulch on your way out. I want these babies to be the most pampered marigolds in town." She blew a plume of acrid smoke over her shoulder, but the wind brought it back to my face.

I smiled while I held my breath, waiting for it to pass. "I have some fertilizer I can leave with them."

"Nah, I don't trust that ol' loon to read the instructions." Judith took a long drag on her cigarette and snuffed it out with the toe of her boot. "You got that ghost woman all set up with a design yet?"

She had to mean Miss Dubois. I started to explain the misunderstanding I'd had with Miss Dubois, but Judith looked nervously at the growing crowd of customers waiting to talk to her. Besides, I knew what I was about to offer Judith sounded too much like excuses. She hated excuses.

"You need to get back to your customers, Judith. Don't worry. I'm just revising a few plant choices."

She pulled me a few paces away from the customers and put her face close to mine. "How's our boy doing?"

"His teacher called last night. He's almost caught up with his work."

"Good for him! Call me before his next game." Judith looked to the western horizon where a curtain of rain swept the lower valley. When she spoke, her voice was melancholy. "I've missed seeing him play."

Throughout history, kitchens have been the chapels where women gather to soothe and fortify one another—chapels with colored wallpaper instead of stained-glass windows. The kitchen table, sticky with rings of juice from breakfast, is an altar of prayer. The soulful hum of the refrigerator replaces the choir.

Rather than deadheading Roseanne's delphiniums, I was in her chapel, waiting and wondering if I was up to the calling. She had invited me in for a cup of coffee, but I knew there was more to the invitation. Her hair had been pulled into a hasty ponytail, and a trail of coffee stains foot-stepped down the front of her shirt. Smudges of mascara were all that remained of her makeup.

While the coffee dripped and Roseanne poured milk into a dainty creamer, I sat at the glass-and-chrome table. Nothing had been spared to create a magazine-perfect kitchen for the Mitchell family. Granite counters. Sculptured faucets. Slate tile. Restaurant appliances. It was cool efficiency through and through.

Roseanne poured me a cup of coffee. "I hope you don't mind. I just don't feel like working in the garden today." She stopped pouring to add, "Of course, I'll pay you for your time."

As much as I needed the money, I said, "Don't be silly. I could use a break."

"Really?"

"Really," I said with more confidence than I felt, then busied myself with sugar and cream. I stirred my coffee and waited.

Roseanne wiped the dribbles she'd made with the carafe and rubbed until the spots were long past gone before returning to the sink. She stood watching something I couldn't see out the window.

"Daniel left me," she said finally.

"Roseanne?"

She joined me at the table and wiped crumbs into her hand. When she spoke, her words were measured out carefully so as not to tip the balance of her self-control. I recognized the technique. I'd used it many times myself.

"Daniel left me. He took Phoebe to his girlfriend's house. The police say they can't do anything unless he leaves the state. He says I'm a terrible—"

She doubled over and convulsed in pain. Even measured words won't let you pass the pain of so great a loss. Roseanne sobbed uncontrollably in my arms. I held her tightly, but her shoulders heaved with no relief in sight. My heart, the mother's heart, awoke. I rubbed small circles between her shoulder blades and sang as I would to Ky.

Jesus loves me, this I know . . .

When I got to the third verse and had to hum more words than I could remember, Roseanne sat up and tried in vain to wipe away the steady flow of tears.

"He's lying, Mibby. He's lying."

"I know. You're a wonderful mother. He's just trying to distract you from the real issue here."

She frowned.

I explained, "It's easier for him to blame you. This has absolutely nothing to do with you as a mother."

Roseanne's chair scraped against the tile and fell over as she stood. She paced with her hands kneading her forehead. "My father told me to get a lawyer, one that's a junkyard dog. Do you know anyone like that?"

I imagined Emilio growling and drooling menacingly in court. "Yes, I do."

But Roseanne needed more than a rabid lawyer. She was as brittle as a moth trapped in a hot car. I wanted to cup her in my hands and carry her to freedom. I wished Louise were there. She would have known what to do.

"Roseanne, let's pray," I said, following Louise's all-occasion disaster plan.

To my surprise, she nodded and bowed her head. I took her hands in mine and studied the crooked part in her hair and wondered if I hadn't offered more than I could produce. I coached myself to keep it simple.

"Heavenly Father," I started, but faltered. "Heavenly Father, this mother's heart is broken, but you already knew that, I know. Mend her and strengthen her. Keep Phoebe safe." I thought I should pray for Daniel, too. But how do you pray for someone who has crushed a friend's heart and stolen her child? "Let the shame of Daniel's actions rest fully on his shoulders—all day and all night until he brings Phoebe back home. Make it soon, Lord. In Jesus' name, amen."

I raised my head, but Roseanne's remained bowed. "Father," she prayed. She breathed deeply and tightened her grip on my hands. "I don't deserve your help, but I need it. I want—no, I need my daughter back. I give you whatever's left of my heart. In Jesus' name, amen."

Roseanne met my eyes. "We are weak, but He is strong," she sang through her tears.

I checked my messages while I tore open a package of Oreos, poured a glass of milk, and peeled an orange.

Beep. "Mibby? Margot. Don't make me come out to the desert to find you. You wouldn't enjoy my company and you know it. Call or I'm making reservations." There was a pause in the tape, and I released a sigh. "This is not an idle threat."

I stopped the tape to allow the dread to leave the room, and then I listened to the next message.

Beep. "Hello, sugar baby. I think you should invite your dearest friend to dinner tonight, because her hunka hunka burnin' love is out of town. I'll bring dessert. Bye."

I didn't want to see Margot anytime soon, so I dialed her number and was put on hold. I didn't recognize the assistant's voice, but it sounded pinched with frustration already. She wouldn't last long, either.

"Whatever you do, don't look like prey."

That was the advice the intrepid television host had offered viewers for that chance encounter with a bear or a mountain lion on a hiking trail. It sounded useful for phone calls to a cantankerous sister, too.

"Make yourself as big as possible and yell or throw things. Whatever you do, don't turn and run. Nothing will make you look more like rabbit stew to a predator than your backside heading for cover."

While I waited for Margot to come on the line, I squared my shoulders and put my hands on my hips, effectively increasing my mass by three percent.

"Talk" was Margot's one-word greeting.

"Hello, Margot." I suppressed a cough in my sleeve. "How are you?"

"Irrelevant. Mother wants to know if you got the package."

I stood taller. "I got it last week."

"Tell me you didn't drink that abominable stuff."

Since I couldn't throw anything at her, I mustered a verbal curveball. "Of course I did. It was delicious."

The line went quiet for a beat and a half.

"Irrelevant."

"Will that be all?" I asked. "I have something important to do."

The phone line hummed its vacant song to me.

"That went better than expected," I told my administrative assistant, Blink. "Shall we share a celebratory doggie bone?"

Louise beamed at me like I'd just taken my first step. "I'm real proud of you. You ministered the love of Jesus to Roseanne."

All of the embroidered cats on Louise's sweater mimicked her approval with broad grins while golden kittens hung from her hoop earrings for dear life. Deserved or not, I took delight in Louise's praise.

"You were able to look beyond your own pain and reach out to the hurting."

Louise had joined Andrea, Ky, and me for dinner, because Manley had to spend the night in Telluride, where he was installing bathroom fixtures for a fading rock star. I'd prepared dinner on the grill and a camp stove. It wasn't bad. But Andrea pushed the rice pilaf around on her plate and looked sideways at me.

She hadn't been around long, but I'd learned to read her. If a face can be an open book, Andrea's pages blew freely with the slightest breeze. It was clear she didn't share Louise's enthusiasm over my accomplishments. I assumed it was the emphasis on Jesus and the power of prayer. She remained quiet through dinner as Ky recounted a lunch hour soccer game and Louise told us about her latest guests, the McGeevers from Iowa.

"They're a whole lot more considerate than those musicians, but one of them snores like a freight train." She raised one eyebrow. "From the pitch, I'd say it was Mrs. McGeever." Louise threw her paper and plastic utensils away. "I'm going to make it an early night, darlin's. If I get to sleep before Mrs. McGeever, I'll have a chance at a good night's sleep."

Ky and Andrea settled into a night of creating the solar system out of balloons and papier-mâché. I suggested that foam balls would be easier but got scolded by Ky for my hostility toward the environment—something about petroleum products. Andrea concentrated on cutting strips of newspaper.

"I'm going up to finish Miss Dubois' plan. If you need me, give me a holler."

Andrea tapped on the doorframe as I slid Miss Dubois' finished plan into a folder.

"Do you have a minute?" she asked. She stepped into my bedroom. "I won't be long."

Andrea closed the door and settled into Grandma's chair. Her eyes narrowed and her voice deepened. "I don't know as much as you do about Christianity, but I'd always thought charity began at home."

"I would agree with that."

She talked faster, each phrase delivered with more intensity than the last. "What about Ky? He's afraid to talk about his father because he doesn't want to hurt you. But he's afraid if he doesn't talk about his father, he'll forget him." She looked at the closed door and lowered her voice. "He needs you to give him permission to talk about his father."

I wanted to tell Andrea how terrifying her suggestion was to me, how very afraid I was of crumbling into a blubbering heap in front of my son. But my comfort wasn't an issue, because her accusations rang with more truth than I liked. If it had come from anyone else, I would have nodded agreement and walked down the hall to Ky's room. From Andrea? Well, I didn't appreciate her attempts to edit my life.

"That's easy for you to say. I'm his mother. He needs me to be strong."

"Are you?"

"What?"

"Strong."

Andrea leaned forward.

"Are you strong?"

"I'm trying to be."

"How hard can it be?"

My heart pounded; I wiped my hands on my pants. "Pretty hard."

She drew her legs to her chest. Her voice softened. "Maybe you could just ask him what he misses about his dad."

She waited a long moment for me to respond and then got up slowly. "I'm sorry. Sometimes I—" she chewed her bottom lip—"sometimes I say things. . . . I'm sorry." Andrea shrugged her shoulders, smiled coyly, and left.

I lay on the bed and watched the fan circle slowly on the ceiling. In no time at all my eyes had filled with silent tears. The next day, or maybe the day after, I would talk to my son about his father.

I had no idea what I would say.

MAY 22

Yesterday was winter. Today is summer, so we have yet another record temperature to celebrate, 94°. Ugh. On a happier note, the Bandera penstemon is blooming happily. Ky thinks the blossoms look like cuttlefish tethered to a pole. Ha! Peeked at montbretia again. Several more sprouts have popped up. I'm impressed. Bought tomato plants finally. Time to plant?

"Where, oh where has my little house gone? Oh where, oh where can it be?" sang Louise. "I thought she'd turn left, but no, she turned right. Oh where, oh where can it be?"

The Daisy Mobile idled roughly at a stop sign, and Louise's saguaro cactus earrings shimmied along in the sunlight. We were several blocks beyond the street I should have taken to her house. Louise smiled knowingly and turned in her seat to face me. I shifted to neutral to wait for the heavy lunchtime traffic to clear.

"Sugar, do you know Psalm 23?"

I sat up straighter. "I memorized it."

"Good for you. Do you remember the part that says, 'Yea, though I walk through the valley of the shadow of death, I will fear no evil: for thou art with me'?"

"Sure." I preferred the verses about still waters and green pastures.

"It's the silliest thing," she said, "but people overlook the *yea,* even though it's out there in front as conspicuous as a fly in the buttermilk. Do you know why it's there?"

I had to admit I'd never even thought about it.

"That's a pity."

A steady stream of cars flowed through the intersection, so I gave Louise my attention.

"Here's what it means: yippee, I can walk through the shadow that death casts over me, and God's nearness will give me courage."

Yippee?

"Mibby, it's fun to see what God can do with us when we let Him, even in our darkest times." Louise's smile faded. "Do you believe that?"

I wanted to believe it, knew I should believe it, so I told her I was trying to believe it.

"Do you want me to drive you through Tenth and Crawford right now? I have all the time in the world."

At the mention of the intersection where Scott was hit, my innards did a double gainer in the pike position and belly flopped. I ground the gearshift into first and lurched into the intersection. "I think that's something I need to do on my own, Louise."

When we stopped in front of Louise's house, she rested her hand on my shoulder. "Don't put it off too long. The sooner you find God faithful in the dark places of your grief, the sooner you'll rest beside still waters in the sunshine." She squeezed my shoulder. "And remember, shadows can't hurt you."

"I never would have hired you if I'd known you were incompetent." Miss Dubois tilted her head, and her bell-shaped hair swung with it. "That's what you are, you know—incompetent."

Her face pinched together like an old leather pouch. If I'd had a mirror, I could have exacted the perfect revenge. Instead, I had three completed plans, representing hours of work, lying rejected on the table between us. I shoved the southwest plan into my satchel and then the alba garden plan. Pinky sat on her lap, his bulbous eyes watching my every move. When I reached for the kaleidoscope-of-passionate-colors plan, Pinky bit my arm.

"Ouch!"

Droplets of blood outlined Pinky's overbite on my forearm. I stood up fast enough to topple the chair. "Your dog bit me."

Miss Dubois' face pulled tighter. "He's a perfect judge of character."

To punctuate her confidence, Pinky bared his teeth at me and growled with malice. I would have found his machismo amusing moments earlier. But now I wondered where Pinky's mouth had been lately.

"Has he had his shots?" I asked.

"You'll have to ask Alfred."

Welts rose around the teeth marks on my arm.

"Let me talk to him."

"Who?"

I was done being professional with this woman. "Alfred. Where is Alfred, for crying out loud?"

Miss Dubois squared her shoulders and talked to me down the length of her nose. "If you're going to speak disrespectfully of the dead, I must insist that you leave."

"The dead? Alfred is dead?"

She stroked Pinky's head, her lips tightly pressed together, but I wasn't about to catch rabies from a pseudo dog. I spoke as calmly as I could. "I'm very sorry about your loss, Miss Dubois, but I must know about your dog's shots. At least tell me the name of his veterinarian."

She rose slowly from the table and walked past the kitchen to a hall, stopping to level a picture on the wall before she disappeared. I assumed she'd gone to a bedroom for Pinky's vaccine record tucked away in a desk drawer or a shoebox on a closet shelf. A door clicked shut. My arm throbbed hotter with my quickening pulse. Miss Dubois wasn't coming back.

I headed for the door. My goal was to reach the Daisy Mobile before I cried, more from anger than pain. I slammed the front door hard. If justice reigned, her Liberty Bell coiffure sported a hairline fracture. Pun intended. Two elderly ladies standing on the sidewalk stopped their conversation to watch me stomp to the truck cradling my left arm to my chest.

"Are you all right?" one of the ladies asked and moved closer.

They both wore shorts and T-shirts touting vacation spots. I doubted Miss Dubois would mix with ladies so engaged with the business of living, but I was desperate.

"Her dog bit me," I said, my voice trilling on the edge of panic. "You wouldn't happen to know the name of Pinky's vet, would you?"

"That dog's bitten half the people in the complex," said the lady in the Cancun T-shirt.

I found out from her that Pinky was up-to-date on his shots. The neighbors had pooled their money to get both dogs their shots in March.

"Both dogs?" I asked.

"Yes," said the lady in the Glacier National Park shirt. "Alfred and Pinky."

My doctor wrapped the wound with gauze and secured it with a knobby band of rubber. "That'll hold it," he said. "But before you go, I want to confirm Pinky's vaccination record with a call to Dr. Kelley's clinic. Wait here."

I had plenty of time to think while waiting for Dr. Fakla to return. Around me, an array of tools I would expect to see on *Old*

Yankee Workshop hung from the walls. Saws. Mallets. Long black tubes with gauges. I hated to think what they'd been used for. So I didn't.

Instead, I revisited my disappointing presentation with Miss Dubois. She had made working at McDonald's look enticing. At least they would pay me for the work I'd done, and somehow, I had confidence that I could apply condiments with enough flair to satisfy the artist in me.

More than likely, I knew, there would be more than one Miss Dubois in my future. I would slave over a plan and he or she would find a reason, any reason, not to pay me. It happened.

But then again, good stuff happened, too. There was the vegetable garden I'd designed for the Wilsons. Nothing had succeeded in getting Twila Wilson out of bed after her heart attack, at least not until her husband told her the peas had grown six inches overnight. From that day on, she went to the garden at first light to see what magic had happened as she slept. Twila Wilson credited the garden for her quick recovery. Besides the check Mr. Wilson wrote, I was paid a bushel of sweet tomatoes, a perk I couldn't expect from McDonald's. And there were others, like June Murdock and the cottage garden she'd commissioned for her mother, and the bride who'd wept over the beauty of her living arrangements, and the aspen grove I'd created for the nursing home. The residents had sent me dozens of thank-you notes.

I made up my mind.

I will not let one bad experience rob me of my good memories, past and future. Sorry, McDonald's, you can't have me yet.

I retrieved a message from Roseanne when I got home from the doctor. Her voice came through the speaker compressed, yet direct.

"Mibby, could you give me a bid for maintaining the whole yard? I can't trust anyone else to do it as well as you. We're putting the house on the market and it needs to look good. I'm staying with my parents." She gave me their phone number and then lowered her voice to add, "Keep praying."

Andrea left the house after dinner to play her cello at a coffee shop near the college. I admired her for making connections in our community so easily. Before she left, she reminded me how this would be a good time to talk to Ky about Scott.

I chose the video from our last Christmas together. It had been just the three of us: Scott, Ky, and me. I waited for Ky to close his math book and fill his book bag with the completed work.

"Ky?"

He buckled the flap of his pack and slung a strap over his shoulder. "Yeah?" he said with just enough interest to spur me on.

"I was wondering if you'd like to watch a video from the Christmas before last."

He let his pack slide off his shoulder to the table. "You mean our last Christmas with Dad?"

"Yeah, I thought it might be nice."

Ky insisted on popcorn, so we threw a package in the microwave and grabbed two sodas from the fridge on the porch. He told me about the presentation he'd given on his solar system project while we waited for the kernels to pop.

"Did you know that the gravitational pull of Jupiter protects earth from getting blasted to smithereens by humongous asteroids?"

"I didn't know that." How nice it was to have that worry crossed off my list.

Ky started the tape and joined me on the sofa. I draped my arm over his shoulders even though Pinky's bite throbbed under the dressing. He leaned against me, and we watched our story unfold. As the official Garrett family photographer, there is little empirical evidence to prove I ever existed. On the other hand, I've captured the people most important to me on film.

We watched Scott and Ky sing happy birthday to Jesus in the glow of the cake's candles, but it was my off-key voice that dominated the soundtrack. Scott divvied up the presents from under the tree until we all had a neat pile of gifts before us. Ky's was biggest, so we gave him a head start. He opened books about baseball, a new mitt, and a computer baseball game. A definite theme emerged.

Scott shook another present and said, "Sounds like clothes to me, bud. Maybe we should let Mom open something." They both turned to me expectantly. Static filled the television screen.

When the picture came into focus again, Scott was opening the briefcase I'd bought him with the meager profits from Perennially Yours. His eyes still muddy with sleep caressed me so warmly the camcorder slipped to record the underside of the coffee table and Blink's wet nose. I recovered in time to catch him saying, "Honey, it's just perfect."

Then Ky asked to read a letter to us. Scott and I sat on the sofa while Ky ceremoniously unfolded the paper and staged a cough. The camera caught the closeness of Scott's leg in the corner of the frame. Sitting there with Ky, watching from a year and a half away, I could feel the warmth of it as surely as I had on that Christmas morning.

"I'm just a poor, pitiful kid, so I had to get creative with my present for you guys," Ky read on the tape. "I figured if I wrote you a letter of appreciation and reminded you of it often, the year could work out well for me, and you'd forget about the little incident with the firecrackers."

Scott said, "Fat chance" from off camera. The sparkle in Ky's eyes said he didn't believe his father.

The letter thanked us for providing him with such a nice house, even though it had holes in it, and for pretty good food, except for mom's unfortunate attempt at haute cuisine.

"Watch it," I warned.

"And most of all, I want to thank you for your support and encouragement for my baseball career. In thirty years, I'll be sure to mention you at my induction into the Hall of Fame." Ky inserted a cheesy grin for the camera at this point. "Now, really folks, I love you a lot and hope you have a really, really, really nice Christmas. Love, your son, Ky."

Scott entered the picture and enclosed Ky in his arms. He looked into the camera and mouthed the words, "We're so lucky."

Ky paused the tape, freezing Scott's image. "Can I ask you something?"

Uh-oh.

This was it. I'd spent most of my time the past couple days anticipating the questions he might be churning around. Where is Dad? Or why did his father have to die? Or the one that I was most sure he would ask, because it was the hardest to answer, did God make Dad die? I needed to do some homework.

I'd dug out the audiotape from Scott's funeral, hoping our pastor had answered the questions for me. Quite frankly, I hadn't remembered a word Pastor Dale had said that day. But on the tape, Dale told Ky, our brimming church, and me that God gives us spouses and children so we can understand His love for us. When we celebrate our children's triumphs, large and small, we understand God's joy over the times we obey Him with love and faith. When we pine for our true love, we understand the longing that unsettles God's heart until we answer His call. We discover the fervor of God's hunt for his children when a toddler plays hide-and-seek with his parents in a department store. And when the ones we love die, and we are consumed by a loss so great that our hearts have been crushed, we understand the grief of God over one of His children who refuses His love.

To know that God slopped around in misery comforted me. But Dale didn't answer the question of God's culpability in Scott's death. Did God blow the whistle when Scott's clock ticked down to zero, and poof, he was dead? I didn't know, so I prayed Ky would stick to my imaginary script.

"What about the father-son banquet at the end of the season? Who's going to go with me?" he asked.

"The banquet?"

"Dad took me, remember?"

I remembered the banquet. It was the question that puzzled me. Logistics. He was concerned over the logistics of being a fatherless son. Problem solving. I could do that.

"Is there someone else you could invite?" *Like me?*

"I kind of thought Coach would take me, since he's already taking Salvador."

"Do you want me to ask him?"

"I can handle it." He filled his mouth with another fistful of popcorn. He flipped the remote over and over in his hands as he chewed. "I have another question."

I dropped some popcorn back into the bowl. "Shoot."

"What if I get, say, strep throat, and I can't go to school for, like, two weeks. Who's going to take care of me?"

"I will, Ky."

"But your clients won't like that."

I mentally flipped through the Rolodex of my clients. I thought of Margaret and Roseanne and Mrs. Pierson. They'd understand. Harlan Chandler? Maybe not, but who cared? "It doesn't matter. I'll take care of you. You're more important than anyone or anything."

His arm went around my waist; his head nestled into my neck. I wondered how long we'd be able to do this. Whatever the answer, it would be too short. He tightened his hold and I waited, for I knew another question was coming. He sat up quickly; his breath came fast and his eyes darkened to the gray of a rogue cloud heavy with rain. Ky threw the question at me, a sinking spitball.

"What if *you* died? I'd be all alone."

I'd forgotten this about my son. He had always saved the real question for last. I pulled him into my arms so he could hear my heart beating. "Your dad didn't want to leave you and neither do I. I promise I will be careful, but I can't promise I won't die."

He squeezed me tighter.

"Ky, let me see your face." His chin trembled but he sat up. In his face I saw the same fear that had owned me since Scott died.

"The world seems very dangerous to you now. It does to me, too. But there's something I want you to always remember. God is good, Ky. Very, very good."

"Louise said that, too. She said to watch carefully, because He makes pearls out of poopy situations." He allowed himself a timid smile.

"She's right. The other thing I want you to know is that Dad and I made plans for you in case something happened to both of us."

"You did?"

"We did. We didn't want you to end up with the carnival or traveling circus, so we talked to Manley and Louise. They said they'd look after you."

The tension in his face relaxed. He looked toward the cobwebs in the corner, and I knew he was picturing himself waking up to Louise's baked goods every morning. "Would that be okay with you?" I asked.

"What about Andrea? She's my sister. Couldn't I go with her?"

"We chose Manley and Louise a long time ago, just after you were born. We thought they'd be good because we saw that they loved you from the moment they met you, and they had stable lives. But most of all, we knew they would teach you the same things we would teach you, especially how very much God loves you."

"Andrea loves me."

"She does," I said and munched on a few kernels of corn, chewing much longer than needed to find an answer to satisfy him. I didn't have to worry. He had it all figured out.

"It would be kind of hard for Andrea to have a kid hanging around," he said. "She doesn't even have a house."

"That could be a problem."

"It would be hard for Blink and me to sleep in her car."

"Louise drives a big Cadillac," I reminded him.

Ever the negotiator, Ky said, "Maybe I could stay with Manley and Louise until Andrea is ready."

Deep in my soul where good intentions sleep undisturbed, I rustled their slumber. I promised myself to eat better, be more cautious, and exercise regularly. Whatever it would take to mother this child into adulthood, I'd do it.

Ky settled back into my arms. His worries about a parentless future had been soothed—for now. He pressed the play button and our Christmas story continued. Packages were unwrapped. Pies were baked. Friends arrived. The plum pudding stuck to the pan.

The Scott I watched in the video was the Scott I'd almost forgotten. He wasn't a cardboard cutout. He loved his family passionately. He had room in his heart for all of us. Ky, me—and Andrea.

MAY

24

Finally planted tomatoes—kind of late. Hope it gets hot and stays that way for a bumper crop. Along with the regulars, Fantastic and Early Girl, I'm adding a Roma and a variety Judith recommended, Sweet 100s. She claims they taste like tomato candy. Ky will be the judge of that. Relieved to see the cilantro still looks good, coming up strong. Also put in six jalapeño plants. ¡Olé!

I had just worked the shampoo into a lather when I heard the heavy rapping of knuckles on the bathroom door and a male voice calling my name. I turned off the water to listen.

"Is that you, Mibby? I'm back."

Suds flowed down my forehead. With my eyes closed, I stepped out of the shower and pulled on my shorts and T-shirt before I felt decent enough to answer him. "Uh, Droop, I'll be out in a minute."

"I don't need nothing," he said. "I just didn't want to scare you again."

The shampoo stung my eyes. "Thanks, Droop. Thanks very much."

"No problem." His heavy boots moved away from the door and then returned. "Mibby?"

"Yeah?"

"We got a problem with the flooring."

A bubble of worry tingled along my spine. Whenever Droop said *he* had a problem, he fixed it and continued working. If *we* had a problem, it meant I would be spending a lot of money. Either way, I wasn't dressed to kill, or to think.

"I'll be right down."

By the time I'd rinsed my hair and dressed in dry clothes, Droop had the remaining boxes of planks opened and splayed across the floor. "What we got here is mislabeled boxes," he said, handing me a cup of coffee. "We got three different types of wood, and nobody at the lumberyard remembers carrying this brand of flooring. Do you still have the receipt?"

I gulped. Receipts were in the filing cabinet, but I'd never even opened it. Receipts had been Scott's job. "I'm not sure. Is there anything else you can do until I find it?"

"Not exactly."

The filing cabinet was tucked under the stairs of the basement. Heavy shadows cast by the bare bulb made the folders hard to read. *Dentist. Gas and Electric Company. Home Insurance*. Finally I found it. *Home Improvement*. It was the fattest file in the drawer. I pulled it out. Another file caught my eye. Loosely hinged from many years of use, the tab read, *Post-Office Box*. Inside, receipts dated back to 1982. The most current receipt showed Scott had paid the rent for one year, ending this July. A small envelope, the kind with string and grommets for fasteners, fell out of the folder. The key to Scott's P.O. box was inside.

I told Droop I couldn't find the receipt for the planks and headed out for a full day of garden maintenance. I considered turning left toward *the* intersection, my personal shadow of death, but I wanted to finish my accounts early that day to do an errand. It seemed like a good excuse.

As a general rule, once the temperature tops ninety, garden maintenance is a lonely, yet efficient, job. My clients waved at me through windows and returned to their chairs near the air conditioner or fan. That day, Mrs. Pierson twiddled her fingers at me from her kitchen window. She had left a message on my machine to tell me it was time to braid the foliage of her daffodils to neaten the flowerbed.

Ugh.

By one-thirty, I'd plaited all of her daffodils—all one gazillion of them. I hated doing it. All they had done to deserve such abuse was stop blooming. Horticulturists have known for years that braiding does more harm than good, which just proves gardening isn't all about science. In equal measure it is about tradition and taste. Gardeners who prefer to keep their gardens tidy rather than mimic nature do so because plants tend to get messy in nature. Like Mrs. Pierson's daffodils, they shrivel up and brown out when they are done blooming to make room for the next round of glorious bloomers.

Mrs. Pierson, with my complicity, was a braider.

She walked toward me through shimmers of heat with a frosty glass. She wore dark wraparound glasses and a broad-brimmed hat with a red gingham bow to shield her face. Jeans, a long-sleeved chambray blouse, and cotton gloves completed her protective clothing.

"You really should cover up out here in the sun, dear."

The flesh of my arms glowed red under my freckles. "I'm almost done."

When I handed her the empty glass, she scurried toward the house and waved over her shoulder. "See you in a couple weeks."

Blink licked my legs as I pushed the wheelbarrow back to the truck, enjoying the saltiness I'd accumulated from a day of sweating.

"Stop that."

He waited until I'd wrestled the clippings bag into the truck to take a quick taste of his favorite place behind my knees. I batted him away. "I am not your pretzel, Blink."

More importantly, I thought, *I'm not Scott*. This was another game he had played with Blink. When Blink moved closer, I threatened him with a day at home with Droop. "Get in the truck." He watched me coax the ignition until the engine drummed out an uneven beat. Blink chewed on a moan that meant he was sorry.

"You miss him, too, don't you, Blink?"

Nose to nose with Blink, I constructed a mental list of all the jobs Scott's death had left for me to fill—father, provider, bill payer, general contractor, pest controller, coach, family stabilizer, decision-maker, future planner, and now, my role as alpha male was being challenged.

"You know the rules, bud. Whoever blinks first loses."

I looked into Blink's eyes, and before I could ask myself what lay beyond those watery pools, I blinked and received my comeuppance, a chin-to-forehead lick. Nobody beat Blink the Wonder Dog. He was now the undisputed alpha male of the Garrett family.

What a relief!

One letter leaned across the viewing window of the post-office box. It was lavender. I pushed the key into the keyhole and quickly pulled it back out. I peered into the window again to see whom the letter was from, but it was tilted with the return address out of view.

"Excuse me," said a man in a business suit. He motioned to the box below Scott's with his key.

"Sorry." I stepped out of his way.

"Thanks," said the man with a disposition as shiny as his head. "Lovely day, isn't it?" He tucked the bundle of mail under his arm and left whistling.

The only way to stop myself from inventing a hundred terrible things the letter could be was to open the box and look. So I did.

I returned to the truck. Blink stood ready for the wind in his face. When the truck didn't move, he looked over his shoulder. The key was still in my pocket. The letter was from Andrea, probably written in her quest to find Scott—the unanswered call of her heart. Blink rested his head in my lap while I scratched his ears and wondered if it wasn't time to invite the girl in, really in. Not the come-on-over-anytime invitation of an insincere neighbor, but the can-you-come-to-dinner-tonight kind of invitation.

"Hey, Andrea," I'd say, "want a family, starting now?"

I allowed myself to daydream while waiting for Ky's turn at bat. The distraction helped me forget my sunburn. I wondered what it would be like to have Ben there, sitting right beside me in the bleachers. Would Ky wave at Ben from the field? Would Ben whisper in my ear that I was adorable even when I was sweating like a pig? Would he buy me a second hot dog?

Judith dug her elbow into my side. "I said, I sold Walled Garden."

She had been fidgeting during the whole game. I thought she was having a nicotine fit but evidently not. I couldn't even imagine Walled Garden without Judith dispensing her gardening wisdom. She had to be kidding.

"You sold Walled Garden?"

"That's what I said, didn't I?" Judith watched the umpire sweep home plate.

"Why? It's doing so well."

"That's the problem. I never wanted to work around so many people. I just wanted a reason to grow more flowers than I needed." She looked at me. "The Realtor found an ambitious kid with rich parents. I'll stay through fall to teach him the ropes."

Judith would have seen my chin tremble if the announcer hadn't called Ky's name. "Kyle Garrett, second base." Ky frowned toward the announcer's booth. *Will he ever forgive me for not naming him Sammy, Mark, or Babe?*

Ky went through his pre-batting ritual walking to the batter's box. A couple of low waggles at the ground, then he windmilled the bat in each hand before he shot a wad of spit into the dust. He settled into the batter's box and let the pitcher know he was ready by holding his position. I held my breath. The first pitch was high and outside.

While the pitcher and Ky went through their between-pitch liturgy, I asked Judith a question. "Does this guy know anything about plants?"

"Not my problem anymore."

The ball slapped into the catcher's glove. "Strike!"

Judith stood to yell at the umpire. "Hey, Batman, where are your glasses?"

"Judith!" I tugged her back onto the bleacher.

"That was a ball if I've ever seen one."

Ky watched the third-base coach. The man swiped the bill of his hat, tugged at his ear, and drew his hand from his shoulder to his waist before he crossed his arm and nodded at Ky, who wiped the sweat off his forehead before stepping back into position.

"Don't worry about the new owner," Judith said, keeping her eyes on the game. "He has a degree in horticulture from Colorado State University and an MBA to boot, better qualified than me by a long shot."

The pitcher reeled back and shot a fastball at the plate. Ky pivoted over the plate to bunt.

Clonk!

Ky sprinted toward first base as the third baseman charged the ball that stopped dead in the grass just beyond the pitcher. He bobbled the ball. I prayed it would buy Ky the time to get to first base. It didn't. Ky trotted back to the dugout, where his teammates slapped him on the back. The third-base coach returned his offhanded wave across the field.

Judith explained that Ky's bunt had gotten a player from second to third, improving the team's chances of scoring. "That was the best bunt I've ever seen," she said.

"Judith, what will you do?" I really wanted to ask her what *I* would do. I'd considered Walled Garden a safety net of employment if Perennially Yours didn't work out—or I bailed.

"Can we talk about this later?"

MAY 25

It's hot. Enough said about that. First water lily opened with two more buds sticking their noses above the water. No sign of false sunflower under the bark. Drat. Also, peony blossoms were already faltering a full week before Memorial Day. Give that plant a calendar! On a happier note, more montbretia are coming up. Andrea's (my ~~friend's~~ stepdaughter's) bonsai looks great. Lots of baby leaves unfurling.

"What on earth happened in here?" Louise asked. She scanned my bedroom from the open door, her jaw slack with amazement. "Did a denim factory blow up?"

I stood before a full-length mirror wearing the last possible contender for the not-too-dressy and not-too-casual outfit to wear to dinner with Ben. Draped over a chair, piled on the bed, and scattered on the floor were those that hadn't made the cut. Some were frumpy, some wrinkled, and honestly, even I knew they were all out of style. All efforts had failed. I looked like a half-empty feed sack.

I hadn't told anyone Ben called to arrange a dinner meeting. He'd said, "I have the payment right here. Let me deliver it to you in person." When I didn't answer right away, his voice had taken on a hint of desperation. "I could really use the company, Mibby."

I said yes to Ben and told Louise, "I'm just cleaning out my closet." Besides, I didn't want Ky to know about Ben. Not yet. I'd seen single mothers parade men in and out of their children's lives to love or to loathe, and I wouldn't do that to Ky.

"Are you telling me you curled your hair and put on mascara to clean out your closet?"

Uh-oh. How had I ever thought I could hide a date from Louise?

"Sweet pea, are you going on a date?"

"Now, don't get all twittered, Louise. I'm just having dinner with Ben so he can pay for the design. It's not a date."

"And to think I felt sorry for you over here all by your lonesome with Ky and Andrea out celebrating." She picked up a jumper I'd worn when I was pregnant with Ky. She studied it with a sneer and dropped it. "Funny, I don't remember you going out to dinner with any of your other clients. And I think li'l ol' Pointer Pixley would have loved to share a combo meal with you."

I flopped on the bed and admitted to Louise what I hadn't admitted yet to myself. "Well, it might be a little date."

"Hot diggity!" She opened the closet door. "Let me help." She slid a few garments across the rod before she turned to me with a frown. "How much time do we have? Allison's dress shop closes at six."

"He'll be here in twenty minutes."

"Oh." Louise sat in Grandma's chair drumming her chin with cherry red fingernails. Hummingbird earrings hovered over her shoulders. "If he's taking you to a demolition derby, you'll be okay."

I groaned. "He made reservations at DiAngelo's."

She spotted the bag of clothes Roseanne had given me and pulled out a sleeveless sheath of flowered organza. "Lucky for you, I'm your fairy godmother." One look at my sunburn and the dress was quickly rejected. "You'd look like a goober farmer headin' to church."

How kind it was of her not to mention the dress's figure-hugging cut. She held up a navy dress with a white collar and piped pockets.

"Is Roseanne a flight attendant? All you'd need with this dress is a pair of silver wings and a pot of coffee to win Ben's heart."

"Remember, Louise, this is a business dinner." I felt odd even talking about a date in the bedroom I'd shared with my husband.

Maybe I should call Ben and—

"You're right, sugar. This should be a time for you and Ben to enjoy each other's company." She dumped the rest of the bag's contents onto the bed. "Any side benefit is just glaze on the doughnut," she said with a wink.

We both reached for a black rayon dress with subdued splashes of cream, apricot, and lavender flowers I couldn't identify. A sage-green crocheted sweater matched the foliage and would cover my sunburn lines. Better still, the dress's full cut would leave plenty of room for my hips.

"This is it."

"I'm not so sure, Louise. Is there anything made out of cotton in there? This is a bit dressy for my Birkenstocks."

"Try it on."

I put my heart in my pocket and opened the door. Halfway down the front steps, Ben turned at the sound of the latch. Behind him dry-brushed clouds caught the rosy glow of the setting sun.

He smiled cautiously. "I thought maybe you'd changed your mind."

"I was just having trouble with these shoes."

He looked down at my feet, and so did I. Thin black patent leather straps crisscrossed my feet like the trussing on two pork roasts. Louise had borrowed them out of Andrea's closet, reassuring me that volume was more important than proportion when it came to shoes. And she had insisted on painting my toenails a rosy red. I hardly recognized my own feet.

"They look tight," he said. "If you want to change, we have time."

I wasn't sure I would come back out if I went in to change my shoes. "They'll stretch out after I have them on for a while."

"It's such a nice evening, and the restaurant is so close, I thought we'd walk. Is that okay?"

Pride goeth before the bleeding blisters. "Sounds good." When Ben didn't follow me down the steps to the sidewalk, I turned to find him smiling at me. "What? Is something wrong?"

"You look really nice."

And so did he, as good as a lemon chiffon pie with a yellow oxford shirt and khaki pants that settled nicely on his slender hips. Aviator sunglasses hung from his shirt pocket. And there was after-shave in the air.

Did I remember perfume? Deodorant?

"Is Ky here?" he asked. "I'd like to meet him."

"No, he went out for dinner and a movie with Andrea." We needed to leave before Louise felt compelled to desert her hiding place in the powder room. "Maybe next time."

Main Street's personality shifted from powerhouse commerce to laid-back entertainment at sundown. Red tulips packed brick planters and nodded their heavy heads when cars passed by. Across the street, moviegoers formed a line at the Independence Theater to see a foreign film, probably something French and full of angst, something Margot would like. Under my sweater my sunburned arms were about to combust.

We joined a small group of people to listen to a sidewalk entertainer play his guitar and sing "Sweet Baby James." When the man finished, Ben dropped some money into an upturned hat, and we continued our walk to the restaurant. As we neared Meeker Street, the scent of roasting coffee beans wafted from Chez Ami, a patisserie where Scott and I had taken Ky almost every Sunday after church. Ami's *chou à la crème* had consistently bribed mostly appropriate church behavior out of Ky. For that I was always grateful to the French and their magic with butter and cream. Ky and I hadn't been to the place since Scott died.

Never in a million years would I have pictured myself walking down Main Street with anyone but Scott. But there I was—with Ben. I looked over my shoulder, expecting, oddly, to see Scott standing in the doorway of Chez Ami looking hurt for being left behind. For a moment I considered telling Ben that our date had been a terrible idea. Cutting our losses and heading for home seemed like the thing to do, but Ben interrupted my thoughts.

"I've been packing my grandparents' things," he said when we stopped to wait for the crosswalk light to change. "And it's a lot harder than I'd thought. I'm under my mom's orders to pack up the mementos to ship home, which makes me extremely nervous, because I've learned the hard way that one man's oil rag is another woman's memento. I gave up sorting and packed everything except the oil rags."

"I wouldn't throw them away, though, just to be on the safe side."

"You think? I better dig them out of the trash when I get home."

We laughed, and the ease of it released the tension in my shoulders and lowered my guard, if only a little.

"And then there's Jenny's stuff," Ben added. "Mom said she'd come . . ."

"But it's something you have to do?" I offered.

"Have you?"

"Cleaned out Scott's stuff?"

Ben nodded.

Someone had told me, probably Louise, that I would feel better if I did; of course, it also would have felt better to cut my feet off at that moment. "No, not yet."

We walked without talking. The thin clicking of my heels made me self-conscious, and the leather straps pinched my feet with each step. I was about to suggest a closer restaurant when Ben asked, "So how are things going with Andrea?"

"Better," I said, meaning it. "She's been great with Ky, helped him get caught up with his homework. They're celebrating the completion of his work tonight *and* his promotion to the eighth grade. Andrea even agreed to go to a hamburger place." He frowned, so I explained, "She's a vegetarian."

"You didn't want to go with them?"

"I thought this would be a good opportunity for us to . . ."

"Enjoy each other's company?"

"Yes," I said, relieved we were on the same page. "That's exactly what I was thinking. Besides, I'm making a special dinner for Ky tomorrow night, stuffed pastry shells. You can never celebrate success too much."

The DiAngelo's sign blinked a welcome two doors down.

"For me," he said, "it's nice to be with someone who understands how I'm feeling without having to explain everything." Ben opened the door of the restaurant, and our eyes met. He smiled sheepishly. "To be honest, this is the third shirt I tried on."

I remembered the debris field of clothing I'd left in my bedroom. "You're an amateur," I said. We laughed again and entered the restaurant.

During the fried calamari, I unbuckled the shoes.

With the soft din of conversation and a mournful mandolin playing in the background, we turned the talk to our families. I asked Ben lots of questions, hoping to save my family story for the uncomfortable time when the bill came and he would have to figure out the tip instead of listening to stories about my mom's multiple personalities and a sister with perpetual PMS.

"I think you better tell me how you got that scar on your jaw," I said.

Ben told me about the summer he'd turned thirteen. He sat in the bushes for hours with a camera trained on his sister Pam, who was sitting alone by the family pool all slathered in baby oil and iodine. He finally got what he wanted when she picked her nose.

"I felt like I'd won the lottery," he said. "I thought that picture would buy me a lot of cooperation from Pam."

What he hadn't anticipated was Pam picking up the photos when she went shopping for their mother. Too bad for Ben; she held a frying pan in her hand the next time she'd seen him.

I was about to tell him that by comparison my family was too boring to talk about when he stopped the waiter to order another basket of bread. I swirled a calamari in cocktail sauce and wedged off the shoes. Ben told more stories about his siblings; most of them included references to mean-spirited pranks and stitches, but his face told the real story. He loved his family.

A bundle of spaghetti slipped off my fork and a spray of marinara sauce dotted my dress. Dabbing it with a wet napkin only smeared the marinara into wider blobs.

"Check out my shirt," Ben said, pointing out a constellation of red spots. He laughed and tore off a piece of bread and dipped it in olive oil. Before he took a bite, he asked about my family. "Sisters? Brothers?"

"One sister, and that makes one sister too many."

"I have a brother like that, born with a chip on his shoulder." He sighed deeply. "We're not sure where he is. Breaks my mother's heart."

"I'm so sorry." And I was. No one disappeared without tearing at the fabric of the people who loved them.

He rolled another length of pasta around his fork. "You can't rewrite history, I guess. What's the story on your sister?"

"Whenever I talk to Margot, I feel like someone has stolen my ice cream cone."

"Ouch."

The waiter delivered coffee and tiramisu. Ben seemed to be biding his time, maybe trying to come up with a more pleasant topic of conversation. I studied the fresco above our table. Chubby cherubs frolicked against a summer sky. Too much tiramisu?

A light breeze stirred the hem of my dress when we stepped out of the restaurant. I carried the shoes in my hand. We agreed that the meal was delicious, but we would start with the tiramisu next time.

Next time?

In front of the Heads Up Salon, he said, "Let me carry those shoes for you."

He held my shoes in one hand and took my hand with the other. All rational thought came to a screeching halt. The whole universe was framed in the place where our palms touched, both a little callused, his strong and warm and alive. Very alive. An alarm went off in my head, but what reason I had left convinced me I was making too much out of some friendly handholding.

Relax!

"Is this all right?" he asked.

Between two pounding heartbeats, I breathed yes.

Ben squeezed my hand. "Good."

I wasn't one bit relaxed. One part of me, and yes, it was the purely physiological part, was performing its responses flawlessly. Rapid heartbeat. Sticky armpits. Sweaty palms. And I didn't want to think about how very red my face had turned. Every reasonable corner of my brain knew neither of us was ready for more than what the evening had started out to be, a time to enjoy each other's company. Had Ben changed his mind?

He asked me how work was going. I spoke as effortlessly as one can with a heart rate of 180. I told him about Miss Dubois and Pinky.

"You should add the cost of the doctor bill to the design charge." When I didn't answer, he asked, "You are charging her, aren't you? You did the work and more."

"I'm not sure she would remember who I am."

"It wouldn't hurt to try."

I remembered how much I disliked the new McDonald's uniforms and agreed to send an invoice the next day. I asked Ben if he'd started flying to Denver yet.

"The plane is still being painted, but I don't mind. It's giving me a chance to make some progress on the house. I will definitely be in the air by the end of the month, plane or no plane."

We walked in silence until Ben handed back the shoes at my front porch steps. The windows were completely dark, and I'd forgotten to leave the porch light on.

"Seems like everyone's gone to bed," he said.

"Yep." I swung the shoes in small circles and tried to avoid Ben's gaze.

"I had a nice time," he said.

"Me too."

Ben bent down to find my eyes. "Can we do it again?"

"That'd be nice."

When he bent his face to mine again, it was the most natural thing in the world to turn mine to meet him. His hands filled the small of my back, and he pulled me closer. Just as I was about to give him the encouraging head tilt, I screamed to myself, *Are you sure about this?*

The answer was no.

"You know what I really like about you?" Ben said. "I can always tell what you're thinking." And he kissed my forehead.

My *forehead*?

"Good night, Mibby."

"G'night, Ben."

Inside the entry, I leaned against the front door. Ben's tenderness had caught the slackened end of my silver thread and strung it instantly with possibilities as shiny as faceted beads. Ben as friend. Ben as boyfriend. Ben as husband, father, and lover. I'd never wanted and not wanted something so badly.

I asked the dark, "How could I have let this happen?"

A lamp snapped on. "What happened?" Andrea asked. She sat encircled by lamplight in Scott's chair. Her eyes were red and swollen. A pile of crumpled tissues had collected on the side table, and several lay scattered on the floor. Scott's Bible rested open on her lap.

Andrea blew her nose. "Did you have a nice time with Ben?"

"Where's Ky?"

"Upstairs. He went to bed about an hour ago."

I leaned against the newel-post. "How'd you know about Ben?"

"Louise came over. It's cool, you know, that you have somebody."

"It was just a business date."

Andrea smiled. "Louise told me all about it. How'd the shoes work?"

I wiggled my toes. "My toes aren't numb anymore."

She smiled, but her faced clouded again.

"Andrea?"

"Actually, I've been waiting for you." She tucked her hair behind her ears and turned her lacquered eyes to me. "Can you answer some questions for me?"

I swallowed hard. "Are they about the Bible?"

"Sort of."

"You might want to ask Louise."

"No, she can't help me. You're the only one who can answer my questions."

I clicked on another lamp and sat on the sofa, waiting to be humbled by my shallow understanding of the Bible.

"Louise told me I should read the chapter that John wrote. She said it would give me the most complete picture of Jesus." Andrea stopped talking to study me. I don't know what she wanted to see, but I must have passed the test, because she said, "I'm trying to decide if I should believe in Him or not."

"Then Louise is right. That's a great place to start." I knew that much.

"I found Dad's Bible in the bookcase, so I flipped through the pages looking for the . . . Gospel of John. I was blown away by all the notes Dad had written in it." Andrea smoothed the pages with her hand. "I thought Bibles were supposed to be sacred or something."

Her composure crumbled as she spoke. "I found a margin note that said, 'For Ky' with a bunch of text underlined." She opened the Bible to a place she held with her finger. She read with tears streaming down her cheeks. "'My son, do not forget my teaching, but let your heart keep my commandments; for length of days and years of life and abundant welfare will they give you.'"

I recognized the passage from Proverbs.

"What does this mean? Why did Dad say this was for Ky?" she asked, the questions shaded by anger.

I had a feeling she knew the answer, but I told her anyway. "It's Scott's blessing for Ky. It was his hope that Ky would live according to God's wisdom so he'd enjoy good relationships with people and God."

"That's what I thought," she said evenly. "There's one in here for you, too, all about satisfying your desires and being like a watered garden."

Really?

Andrea's shoulders heaved. Through sobs she said, "But I looked at every page in this book, and there is nothing—nothing in here for me. He didn't have the time to find a blessing for me?"

I invited Andrea to the sofa with outstretched arms. We cried together, long and hard, mourning the fact we had lost even more than we'd thought.

What had Scott been thinking?

The answer was easy. He had not wanted me—or Ky—to find Andrea's name written in his Bible and ask him why it was there. He had not wanted to chink the lovely façade he had built for himself. But he had never imagined this moment, the very moment when a young girl's life would fracture into slivers because her father had hidden her away. And he had not pictured me left holding the tiny fragments in my hands to caress or to drop. I remembered the broken mirror of my mother's dresser.

I pushed her hair out of her damp face and cradled her cheeks in my hands. "Andrea, Scott really screwed up. He never should have hidden you from me. But now you're here. I know you. I know you're worthy of a blessing."

Her eyes narrowed, and I braced myself for the next question.

"Am I worthy enough to know your real name, then?"

I bent to kiss Ky good-night. The twitching eyes told me he was far away in a boy's dream. I hoped he was watching his home run hit the scoreboard and listening to a stadium full of fans cheering him on his victory lap around the bases. The next day, I would tell him about his father's blessing.

Blink moaned when I jockeyed for my space on the bed but

moved over anyway. That deserved a vigorous scratch behind the ears. I opened Scott's Bible to the place he had marked for me, Isaiah 58:11. "The Lord will guide you continually, and satisfy your desire with good things, and make your bones strong; and you shall be like a watered garden, like a spring of water, whose waters fail not."

I could hear Scott's voice speaking the blessing to me, so I read it over and over. At first, I thought it was Scott's benediction on my obsessive gardening. With each reading, the emphasis fell on different phrases: "The Lord will guide you continually, and satisfy your desire . . . you shall be like a watered garden."

The blessing wasn't about gardening at all.

Blink shifted in his sleep, and my meager allotment of mattress narrowed even more. Perched on the edge of the bed, I checked the clock again: 3:43. I hadn't thought about my evening with Ben for five whole minutes, so I ran it over in my head one more time. I hoped it would lull me to sleep, but who was I kidding?

Laughing over dinner. Holding hands. The kiss on the forehead. The way Ben's hands felt on my back. All that tiramisu. It was hopeless, so I broke a sleeping pill in half and washed it down.

While I waited for sleep to come, I prayed, "Lord, I could use some strong bones and spring water, but I'm not at all sure about satisfying my needs, if you know what I mean. Please connect my heart to my head before I do something incredibly stupid. Amen."

MAY

26

I'm so glad I planted the upright fuchsias in front pots. Blooms remind me of lipstick samples the Avon lady used to leave with my grandmother—and they last forever! Best news yet—not a hint of budworm infestation. Yeah! Declaring false sunflower DOA. So sad. Considering Zagreb coreopsis or gloriosa daisy as a replacement.

"The man said no receipt-o, no refund-o. We'll have to work with what we got." Droop stared at me over his reading glasses. A jumble of floor planks crisscrossed the family room. "Do ya trust me?"

Trust had nothing to do with it. I needed a cup of coffee badly, but Droop had dismantled my field kitchen to lay the floorboards.

"Coffeepot?" I asked pitifully.

Droop led me through the dining room, where Ky's solar system project swayed from the light fixture, and into the living room. The coffeemaker sat on the hearth, where its red light glowed invitingly. That was the easy part. Locating a mug, spoon, sugar, and cream took us another ten minutes.

"What's your plan, Droop?" At that point, I would have agreed to dirt floors. I stirred cream into my coffee.

He grimaced. "You need to learn to drink coffee like a man."

"What's your plan?"

"All I'm saying—"

"Droop, let's talk about your plan."

"Right-o." He hiked up his pants and started his pitch. "There's an old house 'round here where the original owners put oak around the edges of the room 'cause that's what they wanted their hoity-toity friends to see. But they wasn't fooling nobody. Everybody knew they was cheap and that a pine floor was hid under the rug in the middle of the room. You ain't a tightwad, but you got lots of other wood that'll do you just fine."

Droop pushed his painter's hat back to wipe the sweat off his smooth head. "Besides, there ain't no way I'm taking up the stuff I already laid in the kitchen. It's just gonna have to be different in the family room."

"You've never let me down. I'm sure I'll like your plan."

"I 'preciate that, Mibby. I really do." He spoke faster, and the spark in his eye told me he was proud of himself. He told me his plan of concentric rectangles, starting with a border of oak and working to the center with maple, walnut, and alder. "Won't be another one like it anywhere. Sound okay?"

It sounded to me like I'd have a giant bull's eye on the floor, but I could trust Droop. "Sounds great. Go for it." He deserved that.

Ky ran into the kitchen and pivoted wildly searching for something. "Where's the food?" Then he set his eyes on me. "Couldn't you make my lunch just once?"

"Ky?"

He groaned and headed for the last known location of food in the Garrett household, the porch. He found a jar of peanut butter and a box of crackers and stuffed them into his bag. In front of the opened refrigerator, he spoke with a tone reserved for perpetrators of heinous crimes.

"You forgot to buy orange juice."

While Ky rifled through the refrigerator, I took my place in front of the kitchen door, fingers laced nonchalantly before me. My face, I hoped, was the picture of heavenly peace.

"Never mind," he said, slamming the refrigerator door. "I have to go."

He cinched his bag and charged for the door. He stopped just short of plowing through me. "Mom?" He lowered his eyes and bounced like a fighter waiting for the bell. "I'm meeting the guys to play soccer."

Nothing irks a male more than the slightest delay to forward motion. Ky, who tottered on the cusp of puberty, needed coaching to stay connected to his higher mind. The coach, by necessity, was almost always female. That meant me.

"Playing soccer is a healthy choice, Ky," I said evenly. "You may participate when you speak to me respectfully." I held my breath.

He met my eyes. He looked surprised but granted me a crooked smile. "I'm sorry, Mom. I've been waiting forever for these guys to ask me to play. They're so good."

"Is playing with them worth getting up five minutes earlier?"

"Maybe."

"Good. We'll get up early and pack our lunches together next time. Let me pray for you."

I'm not sure if the door slammed or I said amen first.

Droop smiled big enough to show his gold molars. "Welcome back, Mibby."

"Mornin', sugar," Louise said, tapping on the screen door. The scent of warm raspberries followed her into the kitchen. "Droop, do y'all have time to rest from your game of pick-up sticks for some Raspberry Dream Muffins?"

"Yes ma'am."

"Time for a break, then," she declared.

She wore her hair pulled back into a blunt ponytail that

revealed tiny pearl studs in each ear. Her knit outfit, matching beige vest and pants with a white tee, seemed like cruise wear, a bit on the bland side for Louise.

I asked, "Are you going somewhere?"

She shot a furtive glance at Droop. "Doctor appointment," she whispered. "Now tell me, Droop, what on earth are you doing?"

While Droop explained his project, I refilled our cups and wondered about Louise. More than her outfit or her destination, it was the thin veil of worry covering her face that troubled me. No doctor I knew gave Saturday morning appointments—unless it was an emergency. I wanted to scuttle her off to the kitchen to ask her why she even needed to go to the doctor, but she was too involved with Droop's droning on and on about the floor. When he finally finished, Louise suggested he switch the order of the walnut and maple.

"Can do," he said. Louise's muffins have that effect on Droop.

Andrea shuffled in. "Do I smell coffee?"

She sat by me on the sofa and put her head on my shoulder. Louise smiled and winked. The phone rang. I didn't want to move so I let the message machine pick it up.

"Mibby, this is Ben. I really want to see you again, the sooner the better. Call me."

Conversation stopped. All eyes fixed on me.

"Aren't you going to pick it up?" asked Andrea.

"Is that the boy who was over here before?" Droop asked. "What's he doing calling you?"

"It was the dress," Louise insisted.

When I didn't move, Andrea said, "You are going to call him, aren't you?"

"I'm not sure." And I wasn't. Before I'd heard his voice, shimmering before me like a lure dangling on a fishing line, I'd decided to tell him I needed more time. But now?

"You don't need no stranger in here messing things up." This from Droop.

"I think it's great," said Andrea. "You guys should've seen her when she got home last night."

Droop put his mug down hard. "What happened last night?"

I looked to Louise to be the tiebreaker, but she was looking out the window.

"Nothing," I said, "except that I got paid for a design job."

Droop studied me through narrowed eyes. "You be careful, little lady." He scuffed off to work.

Louise gathered the refuse of our breakfast and headed for the kitchen door. I got up to follow her, but Andrea stopped me. "You're entitled to a little happiness. Think of Ben as your reward. Go for it."

I caught up with Louise just as she stepped through the back gate. "Are you okay?"

"Right as rain, perfect as sunshine, that's me," she said over her shoulder. Her iron gate clanked shut behind her. Louise hesitated and then turned to look through the bars. Her voice teetered.

"I don't want you to worry, and I don't want you to come over here and make me cry, do you hear?" Louise swallowed hard. "Manley's taking me in for a biopsy this morning. They found a lump."

I had every intention of waiting by the phone to hear from Louise about her biopsy, but Droop wasn't happy with my supervision. When I suggested a third variation on the flooring, he told me to skedaddle, or something like it.

I headed out to my maintenance clients, and although I spent the day pruning, potting, and planting, I felt more like a cat rancher, and my thoughts were the cats, and feral cats at that. Just as I decided I had my relationship with Ben all figured out, worries about Perennially Yours darted by, and then I was back to debating if I should even see Ben again, which made me feel the crushing weight of my loneliness all over. And since I'd gathered such impressive momentum, I let my worries accelerate. There was Ky's college tuition to think about, and the insurance on the Yukon that was due, and I pictured myself sitting alone at Ky's wedding. That got the tears started, and they only intensified when I imagined Ky living in Barrow, Alaska, with his wife and five children while I celebrated Christmas with a Swanson Hungry Man dinner. And who, I asked myself, would tell me about my chin hairs when I was the oldest living resident in the nursing home? By quitting time, I hadn't managed to herd one cat into the barn.

On the drive home, I cranked up the volume to sing, "I can't get no . . . satisfaction. . . ." I bellowed along with Mick across the Packer Street Bridge and through the downtown shopping district. In the driveway, I laid my head on the steering wheel and asked God for a little grace. My ambitions weren't lofty; I only wanted to enjoy the company of my son and be a good friend to Louise.

Amen.

"This is rough on the knees," I said, kneeling over the bathtub to wash our dinner dishes.

Ky left the bathroom and returned with two sea sponges. "Try these. Andrea uses them when it's her turn to wash."

"Much better."

Blink nudged closer, hoping for a turn at cleaning the baking dish.

"How much longer will we have to do this?" Ky asked, drying

a plate and putting it in a plastic tub with the other clean dishes.

"I've enjoyed this bonding time with you so much that I've told Droop to return the new dishwasher to Sears."

He rolled his eyes. "That's not funny, Mom."

We finished the plates and moved on to the baking dish. Ky scratched Blink's ears while I scraped at the crusty ring of marinara sauce around the rim of the dish. As odd as it was to wash dishes in the bathtub, the normalcy of a whining teenager and a begging dog soothed me. But it didn't last more than a heartbeat.

"Are you going to marry Ben?"

"Am I what?"

"Are you going to marry him?"

"How do you know about Ben?"

"You're stalling, Mom."

Andrea! Just when I'd thought it was safe to trust that girl—

"So are you going to marry him or what?"

"Ky, I . . . I . . ." It was a cliché, but it was true. I felt like I'd been caught with my hand in the cookie jar.

He spoke in a voice so low I had to turn off the water and ask him to repeat the question.

"Have you forgotten about Dad already?"

"Forgotten him? No way. What made you ask such a question?"

"It's just that you never talk about him. And then you go out with that guy."

I considered reminding him about our family video night, but his recollection didn't need correcting. He needed reassurance. "I haven't forgotten your father. Everything I see or touch or smell reminds me of your dad. Just sitting here looking at you—you look so much like him. I remember, Ky."

His voice quavered. "I thought maybe I was the only one who did."

I wrapped my arms around him. "That had to be so scary for you."

He buried his face in my neck, and his shoulders shook with his cries. I tried to hold him tight enough to corral his fears. "I'm so sorry. I'm so very, very sorry."

I prayed for the courage to retrace my steps on the grieving trail as I turned and walked it again with my son. *And, Lord, forgive me for leaving Ky alone in his sorrow.*

Blink pressed himself into the center of our embrace. We both laughed, which Blink interpreted as a sign to start kissing. The next thing I knew, the sudsy washcloth was down the back of my shirt. Boys sure have a funny way of grieving.

I found Louise lying on the bed in the Geranium Room, staring straight up, arms by her side. I took off my shoes and lay on the bed beside her. She took my hand and held it tightly.

After a minute, she said, "I've been studyin' that ol' water stain on the ceiling. Does it look more like a pregnant turtle or clown getting on a bus?"

"Pregnant turtle, definitely."

"I think so, too."

We were quiet for a long time after that. The blush faded from the day, and gray settled around us like a cat coming home after a day of hunting. I tried to think of something to say that would ease all of Louise's fears, but nothing came to mind. Instead, I studied the stain on the ceiling. The pregnant turtle was starting to look more like a clown.

"I can't decide," she said finally. "Should I bake an apple pie or make strawberry shortcake for the missionary potluck?"

"Louise?"

"It's so hard to find really good strawberries this time of year. I bought some from California last week. They were the prettiest things you ever did see, bright red and plump, but darn if they weren't as crunchy as apples and twice as tart. Maybe I should bake the pie, just to be safe. There's nothing quite as American as an apple pie, now, is there? I'm sure the Masons haven't had pie in an awfully long time. There aren't too many apples in Kenya, I suppose. But then, they probably haven't seen a strawberry in a long time, either. What do you think?"

I looked at her out of the corners of my eyes. Yes, there she was, the friend who had had a breast biopsy only hours before. Now she was frowning at the ceiling over what kind of dessert to bake for a missionary's homecoming. And I'd come thinking she needed to talk about the big C.

"I've never tasted a better apple pie than yours," I said. "I'd travel from Africa for half a slice."

"Apple pie it is, then." Louise stared down the pregnant turtle on the ceiling. "It wasn't bad at all, you know. While I waited for the doctor, a nurse—and what a sweet li'l lamb she was—told me all about the procedure. She explained how the doctor would use a vacuum with a needle to extract some tissue for the biopsy. Of course, I pictured a needle as big around as my arm. As if it wasn't enough to be worried about cancer, now there was a chance they'd suck a lung out of my chest with a Hoover vacuum cleaner."

I relaxed. All she needed was someone to listen. Even I could do that.

"It's a good thing you weren't at the hospital, sugar. We would've died laughing. They gave me a paper gown and put me on a table with a hole in it. And y'all know what went in the hole. Before I had a chance to blush, it was over, lickety-split, piece of cake."

Louise played the delicate Southern belle, melodramatic and

breathy. "Woe is me. Why, I nearly faint whenever I recall that beastly ol' machine. A woman with a delicate disposition such as I should never have to touch a vacuum cleaner again." And then she was Louise again. "Do you think Manley will buy that?"

Manley had greeted me at the door with his hands deep in his pockets and doing the hapless male two-step. Now I heard him walking up the steps. I started to sit up, but Louise's grip anchored me to the bed. The footsteps stopped outside the door. I expected it to open, but the next thing I heard was footsteps down the stairs and a door closing. Only the clock's ticking pulsed the silence.

"Louise, I think I just heard Manley come up the stairs. He's awfully worried about you."

She sniffed. "He's the one who sent me up here to feel sorry for myself, said I had until dinner to work it out of my system."

"It's almost eight."

Louise tightened her hold on my hand. "Really?"

I squeezed her hand back.

"It was so sweet of Doc Wilcox to arrange the biopsy for today. Everyone came in special just to get it done. I think he knew every moment would be pure agony until I knew for sure what's inside me—if there is something inside me." Louise's voice faded to a whisper. "Even still, I won't have the results until Tuesday."

No problem. There were tons of chocolate goodies I could bake to get us through the wait—Chocolate Rhapsody, Black Forest Pudding Cake, Midnight Bliss.

She sat up and combed her hair with her fingers. "Enough of that," she said. "Manley needs his supper."

She left the bed to check her image in the dresser's mirror. "Oh dear, I've got to get some color on. I look as tired as a day-old biscuit." Louise caught my reflection in the mirror. "What is it, sugar?"

"Ky found out about Ben. He thinks I've already forgotten about Scott."

"Oh, that precious lamb." Louise sat by me on the bed and took my hand. "He's feeling so alone."

"I've really let him down."

"Not yet, you haven't. But you can't put off anything important, anything you know you have to do for yourself or Ky."

There was a light tapping at the door. Louise smiled. "There's my Prince Charmin' looking for his Sleeping Beauty—and something to eat, not necessarily in that order."

With that, she patted my cheek and went to Manley. And shame upon shame, I envied her his comfort.

MAY 30

Weather station reported .02" of rain from this morning. Hardly worth mentioning, but it sure smelled nice. Catalpas blooming all over town with clusters of blossoms that look like popcorn balls. Some are dropping petals already—just a dusting of snow petals, I guess.

I was making a shopping list for the Chocolate Rhapsody ingredients when Mr. Chandler called. "You need to get here as fast as you can. Things are completely out of control."

The last time Mr. Chandler had called in a state of panic, his euonymus shrub had sprouted a rebellious branch, hardly a reason to alert the garden riot squad—or me. But putting him off would only have fueled his anxiety and the number of times he would call, so I grabbed my pruning shears and invited Blink to join me.

Mr. Chandler met me as I pulled the Daisy Mobile into his driveway. Buttons trailed him, yapping incessantly at the door of the truck. I slid out of the truck, leaving Blink to quiver with anticipation inside.

"Here it is," Mr. Chandler said, gesturing to the shrub. "Right out here where the whole neighborhood can see it."

The mint julep juniper towered above me, and yes, it was covered with white bindweed blossoms, the weed with the taproot that grew to the core of the earth. Mr. Chandler would be disappointed when I left that day. Spraying the bindweed as it clung to the juniper was out of the question. The herbicide wasn't discriminating. It killed everything it touched. That meant untangling the tendrils of the viney weed and laying it out on the ground. Only then could I douse it with an herbicidal brew and leave it in the dirt to die.

As I explained all of this to Mr. Chandler, his eyelids fluttered like the lid on a boiling pot. "I can't be having weeds taking over the place willy-nilly."

Buttons stopped yapping long enough to get a good hold of my pant leg.

The veins at Mr. Chandler's temples pulsated. "Do whatever it takes to kill it."

I heard the hem of my overalls tear. Buttons seemed encouraged and redoubled his effort to capture my pant leg. Blink scratched wildly at the truck's door.

"And another thing, do you see how much growth is on this euonymus?" Mr. Chandler pointed at the same shrub that had dared to break ranks last year. "You're fertilizing it way too often."

Buttons tugged hard, and I nearly fell. He threw up his hands. "For crying out loud, doesn't anyone take their work seriously anymore?" With that, he huffed off toward the house, and Buttons followed him.

The first time Mr. Chandler had called me in a fit of horticultural panic, I fretted over being competent enough to maintain his yard. The second time it had happened, I fumed over the unreasonableness of his demands. Now I did what he asked and happily sent him a bill. The arrangement seemed to be working for both of us.

I waited until Buttons was safely inside the house before I let

Blink out of the truck. Once he had claimed his territory, doggie style, Blink was content to lie near me in the grass, the master of all he surveyed.

A blanket of clouds held the previous day's warmth to the valley floor, so after working for twenty minutes, I removed the gloves and the long-sleeved shirt I'd worn to protect my arms from the irritating oils of the juniper.

The tedious job gave me too much time to think. My heart sagged every time I thought about Louise and what she was facing. The prospect of her having breast cancer fueled the fervency of my prayers but not their reverence. "Hey there, God! This can't be happening. Louise isn't optional. You have to heal her. Amen."

I didn't feel any better when I thought about Ben. The next time I saw him I vowed to tell him we needed to hit the pause button. It was the modern, techie, totally fresh way to tell him I needed room to breathe and think and heal. And so did Ky.

The bindweed vine lay in a sodden heap at the base of the juniper when a red-and-white truck pulled up behind the Daisy Mobile.

Ben!

I turned my back to the street and groaned. I wasn't ready to talk to him. I looked down at myself. The scratches on the insides of my forearms had inflamed into a rash, and my pants were muddy from kneeling in the damp soil. I took a quick sniff down the front of my T-shirt. Not too bad. I smelled like a car freshener thanks to the juniper. The question was, did I look like a woman Ben would wait for? I prayed he would think so.

"You're a tough woman to find," he said, smiling warmly and stepping close enough to make me wish I'd checked my breath, too. I inched away, hoping distance would help me keep my cool. It wasn't easy. He wore newer jeans that fit very well and a button-down shirt. He carried a small ice chest.

"How did you find me?" I asked, but I was thinking, *Keep your heart and your head together, girl.*

"Andrea gave me a list of all your clients."

"That list's pretty long."

"Let's just say I started out thinking we would have breakfast together. Are you hungry?"

Yes. No. I gestured to my dirty knees. "A little, but I'm too dirty to go anywhere."

"I have it right here," he said, opening the ice chest and showing me its contents.

"Tiramisu?"

I followed Ben to a park near downtown. I used an old Taco Bell napkin and the last of my bottled water to wash my face and hands. Then I dabbed my arms with the wet napkin to soothe the blooming rash. The bandage on Pinky's bite needed changing, too.

The park was a city block of verdant green, shaded by an orderly and sensible arrangement of towering cottonwoods, one of the few trees available in the early decades of the last century, when the park was created. Traffic zoomed by on the business loop that channeled highway traffic east and west on either side of the park. This wasn't a park I usually visited. Close to the bus station and the highway, it had become a gathering spot for transients traveling through Orchard City. The play equipment still shone from lack of use.

Ben spread a plaid blanket under a huge cottonwood tree and returned to his truck for a basket. Watching him put such care into preparing the picnic made the whole idea of telling him to hit the pause button seem flippant and cruel.

Blink was in a hot frenzy when I finally attached a leash to his collar and opened the door. Nose to the ground, Blink pulled me toward the nearest tree. I double-handed the leash and dug in my heels.

"Blink!"

And then I was on my face. Blink was too busy following a scent to notice I'd dropped the leash.

"Blink, come!" yelled Ben with authority. I was about to lunge for the leash when Blink stopped, lifted his head, and did the most amazing thing. He went to Ben.

Ben offered me a hand up. "It's an old military trick. Expect the troops to follow orders and they usually will."

"Is the military accepting canine enlistments?"

"Nope, he's four-footed, which makes him four-F."

Ben laughed at his own joke and invited me to sit on the blanket. I had hoped that I'd overestimated Ben's feelings for me; but his morning-long search for me and the way he embraced me with his eyes made what I had to tell him so much harder.

He offered me a generous portion of tiramisu on a china plate.

"Where's yours?" I asked.

"I ate mine somewhere between Mrs. Donovan on Pine Street and the Petersons near the cemetery."

"You should have called."

"I wanted it to be a surprise." And indeed it was.

We talked about the weather and the traffic and the homeless dilemma before Ben, without realizing it, brought the conversation where it needed to be. "I was wondering if you and Ky would like to fly with me to Aspen this weekend," he said. "One of the mechanics at the hangar told me about a great restaurant up there. We could do a little hiking or fishing or—" He stopped to study me. "Would you rather go someplace else?"

"No, Aspen would be great, of course." But there couldn't be a trip to Aspen. "It's just that I haven't had much of a chance to think this all through." *Was that vague enough?*

"What's there to think about? It would be a good way for me to meet Ky and get to know him. If you can't be gone all day, maybe I could bring my mitt over and play catch with him. Maybe shag a few balls at the park."

"He'd like that." *Eventually. Maybe. I don't know.*

"But?" he prodded.

"But . . . I'm not sure it's time to involve Ky with someone I'm seeing."

His smile broadened. "So we're seeing each other?"

His question told me he had missed the point, the same point I'd missed. It wasn't just me. It was me and Ky, inseparable, mother and son until daughter-in-law do us part.

"Well . . ." I started.

"Could you muster a little more enthusiasm?"

"I'm sorry. It's just that I'm not sure I should even be seeing you right now," I blurted.

He turned from me. His profile was expressionless, but I could guess that I'd hurt him. "Ben, you're—"

"Hold it," he said. "If you're going to say I'm a good friend, let me get a screwdriver from the truck so you can drive it through my heart."

"Don't say that," I pleaded.

"Sorry. It's just that . . ."

He beseeched me with his eyes, and I almost melted. Ky would have to understand. I would explain to him that a woman can remember and love with the same heartbeat. His father's memory would always be safe with me.

But did Ben deserve more? I was a woman who still looked over her shoulder for her dead husband. This man deserved someone who knew where the line between life and death was drawn and didn't erase it. And Ky. He was the most deserving of all. He needed a shepherd for his grief journey. I had to make Ben understand. It seemed perfectly natural to illustrate the point with one of my crazy dreams.

"Have you ever had that dream where you're on your way to a new job, and usually for me, it's a waitressing job, and you can't find your shoes, but you go anyway, because you really need the job? And then the manager tells you to wait on tables, and you haven't even looked at the menu."

He shook his head. "No, can't say I've ever had that dream."

Of course not. The man flew jets. Men who controlled massive flying machines didn't have anxiety dreams. But it seemed a shame to waste such a well-developed illustration, so I forged ahead. "That's how I'm feeling—unprepared. I can't find my shoes."

Ben pulled grass out by the root. I wasn't convincing him of anything. I tried again. "You're going to think I'm crazy, but Scott is with me everywhere I go. He's the first person I think of when I wake up, and I'm disappointed if I don't dream about him. The other night I scolded him. I even caught myself asking him for advice about you."

"There you go," he said. "How could I expect a fair shake from your husband?"

A young man strayed from his travels and approached us. "I saw that you were having a picnic. Do you have any leftovers you won't be eating? I wouldn't ask—"

Ben gave the man the remaining tiramisu and a couple bills from his wallet. "Do you need a ride somewhere?"

"No, but thank you. This looks great."

We watched him walk to another tree, where he let his backpack slump to the ground, and he sat heavily. The young man lowered his head for a moment. When he looked up, he took a cloth out of a pouch on his pack and spread it across his lap. Only then did he eat the tiramisu.

Ben picked up where we'd left off. "Do I need to back off a little? Am I rushing you? I won't call you; you can call me."

I heard the frustration in his voice, but I wasn't the one to relieve it. I tried to reassure him. "It isn't you, Ben. It's me. You're too good to be true, and you've been so patient. It's just that I need some time."

Orchard City averaged only nine inches of rain a year. It had twelve months to accomplish such a meager feat, but there was no time like the present. At that very moment, I felt one and then another drop of rain. Ben didn't seem to notice.

"Do you *want* to find your shoes?" he asked.

"Yes." I most certainly did.

"When you say you need time, am I right in assuming you need time without me hanging around?"

No. Yes. No. Probably. Well, yes.

"I think that would be best." And because I didn't want his jet jockey ego to lose any altitude, I added, "You rattle me."

That made him smile, and I let myself sigh silently.

"Glad to hear it. How long do you think you'll need?"

"Not long, maybe a month at the longest. Probably less."

He reached for my hand and kissed it. "Don't take too long. You're good for me."

Ben drove away from the curb, and the rain came harder. Even Blink thought it was a good idea to return to the Daisy Mobile. On the ride home my stomach roiled with regret. I'd chosen a fork in the road that could take me a very long way from Ben Martin. Now that I'd done it, I wanted my road to lead back to him more than I'd ever dreamed.

The weather cleared bright and fresh. I'd gone home after finishing my maintenance clients to find Andrea packing a canvas bag with snacks for Ky's last game of the spring season, the do-or-die playoff game. Inwardly I groaned. Being with people or dogs was the last thing I wanted to do, but I had promised Ky that morning I would go, no matter what.

"Ky wanted to stay after school to sign his friends' yearbooks," Andrea said. "I told him we'd pick him up at school. That way he'll have time to eat before the game."

Thanks, Andrea.

For someone who had eaten tiramisu for lunch, I was very interested in Andrea's bag. "Is there enough for me?"

She patted the sides of the bulging bag. "I hope so."

Andrea was determined to teach me better sun exposure habits, so we sat hip to hip under an umbrella in the bleachers. The canvas bag was between our knees. Around us, parents and grandparents watched the game. Older brothers and sisters huddled with their friends in front of the snack bar, hoping beyond hope for someone of the opposite sex to cover the distance between the two groups, to single them out and make them the most envied person in middle school. I usually enjoyed the mini dramas played out at the field, but today the girls' giggling only irritated me. I cast them a sour glance. They didn't even notice.

I wanted so badly to feel magnanimous about the sacrifice I'd made for Ky, and knowing myself like I did, I felt reasonably sure I would in a day or two. Until then, I needed chocolate. I rooted around in Andrea's bag until I found a puffed rice bar dipped in chocolate, which surprised me. Andrea usually shunned anything refined. She had to have brought it for me. I bit into the confection and discovered that my eyes had deceived me. The brown stuff wasn't chocolate, and the puffed rice stuff had the taste and texture of beaver food.

I interrupted Andrea's conversation with a woman holding a sleeping infant. "What is this?"

"It's a FemBar, and it's good for you. It's totally what women need—vitamins, calcium—"

"Wood?"

"You're impossible! You would feel so much better if you ate unprocessed food."

To appease her, I ate the woody thing and hoped none of my tree friends found out about it.

The air had been warm, but a spring warm, tenuous and thin. As the sun moved to the horizon, its warmth dissipated. We shared a blanket over our legs.

"Colorado is crazy," Andrea said. "One minute you're boiling hot and the next you're practically frostbitten."

"It's not for wimps."

The players on the field were hoping for a taste of glory. You could see it in the way they leaned into their stances and the hard, fast swings of the bats and hear it in the grunt of the pitchers. They held nothing back, so naturally, few balls were hit. We had plenty of time for pleasant conversation.

Andrea told me about one of her elderly customers at the Pampered Cow. He came every day and ordered the exact same thing, organic rolled oat pancakes. A small frown creased her forehead. "He ordered the eggs portabella today. He never orders eggs. I hope he's okay."

The more I'd gotten to know Andrea, the more humble I grew. She had an expansive heart. No one was beyond her caring.

The opposing pitcher stepped into the batter's box. Andrea commented on his height, saying she doubted he was only thirteen. Then she asked me, "Can, like, anybody go to church? Do you have to be a member or something?"

I almost laughed at her question. She made attending church sound like a health club. And then I wanted to cry. How had it happened that an educated woman living in America thought of church as an exclusive club?

"You can go to any church anytime," I told her and prayed it was true. "No charge."

"Cool." Andrea turned her attention back to the game.

The opposing team struck out and took the field. Ky was up first. Andrea clenched her fists into tight balls. "I hope the pitcher doesn't throw a curveball. Ky will swing at a curveball every time." And then she yelled to him, "Hold out for the fastball!"

Ky watched a fastball whiz by. When it slapped into the catcher's mitt, he backed away from the plate and rolled his shoulders.

"Ball one!"

"Way t'go, bro!" shouted Andrea.

The next pitch came in low. Ky held his stance.

"Ball two!"

Andrea stood, and the blanket dropped to her feet. "Hey, man, you know what you gotta do! Oh yeah, oh yeah!"

A man sipping coffee from a Starbucks cup turned around to look at Andrea and rolled his eyes. It was true. She was as unlikely a cheerleader as you would ever meet with her pale skin and black on black outfit. At least her starry tattoo matched Ky's team colors.

I stood up with her to show our solidarity. "Don't let him rush you! Take your time!"

The pitcher threw the ball into the strike zone, and Ky swung fast but only tipped it outside the first baseline.

We cheered him with chants of "Good eye, Ky" through another foul and ball three. The man with the coffee moved to the visitors' bleachers. Andrea mouthed to his back, "Good riddance."

Ky knocked the dirt off his cleats with his bat.

"He's making the pitcher wait to disrupt his rhythm," I told Andrea. "Scott taught him that."

Her voice was breathy with wonder. "Really?"

I wanted to tell her about all of the other things Scott had taught Ky and how they had somehow accumulated into a primer on manhood. The weight of promises. The supremacy of faith. The wisdom of maintaining his equipment. What makes a friend and how to remain strong in the presence of his enemies. And, of course, spitting, which Ky demonstrated on cue.

What would Scott have taught Andrea?

Andrea started a chant and I joined her. "Way t'go, bro! Good eye, good eye!" By the second repeat, we had added hand motions and a slide to the left and to the right.

The pitcher reared back and grunted with the effort of throwing a shallow curveball. Andrea and I watched breathless. Ky twitched but held his stance.

"Ball four!"

With Ky safely on first base, I asked Andrea if she wanted to go to church with us that Sunday.

"Will there be snake handlers?"

"Only one or two."

I waited for Ky and Andrea in the Yukon. Andrea passed out treats from her bag to the players on Ky's team, and I hoped she hadn't brought them anything healthy. An unreasonable joy fluttered within me. I'd come to the game weighted by my talk with Ben and the loneliness it had underscored, yet spending two hours with Andrea on hard bleachers had somehow lifted my mood, and I couldn't credit chocolate. It didn't hurt that Ky's team had won their game. That was why his sour attitude surprised me.

"Can we go now?" he demanded.

"Sure, as soon as you ask me with respect."

"You two are not allowed to sit together ever again. You don't yell cheers at a baseball game." He scowled.

Andrea and I did the least helpful thing possible. We laughed. And then we chanted our cheer all the way home.

"Way t'go, bro! Good eye, good eye . . ."

Louise came to the garden dressed for rustic living, which meant a bandanna tied around her neck and a designer denim jacket. Her jeans were tucked into Doc Marten high-tops.

"Mibby girl, I've got some good news and some bad news. The good news is that we caught it early; the bad news is that we didn't catch it early enough to avoid a mastectomy and chemotherapy." She sucked in a breath. "That wasn't so bad. I'd dreaded telling you all day."

"Oh, Louise—"

Her hand on my arm stopped me cold. I didn't know what to say.

"I know this is a lot to take in. That's why the ol' teddy bear and I are going up to Columbine Lodge to regroup and prepare for battle."

We sat arm in arm listening to the night song of crickets. Louise finally broke the quiet. "I've had a day to think about this, and God is still good even if I have cancer. He hasn't changed a bit. He still loves me, and that's what I'm dependin' on. Do y'all remember reading Zephaniah in Sunday school? I read it again today. The Israelites were facing a terrible time and knew it. Like me with surgery and chemo, the anticipation had to have been awful. The prophet comforted the Israelites by telling them God was their victorious warrior. He'll be my victorious warrior, too. His love will quiet me, and He will rejoice over me with singing. Imagine that, God singing over me. And not just any song. It'll be a love song for sure."

Louise rested her head on my shoulder. "You have to know, sugar, I am not looking forward to surgery and chemo and losing my hair and feeling sick and—" She stopped and took a deep breath. She sat up to look me in the eyes. When she spoke again, her voice was strong and clear. "My peace is His presence; my hope is His might. Period."

After a short prayer, she left my garden whistling "Dixie." She called from across the alley, "The South shall rise again!"

JUNE

6

Too windy to run sprinklers, but things are awfully dry. Hopefully tomorrow will be calmer. Despite onslaught of heat and wind, great things are happening in the garden. Hydrangea blooms are starting to pink around the edges, and the first clematis blooms have appeared on the Jackman & Hagley vines, and Comtesse de Bouchaud is covered in blooms. By the pond, daylilies are unfurled and a Japanese iris—a slender needle of green tipped with deep purple—will bloom any day now.

Officer Ortiz studied my license and registration and checked my face against the picture.

"Mrs. Garrett?"

"Hello, Officer Ortiz. Nice day, isn't it?"

"Your license tabs have expired," he said flatly and looked around the interior of the SUV. "Is that your baby?"

"Friend's baby. I'm helping her move."

He watched the oncoming traffic as he talked. "Mrs. Garrett, my father died when I was fourteen. He had taken care of everything for my mother. When he was gone, she was completely helpless. She didn't even know how to write a check, had never paid the bills or learned how to drive. We almost lost our house to the bank."

Officer Ortiz did a convincing impersonation of Mr. Rogers, but he had me all wrong. I knew how to register a car, for crying out loud. It was more an issue of having the time. There was so much to do, and there was only me to do it. *Give me a break—not a ticket.*

"Some very nice folks work down at the DMV who can help you take care of this. Do you know where to find the county clerk and recorder's office?"

"At the county courthouse?" *At the neighborhood of make-believe?*

"They're not there anymore. They have a new location at the Aspen Grove Shopping Center. There's plenty of parking, and the office is open from eight to five." He handed me one of his cards. "Tell them I sent you."

"Thank you," I said, tucking the card into the console. *First thing tomorrow.*

"Better yet, why don't you follow me there right now? Then I won't have to worry about you being pulled over and cited by one of my fellow officers."

"It's just that I have my friend's baby here—"

"It won't take ten minutes."

Officer Ortiz returned to his patrol car and pulled into traffic, and I followed.

Phoebe, Roseanne's daughter, woke up when I started the Yukon. She looked at me with her big round eyes and strained against the straps of the car seat. I wasn't her mother, and she knew it. Roseanne didn't answer her cell phone. I hoped she hadn't gotten into another shouting match with Daniel's girlfriend. By the time I parked in front of the Vehicle Registration Office, Phoebe was screaming. Officer Ortiz saluted from his car as I walked into the building carrying her.

Every eye was on me when I took a number, forty-eight. The *Now Serving* sign lit up thirty-one. All of the seats were taken. I rummaged through the diaper bag to find something irresistible to babies. There was some powdered formula but no bottle. Phoebe screamed louder. I tried Roseanne's cell phone again. No answer. I bounced Phoebe gently and paced the crowded office. As long as we were moving, her crying was a plaintiff moan. A clerk called out thirty-two and thirty-three.

"Hang in there, baby girl. Only fourteen more people ahead of us," I cooed.

I pushed the redial button on my cell phone, but Roseanne still wasn't answering. Phoebe had another problem. I headed for the ladies' room. When I returned to the waiting area, they were helping number fifty-one. The nice clerk wasn't moved when I showed her Officer Ortiz's card.

"You'll have to take a new number."

My cell phone rang. It was Roseanne. "Where are you?" she asked.

I explained our ordeal, but it was Phoebe's wails that she heard. "I'll be there in five minutes."

With legal tabs firmly in place on my license plates, I knocked on the Bishops' door. Roseanne greeted me with her finger to her lips. "I finally got Phoebe down," she whispered. "I made some lunch."

Roseanne's parents lived on a tree-lined street in a low-slung brick ranch house. The Bishops had furnished their home with an eclectic collection that spanned the decades of their marriage. There was a Danish modern chair from the sixties, a faux Mediterranean étagère from the seventies, and a reproduction curio cabinet like those popular in the eighties, where Mrs. Bishop displayed her collection of porcelain bells. A nineties-esque sofa billowed with cushion upon cushion in variegated shades of blue. The glass-topped coffee table was probably the latest addition. Not one picture tilted off plumb; every pillow was fluffed, and the dust motes hovered in rays of light, not daring to land. It reminded me too much of the mortuary where my grandmother had lain for her viewing.

Roseanne found me looking at her mother's bells. "It's like a museum in here, isn't it? I offered to buy Mom new furniture when they retired here, but she wouldn't have it. These are her trophies, or her booty as she calls it, from following Dad from one army base to the next. She can tell you about every dent and on which move it happened." Her voice got husky. "I didn't appreciate what all this meant to her until now."

I helped Roseanne fold the sheets of plastic that covered the sunroom's chairs. While I ate a tuna fish sandwich, she filled me in on what had happened after I'd left the girlfriend's house.

"I can't thank you enough for helping me today. It's a blessing my folks are out of town. They've never gotten along with Daniel. My father knew what he was capable of long before I did. That shouldn't have surprised me. As a military officer, it was Dad's job to read men. And my mother? She would have eaten that woman alive, especially when she said that Phoebe was a bad baby."

Roseanne stifled a cry with a fist. When she'd regained her composure, she continued. "As it was, I screamed at her like I'd never screamed at anyone in my life. I'm still trembling." She held her hands out to prove it. "I'm so glad you took Phoebe with you. The thought of that woman . . ."

The orderliness of her face collapsed once again into sobs. I put my hand on her arm and waited. She blew her nose. "I guess I should thank that woman for being so inept. She must have harangued Daniel day and night over having to stay home with Phoebe. At least Phoebe's back with me now."

I helped Roseanne unpack the Yukon and set up Phoebe's crib at the end of her own bed. She spoke manically of the day's events as if she was trying to purge them, but it seemed only to fuel her anger. I left when Phoebe woke up, knowing the baby would soothe Roseanne like I could never do.

The afternoon with Roseanne and Phoebe left me parked in a dismal place, somewhere between despair and foreboding. If the life of someone as smart and wise as Roseanne crumbled so easily, what were the chances that I would fare much better? More and more, the future I envisioned for myself was bleak—very, very gray. And the longer I sat on the sofa watching the afternoon talk shows, the bleaker it got. If I sat there for one more minute, I would implode.

I counted to twenty and hefted myself from the sofa. Louise would be home late that night or the next morning from her retreat with Manley, and nothing expressed camaraderie quite like layers of sponge cake and raspberry mousse topped with a thick covering of chocolate and whipped cream. I headed for the kitchen to bake the Chocolate Rhapsody.

Droop backed down the driveway on his way home to Honey, and I had to stifle a tickle of envy. Soon after, Ky thundered down the stairs carrying his supplies for Salvador's birthday party, the first sleepover of summer vacation. He dropped the sleeping bag loaded with whatever young men can't live without for twelve hours. It seemed excessive.

"Do you have a toothbrush in there?"

"Oops."

He stepped aside to let Andrea pass and gave her an appreciative whistle before continuing up the stairs. Her black sheath followed the slight curves of her body, ending several inches above her knee. At the end of her bare legs, she wore the shoes I'd worn to dinner with Ben the week before, only the slender straps crisscrossed her feet with gentle precision; no circulation problems for her. A car honked at the curb.

"We can drop Ky off at Salvador's," she said. "Save you a trip."

I parted the curtains. Andrea's friend drove a newer sedan. "Looks dependable."

"It is. It belongs to my friend's dad. We're going to the concert with her parents."

Andrea swung a lace shawl—black, of course—around her and let it collect in the folds of her arms, leaving her pale shoulders bare. No freckles or moles or even a polio vaccination marred their perfection.

"I'll have Ky call you when he gets there. How's that?" she said in my ear as she hugged me good-bye.

"No need," I said. I wanted to ask her what time she would be back, even hoped it wouldn't be too late. "Have fun."

The car honked again. She yelled up the stairs. "Come on, Ky. You're coming with me!"

I slid down the wall to sit on the floor with Blink as the house resettled itself from Ky's boisterous departure. Shadows lengthened; a prism of color passed over my toes and disappeared into a dark corner. The house ticked off a cadence as the day cooled until it slowed and stopped. The weight of the silence crushed me.

Ben! His name startled the silence like a firecracker.

"Come on, Blink. We're going for a ride."

Past the hospital and the college, I explained our outing to Blink. "Guys like Ben don't come along every day. No, really, they don't. Just look at Roseanne. She'd agree. Besides, Ky needs a man in his life."

Blink's ears fell back.

"Stop that. You know he does. And besides, it's been a whole week. I've had plenty of time to think about it. Maybe I'm not completely ready—and what does ready really mean?—but if I wait to be all the way ready, I'll be an old, bitter woman sitting by myself in a home for hapless widows."

At the stoplight in front of the Baptist church, I changed the subject to talk about my resolution to exercise. Past a strip mall and through the subdivisions, my heart rate increased enough to make me cough.

"Maybe Andrea was right. Just go for it. Yep, that's right. Go for it."

Once we entered farmland, Blink was off the seat, face to the wind. I talked to his listening half. "You won't be able to argue with this—I can help Ben. He acts all strong and together, but really, I think he's hurting. I know all about that."

Blink sat down and leaned against the door with his chin resting on the windowsill.

"I know, Blink. I think about Scott all the time, too. How would he feel about Ben? Would he like him? Would he approve of Ben as a father? There's only one way to find out."

Moths flitted wildly around Ben's porch light, scorching their antennae when their ardor overwhelmed their survival instinct as they dove toward the bulb. I was parked across the road wondering if the same fate awaited me. The parallel was all too clear. Whether it should have or not, it comforted me to know that unlike the moths, I knew the difference between a man and a light bulb. I zipped up my jacket and invited Blink to lie on my lap.

"Ouch. Keep your claws to yourself."

The dancing light of Ben's television flickered against the shade. I pictured him lounging in his grandfather's chair, probably watching *SportsCenter* and hopefully thinking of me, but maybe Jenny. It was all I could do to keep my seatbelt on.

What was it about Ben? Was it his approval or was it his touch?

Either way, I drank it up like a woman dying from thirst—and wanted more. But if I released the seatbelt, walked up the driveway, and knocked on his door, Ben wouldn't offer me a glass of water.

Blink pawed at the door and whined.

"Let me think, Blink."

I looked to the sky for permission to go to Ben. Instead, it reminded me of my grandmother's twist on astronomy. She had first told me about it on a blustery spring day when I'd helped her hang the laundry. When we finished, we lay in the grass watching the clouds glide by. Grandma told me that the sky was the floor of heaven, like God lived in the apartment upstairs. By day, He unfurled his flags of faithfulness, the clouds, to remind us of His everlasting love.

"How do you know the clouds aren't dust bunnies under His bed?" I asked, giggling at my own cleverness.

Grandma rolled on her side to face me, and I turned to her. She was so close I could smell the eucalyptus candy she held in her cheek. "Oh, He never sleeps. He's always using His creation to show us His loving presence. And by night, the glory of God shines bright through the pinholes in heaven's floor."

"Those are stars," I protested.

"Yes, I know." She rolled to her back again. "But pretending they're as low as my ceiling makes God seem so close."

I rolled up the window of the Daisy Mobile against the cooling night. *You see me sitting here, Lord? Do you even get how alone I am?* And the biggest question of all: *Do you care?*

The Lord will guide you continually, and satisfy your desire with good things . . . you shall be like a watered garden.

"Move over, Blink. We're going home."

As if I needed it, the traffic light blinked yellow, cautioning me that I'd arrived at Tenth and Crawford, the intersection where Scott had died. I pulled to the curb; my heart raced.

"What am I doing here?"

I considered my options. I could back up to Carpenter Avenue and detour as usual, or I could continue on through the intersection. I looked at the stars again. The city lights dimmed their brilliance, but it wasn't the stars I needed anyway.

I sounded my charge, "Yippee," and shifted into first.

You are here, Lord; I know you're here; yes, I know you're here.

I shifted into second and then third gear.

Nothing had changed in the almost seven months since Scott had died there. Trees still lined the street where historic homes stoically stood. Beatrice Carver still had a flock of flamingos in her yard, making a statement only she appreciated. And Günter still had his Christmas lights blazing. A car full of teenagers passed and looked over curiously. I couldn't blame them. I drove fifteen miles an hour under the speed limit.

Through my tears, the lights from houses and streetlights dilated into radiating glitters. In my dark valley, light swam with a watery peace. "You are here," I said out loud, believing it even more.

Movement on the pavement caught my eye. I braked hard and cranked the wheel. Blink barked. The Daisy Mobile jumped the median curb. The tire popped, and the truck slid into a lamppost hard enough to tilt it slightly. Blink had slipped to the floor but was back at his window barking fiercely at the fleeing cat, but it was long gone.

Lights came on in the houses. A man in his bathrobe ran across the street with a satchel. It was Dr. P, a retired doctor with an impossible Greek name. He had been the first on the scene of Scott's accident, too. I really didn't want to face him. I tried the ignition. Nothing. Behind me, the flashing blue and red lights of a police cruiser stirred my emotions.

You are here, Lord. I laid my head on the steering wheel and let the truth of it saturate my thoughts. *You are here to walk with me in my humiliation. You are here to bring light into the darkness. You are here to love me.*

By the time Dr. P and Officer Ortiz came to my window to ask me where it hurt, I was crying. Not a self-pitying cry that found fuel in every shadowed place of the soul, but the refreshing cry of surrender. From the concerned looks of my audience, they didn't recognize the difference.

"Mrs. Garrett, is that you?" asked Dr. P.

Blink bared his teeth at Officer Ortiz. "Could you restrain your dog so the doctor here can take a look at you?"

"Blink," I scolded. "Sit down!" He did even better. He lay down and put his head in my lap. "Good boy."

The doctor leaned into the window to shine a light in my eyes, and then he reached in to take my pulse. "I want you to sit quietly, Mrs. Garrett, and keep your head absolutely still until the paramedics come."

"It doesn't hurt," I told him.

A crowd gathered on the median and on the sidewalks, faceless in the darkness. Was Ky among them? Dr. P handed me a length of gauze. I wiped my eyes and blew my nose. "I wasn't going very fast. Probably less than twenty."

He whispered in my ear. "Did you do this on purpose, Mrs. Garrett?"

I saw it in his eyes, a grief-stricken widow who wanted to follow her husband into eternity. I couldn't blame him; the thought had occurred to me in the early days of my grieving, but not now. It was my turn to reassure him. "Dr. P, a cat darted in front of me. I swerved to miss it."

"Good," he said. "That's very, very good." He patted my hand. "The missus and I, we meant to come and see you and the boy." By way of excusing his neglect or keeping me occupied, he told me about his trips to Haiti and Guatemala to treat the poor. "That's just about everyone down there."

After the paramedics finished their exam and the tow truck left with the Daisy Mobile, Officer Ortiz insisted Blink and I ride with him down to the station. "I don't want you to be home alone. When your stepdaughter gets home, she can come get you there." Gone from his voice was the condescension of our last encounter. With the police radio chattering in the background, he said, "I was called to your husband's . . . accident last fall. I'm sorry for you and your son."

The woman eyed my purse sitting on the seat between us, so I picked it up and opened it to get it out of her reach. I rummaged through its contents for something useful in a police station lobby. No gum. An empty lip balm tub. Not even a nail file. I hugged the purse to my belly and stared at the Wanted posters on the opposite wall.

"You got a cigarette in that purse?" she asked. The fluorescent lights mottled her skin and deepened the circles under her eyes.

"Sorry, no."

The woman covered her face with cracked red hands and then ran them through her oily hair.

"I'm here to bail my son out again," she said. "I should just leave him here to rot."

I tried to picture myself there to bail Ky out of jail for the umpteenth time. Happily, the vision was too implausible to materialize. From the woman's posture, it was evident she knew the scenario all too well. She kneaded her temples while looking at the floor. Her stringy hair lay lifeless down her back. I supposed some conversation would help both of us in our waiting. I asked her how old her son was.

"Twenty-eight going on stupid," she said without looking up.

An officer with a clipboard called out a name, and the woman pushed herself up from her chair and lumbered down a hallway after him. Blink whimpered. I scratched his ears in agreement. Louise and Andrea found me watching the woman and the officer go into a room.

"Oh, sugar," Louise cried as she sat and pulled me to her bosom.

Andrea sat on my right. "Are you all right?"

I told them both how happy I was to see them and apologized for interrupting their plans. I was ready to leave the night behind. "Can we go home now?"

"Not yet, sugar. You have some explaining to do. Did you do it?" Louise asked, her nose almost touching mine. "Did you go to your dark valley?"

The front doors of the station swung open. A group of men dressed like modern-day pirates strutted past yelling obscenities at the desk sergeant. Blink pulled at his collar and barked ferociously. Without breaking his stride, one of the pirates spat at Blink.

"Let's talk in the car," I said.

I expected to find Louise's white Cadillac. "You brought the Yukon?"

"We needed something stealthy," said Louise.

"Why?"

"For heaven's sake, we can't go on a stakeout in a white Cadillac. The hoodlums would spot us for sure."

Oh no, the rose-killer stakeout! "I don't suppose there's any chance of letting you and Andrea have all the fun?"

"Not for all the peanuts in Georgia," said Louise.

"And not for all the nose rings in San Francisco, either," added Andrea.

Louise hefted herself into the driver's seat. "Are y'all coming or not?" she demanded. "If you are, you better get in the car. It's a long, lonely walk to Margaret's." Nothing like a little extortion between friends. Andrea motioned me into the shotgun position.

"Okay, I'll go, but don't expect me to tackle anyone. I'm just an observer."

"That's just fine, sugar lamb. We brought you some black clothes to wear, too. And don't you worry. We brought the hot chocolate and marshmallows."

Andrea spoke up from the backseat. "Don't forget about the chocolate cupcakes, toffee, Snickers, and tiramisu."

"You brought tiramisu?" I asked.

"That was Andrea's idea. She knows how much you like it."

Andrea reached over the seat to squeeze my shoulder.

"Good thinking," I said. Maybe this wouldn't be so bad after all. And the next morning, we could have the Chocolate Rhapsody for breakfast. I decided to keep that a surprise.

As we drove through the deep darkness to Margaret's house, I told them about my intersection adventure. Louise cooed and raised her eyes to heaven. I intentionally left out the part about going to Ben's house. I wasn't proud of that. Instead, I asked Louise about her time on the mountain.

"It was glorious. Me and Manley had a wonderful time of remembering and planning and, of course, eating. It was like being on God's front porch, just a lazy time of togetherness. No more frettin' for me. Besides, there's always time to fret, but there's never enough time to eat brownies."

Louise parked the Yukon in front of Margaret's house. "Y'all go on in to get the brownies from Margaret. She's going to stay in the house to turn lights on and off so her house looks like any other night. We don't want to tip the li'l monsters off."

When I rang Margaret's doorbell, she yelled through the door, "Wha'eber you're thelling, I don' wan' any." She sounded like her lips were numb.

"Margaret, it's me, Mibby. I'm here for the stakeout."

Margaret opened the door a slit and slipped on her glasses. She smiled broadly, then clamped her hand over her mouth. "I left my deeth by da bed. Be right back." The door slammed shut.

I looked into the darkness for any lurking vandals. When the door opened again, Margaret's smile was toothy, her speech sharp. Gentle waves of gray hair fell across her flannel robe. Best of all, she held a brimming plate of brownies.

"Don't do anything stupid, Mibby. If you see anything, call the police on one of them Dick Tracy telephones. You got one of them?"

I assured her we weren't feeling heroic, just silly. And yes, I had a cell phone. I was even pretty sure I'd charged it. With that, Margaret released the plate of plump brownies. My mouth got all juicy just smelling the rich chocolate.

We parked half a block away from Margaret's house, far enough from a streetlight to hide in the shadows but close enough to see any action. Such were the concerns of our near-sighted detective agency. I wiggled into one of the black sweatshirts Louise had brought. It was adorned with a sequined snowman with a red top hat.

"This doesn't seem too stealthy, Louise."

"No matter. Just slouch and wear this."

We pulled stocking caps down to our eyebrows.

"Do you think we need to blacken our faces?" asked Louise.

"No," Andrea and I said in unison.

"Let me sit in the back with the beast for a while," Louise said. "You have better vision, Andrea."

It had been a ruse. Within moments, Louise was snoring with Blink while Andrea and I raced to the bottom of the brownie plate.

"Mibby, I reread all of the letters today. He—Dad, Scott—never says that I'm his daughter, not really."

This would have been a good time to exercise my gift for raising doubts, but I was just getting used to the idea of Andrea as my stepdaughter. One more mental U-turn might send me into a skid. Besides, better than most, I understood the blessing of belonging.

"Andrea, you'll have a better idea of who you were to Scott by what he did than what he said or wrote. He sent you words of love and encouragement every month along with a check to help meet your needs. That's more than many fathers can give the children they live with. He loved you, Andrea. And it sounds like he loved you enough to sacrifice being your in-person dad so you could have some stability."

"Are you all right with that? With me?"

"I am."

Andrea flashed a brownie-stained smile. She reclined her seat just far enough to see out the driver's window. The darkness deepened to murkiness as lighted windows blackened. I shrank from the menace by joining Andrea in a reclining position. Louise's and Blink's snores resonated through the Yukon.

"I took my car in today," whispered Andrea.

"You did?"

Andrea explained how working for Louise had helped her get the money faster. "With the parts the mechanic has to order, it should be ready in a week."

"A week?" I reached for another brownie. "Where's the tiramisu?"

I scraped the last remains of tiramisu from the plate. "I hope you know you can stay as long as you like."

"I know, but I can only teach in California, and I really have to work. Student loans and all."

How had she done it? How had she made a place in my heart for herself and then made plans to escape with such ease?

"I wish I could stay," she said. "It's the first time in months and months that I haven't felt suffocated by loneliness."

"Really?"

"Really."

She turned toward me. "I have a favor to ask."

I said okay, but my pulse quickened and my armpits got clammy. She wanted one of my kidneys. I was sure of it.

Even in the blackness of a moonless night, Andrea's eyes caught enough ambient light to sparkle. "Can I see your tattoo?"

"Now?"

"Why not? The windows are totally tinted. No one can see us."

I was sure Andrea's expressive eyes had swayed many to her appeals. Why shouldn't seeing my tattoo be one of them? I shifted in my seat and lowered my jeans to reveal the pasty skin just below my waist.

Louise snapped on a flashlight.

"Show's over," I said, hiking my waistband into place.

"That's it?" complained Louise. "No rose? No heart? Not even a sinking ship? Just M-I-B? Why, you didn't even put periods between the letters. And it's awfully small. I wouldn't call that a tattoo at all. I've had bigger mosquito bites."

"I sure hope our perpetrator is deaf and blind," I said. "With all the noise you're making—"

A figure shuffled down the sidewalk toward Margaret's roses carrying something that looked like a gas can.

"Get down," I whispered. "Someone's coming."

I needn't have worried. There was no mistaking the silhouette. Our suspect, I knew for a fact, *was* nearly deaf and blind. I jumped out of the car and ran to intercept him.

"Walter, put that can down this instant!"

"That will be enough, Mibby," scolded Louise. "I think Walter knows how you feel."

"But—"

"I think it would be best if you went to the living room and waited for us."

I sat on my hands while Louise and Andrea debriefed Walter. I could see why Margaret wouldn't want to live in Walter's house, besides the fact that he killed roses. The drapes, the tables, the porcelain figurines were all dulled by a gray mantle of dust. I sneezed, and Louise blessed me from the kitchen. Then she asked Walter why he had poisoned the Don Juans.

"I'd tried everything to get Margaret to notice me," he said. "It seemed like she couldn't see nothing past them roses. I wanted her to need me, to give me a chance to . . ." Walter faltered.

"Go on," urged Andrea.

"I wanted her to let me love her. It seemed to make sense until the gardener . . ."

"Garden *designer*!" I called from my exile.

"Did she say something?" Walter asked Louise.

"Don't mind her just now," Louise said. "Let's talk about you and Margaret." To my disbelieving ears, Louise coached Walter on how to win Margaret's heart without killing any more roses. When I started to complain from the living room, Louise explained, "The quality of Walter's love isn't the question. Its expression is what we need to work on."

JUNE

7

Tomato plants look like heck. Wind? Heat? Cold? Yes! Hope we have enough growing season for a good harvest. It would be a long winter without salsa. If only the weather would make up its mind. On a lighter note, Japanese iris popped open. What a showoff!

Droop ran his hand over the Daisy Mobile's front bumper. "That ain't bad. Makes it look like a working man's truck." From Droop, that was a high compliment.

"It was either get a new tire or straighten the bumper," I said. "Thought maybe I'd get more use out of a tire."

"Good thinking. Hey, I got a lot done today. It kinda looks like a kitchen in there. I'd love to show it to you, but Honey's got special plans for me. Sure hope it ain't got nothing to do with them cousins of hers." Droop closed the garage door for me and walked off, hitching up his pants. He turned and said, "Oh yeah, Andrea and Ky went somewheres. Said they'd be home 'bout suppertime. Bye now."

Ever the master of understatement, Droop's comments hadn't prepared for me for what I saw when I walked into the kitchen. It was a kitchen. When I'd left that morning, boxes of kitchen cabinets had lined the room like a child's toy blocks. Now the cabinets were in their appointed places, attached to the walls and floors. The island cabinets still stood in a looser configuration waiting to be secured into place. I never would have been able to predict my response to seeing my dream kitchen almost realized.

Whammy!

Grieving is an odd occupation. Fears seeded deep in the brain germinate and sprout in the most unlikely places. Somehow the unfinished kitchen had kept Scott alive to me. Leaving the sink suspended from two sawhorses had meant we were still in something together. Completing it meant my life without Scott would officially begin. And the question would have to be answered—can I do it?

The kitchen was our last project, the grand finale of the restoration. We had planned it that way. It was to be the most expensive and most important room in the house, and we wanted to do it right—no skimping. When we had finally saved the money for the project, we started tearing pictures out of magazines and collecting brochures from kitchen shops. We obsessed over the minutiae of kitchen design. White on white? Stainless steel? Soapstone or tile? Granite? Secretly, I was terrified we would mess up. I'd asked for Louise's opinion so often, she had threatened to cut off my muffin supply. Scott saw the project as problem solving—no big deal, just do it. Typical man-think.

Catalogs, brochures, paint chips, and flooring and countertop samples littered the kitchen table all through the process. Scott had suggested that we each design the kitchen separately, then pool the best ideas from both plans. I finished my plan first. I even painted a rendering. With all the pieces in place, I was ready to show Scott my work.

He had come to the kitchen dressed for work, a picture of confidence in a gray worsted suit and shirt and tie. He checked his watch. "Better get going."

"Do you have time to look at this?" I asked, holding up the portfolio with the plans and color samples.

His frown told me he didn't, but he said sure, smiled, and took off his jacket. I brought his coffee to the table while he studied the plan. "You want two different colors for the cabinets? I don't know, Mibby. And the drawer pulls—you don't want brushed nickel. Everything else in the room is warm."

Scott's mistake had been thinking I had plenty of emotional distance between the kitchen design and my ego. It wasn't his fault; he'd expected the same objectivity I had with my clients. This was different. This was my dream kitchen, the one I'd been obsessing over for weeks, the one in which I'd envisioned myself making crème brûlée and roasting the Thanksgiving turkey. He couldn't picture mixed cabinet finishes? The drawer pulls were a mistake?

"Nope," he said, shaking his head, "these drawer pulls are all wrong."

Really?

I'd been to every home improvement store in the valley and along the Front Range, surfed the net, combed catalogs, and scrounged through architectural salvage yards. I'd finally found the drawer pulls in an upscale hardware store in Telluride. They were perfect, and yes, expensive, but they were the ones I wanted; they were my prize. What Scott didn't know was that I'd already bought them.

"Take it back," I said, hoping to tease him into compliance.

His mouth said nope, but his dimple, the left one, the one that betrayed his mischief, puckered slightly.

"Take it back," I pressed.

On his way to the coffeepot, he smiled and said, "Won't do it."

I lobbed a drawer pull at his back the only way I knew how,

like a girl. He turned to smile, probably to acquiesce, just as the hardware struck him square in the forehead. We laughed so hard we ended up on the floor with Blink barking along. With a sigh, we leaned against the wall, Scott's arm around my shoulders.

"I really love the design, Mibby. You've done a great job. I don't see why I should even bother. It's perfect. Order the cabinets today." And so I did.

Now I wanted to be back at that day when the warmth of Scott's touch was more than a memory. I was ready to deal. I would trade anything I owned to reside in the past with Scott forever, but nothing I owned had value to me anymore. That was the dilemma. I couldn't recover what I'd lost, and the future only taunted me. It had been less than twenty-four hours since I'd felt God's presence in my pain, and I was back in the same crushing place without Him. But this time, my soul reached out to touch the hem of His garment, and He was there.

It was then that I finally accepted that one night of bowling for lampposts wouldn't be enough. I'd find myself in the dark valley again, and again I would face the same decision—turn to despair or turn to Jesus. I had no idea where the journey would take me. Would the valley become lighter with His presence, or would I leave the valley to walk on the mountaintops? My estimate of a month to reach my destination had been naïve. Ben needed to know that.

"I wish you'd come in last night," said Ben.

"You saw me?"

"Your truck's a little hard to miss." His beard was at least three days old, and his voice about as scratchy. "You were out there a long time."

"I was thinking about why I'd come and what I wanted—" I stopped short. This conversation had to be about what I needed or I would be right back where I'd started. "I remembered something I had to do."

He invited me into the house, where several boxes marked *Photos* and *Dishes* and *Knitting* stood in the living room. Only shadows were left on the walls where the family photos I'd seen on my first visit had hung. My mouth went dry.

"Are you going somewhere?"

"I'm taking a load of stuff to my parents'." Ben picked up two boxes. "Did you find your shoes?"

"Wha—?"

"You said you needed some time."

"Yes, I do. I mean I still do, and most likely, it will take longer than a month."

"Oh."

I picked up the box marked *Knitting* and followed him to his truck. When he'd loaded the last boxes onto the truck, he narrowed his eyes.

"And what exactly do you need all this time for?"

I hadn't expected his anger, but I should have. After all, I'd accepted the date. I'd welcomed his affection. I'd even parked outside his house and inflated his hopes. He deserved an explanation.

I told Ben about going to the intersection and hitting the lamppost, even my trip to the police station.

He spoke so softly I had to move closer to hear him.

"I was pretty upset when I left you in the park. I mean, I've lost someone, too. In the days after the accident, I cried like crazy. Couldn't stop. Went to my parents' place for a while. Spent a lot of time in the hills. And then I just had to stop. All the crying in the world wouldn't bring her back."

I didn't know what to say, so I helped him spread a tarp over the truck's contents. He fastened a rope on his side of the truck and threw the rope to me. I looped it around a hook and threw it back, but it didn't return. I went to him. He was leaning against the truck with his chin tucked to his chest.

"Ben?"

"I can't remember our first anniversary or her last birthday or where we spent Christmas. I can't even remember where we went on vacation or what kind of cake she baked for my birthday. The memories are gone like they never happened. Where are they?"

"I don't know."

"It doesn't matter, I guess," he said. He cinched the load tightly and tied the rope off on the bumper.

I followed Ben through the house while he turned off lights and locked doors.

"Before you came last night, I was sitting out in the garden watching the sunset," he said. "It was really nice—lots of colors and it kept changing. I was just sitting there enjoying it, and the scent of the roses got so strong, and then this . . . I don't know, it was a darkness. I couldn't see it, but I felt it. It covered me. It was so heavy. Man, it scared me so bad. I fell to the ground and cried like a baby. It was like I'd never cried at all."

Ben scanned the living room. When he was satisfied he hadn't forgotten anything, he locked the front door and we walked to the truck. "I was okay when I was flying," he said, "and it helped a lot to have the house to paint and the garden to plant. The roses were my mother's idea; she said it would help to have a place to remember. I don't know. Maybe it did. Anyway, it's too quiet here. I have some time before the plane's ready to fly, so I'm going to help my dad put a new roof on the house."

It would have been so easy to walk into Ben's arms, tell him I'd go anywhere with him, tell him everything would be all right, but anything I offered him would only delay his grief, for that was all the power I had.

"Mibby, I want you to know that you've been good for me. It helped to be with you." He raked his hands through his hair. "Listen to me. I'm rattling on like a . . ."

". . . man whose wife has died?"

"But I thought I was all done with that. As long as I kept busy, I could handle it."

"I don't think it works like that, at least not with me it hasn't. It's like I'm being stalked. The pain always finds me, usually when I least expect it." He smiled when I told him about my whammies o' grief.

"I likened mine to a baseball bat to the gut."

"Ouch."

Around us, the crickets warmed up their night song, and the earth sighed with the fading light.

"What's your plan?" he asked. So much like a man to strategize and prepare, like grief was a city on a hill to be captured.

"I have to get a lot smarter about dealing with the pain. I have Ky to think about. Whether I'm a worthy model or not, he's watching me. I can't run and hide anymore. There's only one way out of grief, and that's through it, that whole valley of the shadow of death thing. I'm counting on God walking with me—us—Ky and me."

He smiled and kissed me on the cheek before slipping behind the steering wheel of his truck. I made him promise to stop if he got tired and to call me when he arrived at his parents' home.

"My mom wants me to talk with my old pastor. I'm thinking it might not be such a bad idea."

The warmth of his kiss lingered on my cheek as he backed down the long driveway. But I couldn't watch him drive out of sight, so I checked the rose garden. The new plants had produced burgundy-tinged leaves and a profusion of buds. When he called from his parents', I'd offer to water them until he returned. Behind me, Ben's truck roared back up the gravel driveway and skidded to a stop. We met at the garden gate.

"I knew you'd worry about the roses," he said. "I've arranged with my neighbor to water them until I get back. Okay?"

"Okay."

Ben hesitated, then asked, "You're not saying never, are you?"

"No, just hitting the pause button."

"Excellent."

And he was gone.

JUNE 16

The heat has sped everything up in the garden. Hollyhocks in full bloom—yellow, fuchsia, peach, burgundy, and white. Doubles showy, but I prefer the singles. They must be 6 feet tall! Just like grandma's! All the summer usuals are here—Shastas, penstemon, gaura, pincushions, and more. And it's snowing cotton from all the old cottonwood trees. Hate to admit it, but I enjoy their feathery flights.

The song of Andrea's cello danced on the gossamer wings of twilight. An opaque shade had been pulled on the day. Colors softened, and the valley exhaled, suspended between day and night. House sparrows dove overhead, catching mosquitoes and moths for their evening meal, plus a little extra for the kids in the nest. Summer was only five days away. As the days lengthened, the evenings ripened and sweetened.

It was Andrea's idea to have a party to celebrate the completion of the kitchen and to say good-bye. She played something by Bach under the locust tree while the lacy shadows of its leaves mottled her white dress. The casserole dishes and platters had been taken inside and filled with soapy water to soak. Blink ate the only surviving hamburger.

Our guests lounged in the grass of the poop deck and sat on

the railing of the porch and in clusters of chairs around the garden. Louise, fatigued from surgery and socializing, slept in a chaise lounge. But then, Andrea's music had had that effect on Louise all along. I watched her slow, even breaths and thanked God for her good prognosis. Since Manley preferred baseball to Bach, he'd long since tiptoed home to watch a Rockies game.

Margaret and Walter sat companionably in the glider under the Bechtel crabapple tree. Margaret patted his knee to keep time with the music while Walter ate his second helping of cherry pie. They'd surprised us at dinner by announcing their engagement. Love looked good on Walter. It softened him like a pair of jeans fluffed in the dryer. At their feet, Roseanne played peek-a-boo with Phoebe on a blanket. Resilient didn't come close to describing that woman.

By the back gate, Ky and Salvador, coiled as tightly as springs, waited for the last note of the movement. Escape was imminent. Mrs. Friedlander had stopped by earlier at our invitation to celebrate Ky's promotion to eighth grade. She'd pushed Andrea's lentil and sprout salad around her plate and left for an early movie.

Droop's wife, Honey, plump and golden, sat alone, sipping an iced tea and swaying with the music. Had Droop followed Manley home?

Andrea's friends sat heavy-lidded on the grass, a sort of gem and mineral show for all their bangles and metal. Even Mr. Stewart, my neighbor, leaned over the fence to listen. The scene was a Seurat painting, fleecy and amicable. I wanted to frame it and hang it above the mantel to warm the gray days of winter.

I found Droop alone in the kitchen leaning against the sink and fingering one of the kitchen's door pulls. "Is that the pull missing from the cabinet over the fridge?"

"Yep."

"Is there a problem?"

"Nope." He turned the pull over in his hands. "Well, maybe."

"Is it something I can help you with?"

"Nope. Well, maybe." He sighed deeply. "Putting this here handle in place is the last thing I gotta do to finish the kitchen. When it's done, I won't have no reason to come no more."

"I can help that."

I took the door pull from him, opened the cabinet under the sink, and tossed it in the trash.

"Much obliged," he said. "See you on Monday. Make sure the dangburn coffee's hot."

When all the guests had gone home and the dishes had been washed, I grabbed a flashlight and asked Andrea to come with me into my garden.

"I told my friends to come back for me after the movie. They'll be here pretty soon," she said.

"This won't take long. I want to show you something." I shined the flashlight on the *Crocosmia*. The flower stem had unfurled and set opposing buds along its length. It was still two weeks from blooming, but the buds hinted at its fire.

"Is there a reason why we're looking at a flower in the dark?" she asked.

"You never know what you might learn. This was my mother's favorite flower. It grew like crazy around our home when I was a child. My mom always referred to it by its common name, *mmmm*ontbretia."

Hint, hint.

"That's nice, but it isn't even blooming."

"Don't miss the point, now. Remember, my mom lo*oooved* them."

Hint, hint.

"You can be so weird sometimes."

A horn honked, and Andrea excused herself. "I'll be back kind of late, so I'll see you in the morning."

I startled awake when someone tapped my shoulder.

"It's me," Andrea whispered. "Good night and sweet dreams, Montbretia Iris Brown. I love you." She kissed me softly on the cheek and left.

JUNE 17

Supposed to peak at 90° today. Grand Mesa, here we come! Should be a great year for wildflowers. Hoping the elephant heads are blooming in the marshy depression we found a few years ago. It's probably early, but who knows? Should at least see some wild irises.

Parked at the curb, Andrea's Toyota stood at the ready to take her back to California. Sadly, it didn't look any better for the money she'd spent fixing it. But if it was possible, it was fuller than when she'd come. The back seat bulged with contributions Louise and I had gathered for her new apartment, and baling twine held her trunk closed, but just barely. Her cello reclined in the passenger seat. There had been a time when I would have been happy to see Andrea go, but now that the moment had arrived, I delighted in watching the grass grow in the cracks of the entry walk. Anything was better than saying good-bye.

The midmorning sun beat down on us. I was wet with sweat; Andrea's shoulders blushed pink. Even so, we sat unmoving on the porch steps, watching an occasional car go by, listening to a robin family chatter encouragement to their newest fliers, avoiding the inevitable.

"I hate good-byes," she said.

"Me too, but we'll see you in August," I reminded her. "And I promise to get your bonsai there healthy and happy."

"I'll definitely be out of scones by then. You better bring Louise."

"If she's done with her chemo . . ."

Our eyes met.

Andrea changed the subject. She pointed at the gift on the step beside me. "I hope that's not for me. You've done too much already."

I said a silent prayer and handed her the present. "It's from Ky and me."

Andrea flashed a sideways smile. "It's pretty heavy. You didn't bake anything, did you?"

"I like you too much to do that."

She stopped unwrapping the present long enough to squeeze my hand. My heart fluttered at her unguarded smile. With the baseball-themed wrapping paper folded neatly, she opened the box and removed the Bible. Her fingertips played with the embossed letters of her name and then rested there. Louise had promised me that Andrea would love a Bible, but she sat as still as a rock. Had I crossed a line that still remained between us?

"Andrea?"

"I don't know how to thank you," she said. "It's so beautiful. My name . . ."

"Let me show you something." I took the Bible and opened to the psalms. The gilded edges stuck together, making it difficult to turn the pages without wetting my fingers, but Andrea should be the first to pucker the pages with her licked fingers. I scooted closer and read the verses I'd underlined in Psalm sixty-eight.

"Sing to God, sing praise to his name,
extol him who rides on the clouds—
his name is the Lord—
and rejoice before him.
A father to the fatherless, a defender of widows,
is God in his holy dwelling.
God sets the lonely in families. . . ."

"I hope you don't mind," I said as I wrote a dedication to Andrea in the margin. Then I said the line I'd rehearsed while staring at the ceiling around two that morning. "I believe with my whole heart, Andrea, that God has set you in our family."

We had a good blubberfest of togetherness until Blink tried to dry our tears with his tongue. Andrea laughed as she wiped her cheeks on the hem of her blouse.

Something in my face must have given me away.

"There's something else, isn't there?" she said.

I pulled the unopened envelope from the San Diego Superior Court from my pocket. Blink's kiss had mussed Andrea's hair into a wild arc. I considered telling her, but I was only stalling. Besides, on her, it looked good.

"What's this?" she asked.

"When you first got here," I started, "I didn't trust you. I was afraid you'd tarnish all I remembered about Scott."

"Mibby—"

I didn't want to lose my resolve, so I rushed on. "After I saw the documents in the box, I knew I had to share Scott with you, but I didn't want to share very much, especially not his estate."

"I hope you don't think—"

I held up my hand to stop her. "I don't. You don't have to worry."

She looked at the envelope again. "What is that?"

I explained to her how I'd written the court to find out when or if Scott and Tina's divorce had become final and how I'd wanted to distance her from Scott any way I could. "I'm ashamed of that now."

Andrea stared at the envelope a long time. "How long have you had it?"

"A week. I was too scared to open it."

"Do we really need to know what it says? Will it change anything?"

"If Scott never divorced your mother, she would be his legal heir and then you."

"Let me see that thing."

I expected her to open it, so I braced myself for what lay inside. Instead, she tore the envelope into tiny pieces and threw them into the air. She brushed off her hands.

"There."

"Worm?"

"No thanks," I said. "I like the rubbery stuff, the kind with the glitter. Maybe green, or the pink is nice."

"Nice don't catch fish." Ky pulled a plump earthworm from the paper carton. "Besides, Droop said they're biting on worms."

"Only because Droop didn't offer them glitter."

Ky rolled his eyes and worked at getting the worm on the hook. To keep from watching him impale the poor thing, I concentrated on kneading the glittery pink stuff into a ball.

"I'll even put it on the hook for you," he said.

"That's a kind offer, but the thought of a little wormy writhing under the water, waiting and knowing that a fish is going to swallow him at any moment . . . no, thanks."

"Mom, it's a worm. It doesn't think. It wiggles and digests food. That's it."

"How do you know he doesn't have pictures of his kids in his wallet? Maybe his wife is making dirt salad to go with the dirt burgers for their neighborhood barbecue. And what about his kids? How will they feel when he never returns? Boy, are they going to be disappointed."

"You're hopeless."

I rolled my pink ball between my palms to make a long rope. "See? I made a synthetic worm. No wife, no kids, no guilt."

"While the fish are laughing at your worm, they can snack on mine." Ky cast his line out to the deep waters of the lake. I chose the shallows off to my near right.

"Do you want me to cast for you?" he asked.

"It's in the water, isn't it?"

That earned me another eye roll.

Ky crouched with his pole, waiting. I wondered if he saw the scene beyond the spot where his line entered the water. We had come to the Grand Mesa to escape the heat. We sat in the bottom of a deep bowl. Spruce trees stood shoulder to shoulder from the mesa's rim all the way down to the rocky shoreline. Before us, the lake sparkled like a sapphire set in emerald velvet. Behind us, the wind excited the leaves of the aspen trees, and then it was at our backs like a friend's strong hand. It blew past us to rile the lake's surface and to rouse the spruce into a wild dance. And then it was gone. The aspens stilled; the water relaxed into a glossy picture of sky and trees and clouds. The scene, like its Creator, drew me to the now, where the regrets from yesterday and the fears of tomorrow lost their power. I wanted to set anchor, to be lulled into restfulness by the lapping of the lake.

"Did you bring anything to eat?"

Behold, the stomach called. Inspiration would have to wait. I propped my fishing pole into a forked branch left behind by another fisherman and made Ky a plate of grapes, cheese with crackers, and the official snack of the fishing Garretts, gummy worms.

A mosquito whined in my ear, so I slathered Ky with enough DEET to qualify him as a superfund site. "And where's your hat?"

"In the car."

I had just swiped his forehead and cheeks with SPF 45 when his pole jerked and bent. The lopsided battle ended with Ky holding the trout for a picture.

"Aren't you going to smile?"

"I'm smiling on the inside."

"Can you prove it?"

"Mom, the fish is going to die."

"Not if you smile now."

He bared his teeth. Close enough.

Snap.

Ky cradled the fish just under the surface until it regained its senses and swam away. "Can we stay longer?" he asked.

"Sure, but I want to take a hike up to the marsh before we go."

"Let me guess. There are flowers in the marsh."

"That's right, and we're not leaving until I find an elephant head."

He plopped his hook dead center into the same hole and reeled in the slack of the line. He flashed a cocky grin. "Are you sure you don't want a worm?"

"Positive. Rub in your sunscreen."

Another breeze stirred the aspen leaves into a shimmery dance and pressed against my back. "Ky, have I ever told you about the first time your dad took me fishing?"

JULY
4

The valley is hot, which isn't a complaint, just a statement of unwavering truth. Ugh. Ironically, Lucifer montbretia is blooming boldly in the garden. Petunias and dahlias providing dramatic color. Glad something thrives in the heat. Don't forget to plant more dahlias in the front next spring. They love to show off.

The hummingbird snuggled into the waterlogged rose, flared his feathers, and shimmied in the morning light to create a spray of droplets. Again and again he lowered himself into the swollen blossom and shuddered the water away. I expected each dunk to be his last, but on and on he went. Finally, an inaudible signal sounded, and off he flew. I stared at the disheveled rose for a long time, but he didn't return.

I finished my coffee in one gulp and returned to Andrea's birthday note. I told her about the design work I'd done for the historical district—pro bono, of course—and how Ky had attended a Rockies baseball camp, and that her bonsai continued to set new leaves. Then I told her the story about the montbretia bulbs Scott had sent before he died.

They're blooming now, I wrote, *a row of flames on each stem.*

I enclosed a picture of Louise and me. In the photo, Louise wore a red wig styled by Virginia to match my hair. Of all the colors and styles she had tried, Louise had insisted she liked the Mibby-do the best. What a friend.

I sealed the envelope but quickly reopened it. I scratched out my signature and changed it to *Love, Mom.*

Acknowledgments

This book was written in the fellowship of many generous and nurturing people. My heartfelt gratitude goes out to them all.

Janet Kobobel Grant, my intrepid literary agent. Thanks for knocking on so many doors to find the perfect home for *Like a Watered Garden.*

Charlene Patterson, my hardworking and always accessible editor. This is a much better book because of you.

Sharon Bridgewater, Darlia Hill, and Muriel Morley, my long-suffering critique group. You never flinched from saying the tough things with love. Thanks, wonderful ladies!

Lauraine Snelling, writer and teacher extraordinaire. Thanks for showing me where to put my first step.

Nancy Leane, my very own Louise. Thanks for tying my boat to the dock.

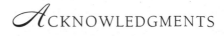

Carol Drake. Before she introduced me to lemon scones, I hadn't truly lived.

Deanna Strand, the most able pilot I know. You gave me the perspective I needed. I would fly anywhere with you in an itty-bitty plane.

Don Isaacs, my high school writing teacher who quoted Shakespeare often. "Brevity is the soul of wit."

Bart D. Allen, Colonel, USAF (retired), and Major Scott Oskvarek, USAF Reserves, 557 Flying Training Squadron, my military experts. Thanks for answering all of my questions about life in the military and, most importantly, serving our country.

Françoise Evans, my French connection to all that's buttery and sweet.

Early readers of the manuscript—Dennis, Janet, Kathi, Kimberly, Marilyn, Mom, Sherry, Sue, and Cherry. Your kind enthusiasm kept me writing.

Thanks to all of my friends who asked me what page I was on. That *really* kept me writing.

Dr. Mohler, Dr. Dean, Dr. Griffith, Pat Riley, RPT, and Lynn Vrany, CMT. Thanks for helping me get back to my dream.

And most of all, Dennis, my beloved husband, cheerleader, and technical advisor. Anything I know about plants, I learned from you. Anything I got wrong about plants, I read somewhere else. More than anything, I want to be the person you believe me to be.